My Chameleon Mate

SUSAN TROMBLEY

Chapter One

Vera

Everything was going wrong on my honeymoon!

Though the space-cruise ship, the Relativity, was nice enough —certainly not top-tier—my new husband had hired the cheapest and most questionable transport ship to take us to Nebula Watch Port for our week-long stay. In fact, *everything* he'd booked other than the on-ship activities had turned out to be through cheap, fly-by-night operations.

I'd thought we'd be living it up at the Paradise Nebula resort, complete with waterpark, full-service salon, and a promenade of restaurants and shops offering the most intriguing items from all over the civilized galaxy. After all, he'd insisted upon a Justice of the Peace wedding so we could spend all our money on the honeymoon.

Instead, Nathan had booked us a room at a ramshackle hotel located twenty miles from the port and even further from the resort.

I would have found a way to get out of this trip if he'd told me we'd be staying for a week in a cramped room with gray walls that

I was certain had once been white, a threadbare comforter on the hard slab of a bed, and a bathroom that looked like it barely ever saw a cleaning cloth.

I'd had misgivings when the rental cruiser had pulled up to the place, and they'd only been confirmed when we'd entered the room. Now, I looked around speechlessly at the room where we'd be spending the next seven Ubaid Standard days.

Nate brushed his palms together after he set down our luggage, glancing around like he was admiring the accommodations his penny-pinching had gained us. "This isn't so bad, now, is it, Vera?"

My mouth fell open to tell him what I really thought, but I quickly closed it and turned my back to him before he looked my way and saw my expression. I blinked back the tears of disappointment that prickled at my eyelids as I quickly shook my head. How foolish of me to think this honeymoon would be all that I'd hoped and anticipated.

"N-no, of course not, darling." I struggled to think of the best words to use to compliment this room without outright lying. "It-it's...." I spun my hand as the wheels in my mind turned. I glanced around desperately, avoiding his expectant brown eyes.

"Cozy?" I turned back to him with a weak smile.

His manicured brows lowered, and he stiffened, his broad shoulders squaring as he crossed his arms. "You don't sound very enthusiastic, Veer." He frowned at me, his finely shaped lips thinning. "You *could* show a little more excitement about our honeymoon. You've been a real wet blanket since we boarded the shuttle in Denver. You've complained constantly."

His eyes narrowed as his strong brow creased in a frown beneath glossy, artfully tousled, brown locks that framed his face.

I tensed, bracing for a familiar refrain.

"You're always so unappreciative," he continued, slipping right into his favorite groove. "I work hard, day in and day out, so I can provide for the both of us while you do," he gestured dismissively with one hand at me, "*whatever* it is you do all day."

"Nail art," I said faintly.

I had a growing clientele, but I was still building up my business, so I wasn't bringing in the kind of money he was. But I had enough clients now that I was working daily. I was far from needing the Akrellian help center where I'd been living when we'd first met four years ago while he'd visited in his official capacity. I wasn't that same lost nineteen-year-old that I'd been back then, desperate for an escape from a rather grim institutional building, surrounded by other humans who'd lost everything to the Menops invasion or the plague that had followed on its heels to devastate our world.

He'd seemed like Prince Charming to me back then, flashing an easy smile with brilliant and straight white teeth, his eyes warming with interest when they alit on me while I cleaned one of the eating halls as part of my duties. I'd thought he was just like a handsome prince from a fairy tale with the naivety of a young woman looking for a hero. I'd felt unbelievably lucky to gain his attention. Even though he did turn out be fifteen years older than me, I'd been certain we were meant to be together.

His tone now was so different from the kind and encouraging voice he'd used back then whenever he'd spoken to me. "All I want is some damned downtime to enjoy myself once in a while, but you're always whining about something, Vera." He didn't bother to acknowledge my profession at all, having referred to it multiple times as a "hobby." "Nothing is ever good enough for you! No matter how hard I work to earn money so I can give you the world, you can't ever be grateful for my sacrifice. All you really care about is how much more you can squeeze out of me for fancy resorts and steak dinners."

The fact that I was still with him even though I could now afford my own place should have convinced him I wasn't a gold-digger, but he remained suspicious, and I felt like I was constantly having to remind him that I loved him, and I wasn't with him to get out of the help center. All because his "gold-digging" ex-wife had "milked every dime she could get" out of him.

I suspected now that she'd merely asked to have steak instead of hamburger once in a while, and that seemed to him to be demanding endless luxuries.

"This room," he held out both arms, continuing to speak without seeming to note that I was fighting tears at him berating me and had turned my head to swipe at my eyes, "is plenty good enough for sleeping in. We won't even be in the room most of the time." He rubbed his palms together. "I've booked all kinds of excursions for the week."

My heart sank even further at that announcement as I tossed my purse on the comforter, cringing a little at the puff of dust that rose from it. "I was really hoping we could spend some time relaxing and sitting by the pool," I said after clearing my throat, giving my voice a chance to steady. "Especially at night, when we can really see the nebula."

"Nonsense!" He waved my words aside. "We're on vacation! We need to pack in as many activities as we can while we're here. We'll never come this far from Earth again. We need to do everything before we leave. Like we did that spacewalk." He gestured to me with a happy grin. "You loved that, right?"

No. I'd hated it. I'd told him as much, through tears actually, begging to return to the safe interior of the ship, and later that night, he'd railed at me for embarrassing him as all the other vacationers on the excursion had stared at me in pity when I'd broken down and sobbed in my spacesuit.

"You know I didn't," I whispered, still humiliated and depressed about that experience. Not to mention vaguely terrified about the fact that we'd be back up in the vacuum of space in seven days.

He shrugged. "So, you panicked when trying something new. It happens to the best of us." His tone implied that I wasn't in that category. At least, not in his estimation. He clapped his hands together. "Now, let's get settled in and get ready for our dinner tonight. I hear the restaurant at this hotel has hamburgers. Your favorite."

I hated hamburgers. He knew that.

~

Several hours later, I sat alone at the dining table in a restaurant as dumpy and questionable in cleanliness as the hotel room. I was alone because Nate had "taken a call" about something work-related and thus had to leave the restaurant to stand in the lobby on his communicator because, despite us being on our honeymoon, it was super important and couldn't be put off until he returned home.

Whenever I complained about him interrupting our leisure activities with work stuff, he reminded me that *his* job paid our bills, and unless I wanted to contribute something useful to the relationship, I shouldn't keep griping about it.

I knew how hard he worked, and how stressed out his job as liaison to the Akrellian Regional Advisor for Colorado made him. He had to work long, thankless hours, often staying after work until late into the night. He was exhausted most work days, which was one reason he'd really looked forward to this vacation, determined to plan every single detail himself, despite my offers to help with that. He hadn't let me plan the wedding, either, but then again, it hadn't been much of one.

Still, even with my nail art to keep me busy as I practiced the huge variety of designs that new clients—both human and extraterrestrial—kept requesting, I felt lonely when he wasn't there in our townhome. It was decorated in a very austere, ultramodern and nearly colorless fashion, gray and white and beige, with just a few stark slashes of black here and there. His ex-wife had chosen the décor, and he'd been too cheap to change it, or let me even add a few pictures to the barren walls or some colorful throw pillows to the sofas. It was a waste of money, he'd insisted, and it would clutter up the place, even worse than my "nail crap" did.

I felt eyes on me, my skin prickling and my head hunching

low as my shoulders rose defensively, embarrassed to still be sitting by myself as the waiter bot clanked past our table. Nate had now been gone for thirty minutes, leaving me to pick at the stale breadsticks as I waited for him to return so I could call the bot over to order.

I glanced around surreptitiously, then pulled my compact out of my purse and opened it to ostensibly check my makeup, which I'd spent a great deal of time perfecting before dinner, much to Nate's annoyance. He would always point out when it was flawed but hated how long it took to get it just right.

Covertly, I turned the mirror so I could take in the other diners, looking for whomever was staring at me so fixedly that I could feel their eyes on me.

A pair of ovoid black eyes in a gray face met mine in the mirror as I tilted it a little further to the right of my face so I could see the reflection of the table behind mine. I gasped and snapped the compact closed, my shoulders lifting higher as I huddled over the table. My hands toyed nervously with the bread plate in front of me as the hair all along the back of my neck stood on end.

I could sense the Lusian now as it got up and approached my table. I froze, swallowing my whimper of terror.

They had that kind of effect on people. Especially us humans. We all recalled the tales of the grays abducting and experimenting on humans before the Akrellians arrived to save us from an invasion of the ant-like Menops.

Some of those tales about the grays had proven to be true, and the Lusians, from the four-foot-tall ones like this one, to the slender and towering ones that dwarfed Nathan's six-foot two frame, made no attempt to deny those accusations—or even defend their actions.

They simply didn't care. Not about whether people liked or trusted them. Nor about whom they hurt.

The short Lusian paused next to my table. I could still feel its eyes upon me, though I avoided looking directly at it as it peered over the tabletop at me.

"C-can I help you?" I asked when it failed to move on after a long, tense silence. I slowly released my bread plate, so it didn't clatter against the table because of my shaking hands.

Lusians didn't approach people for idle conversation. If they spoke to a person, then there was some potentially nefarious intent behind their words.

"You must agree to take the trip," the Lusian said without any greeting. "It is your destiny."

I supposed I should be grateful it spoke aloud, as I'd heard they often just projected their thoughts into a person's head.

My terror was suddenly tempered by confusion as I gaped at the emotionless features of the eerie extraterrestrial.

I gestured hesitantly to the restaurant surroundings. "I already agreed to the trip. That's why I'm here."

The Lusian didn't turn its head. Instead, the fathomless black eyes remained fixed on my face, making me want to gulp past the lump in my throat. "The trip you will be offered. You must take it."

Those eyes shifted away from me, the Lusian's gaze turning towards the exit doors into the lobby, where Nathan had gone to take his call in private. "You must claim your destiny." The soul-searching gaze returned to me. "Or you will remain with *that* male for life." I detected no emotion in the almost robotic voice of the Lusian, but I still sensed the stress put on the word "that."

With those cryptic words, the terrifying alien with the child-sized frame turned and walked away in an odd loose-limbed gait, passing all the staring diners without a single pause or glance in their directions. It left through the same lobby doors that Nathan had gone through earlier.

A few minutes later, as I still sat stunned and confused, staring at those doors, Nathan stalked through them, striding towards me as if *he* was the impatient one, even though he'd made me wait for over forty Ubaid Standard minutes, judging by the holo-clock on the wall.

"Guess what," he said as he pulled out his chair to flop into it without a word of apology. When I remained mutinously silent, my lips compressed in irritation, he frowned, setting his hand on the tabletop to drum his fingers loudly. "*Well*? Go ahead. Guess."

"What?" I crossed my arms in front of me, regarding him through narrowed eyes, suddenly completely over his bullshit.

Not even a whiff of an apology on this man's lips! Because of him wandering off, I was accosted by a Lusian. Well, maybe not *accosted*, but still, speaking to one had been terrifying, especially since I'd been alone at the time. It was unlikely the few other diners in the restaurant would have come to my aid against one of *those* extraterrestrials.

Nathan sat back in his seat with a surprised expression, like he wasn't expecting me to be angry. "Hey, Veer, don't look at me like that!" He held out both hands in a shrug. "I know I took a bit of time with the job, but while I was in the lobby, I ran into a really friendly concierge. She told me—"

"She?" I snapped, my entire body tensing at the way his tone had changed when he mentioned this "concierge."

Nathan rolled his eyes and again drummed his fingers on the tabletop. "If you'll let me *finish*?" He glared at me until I sagged in my seat, my fire burning out. I was too tired and depressed for this crap.

The Lusian had left me shaken, and nothing about this trip had been enjoyable so far. Not a single thing.

"Right," he said in a smug way that made me want to beat him with my stale breadstick, "so, anyways... Crystal," he practically purred the woman's name, "told me all about this special excursion to the CivilRim," he quickly held up both hands as I opened my mouth to immediately reject the idea. "Not the region with all the pirates, Veer!" He shook his head firmly. "No, it's *another* part of the Rim. There's a solar system that was just mapped there, and this excursion will take us to the edge of the system. We'll be on one of the first starships to travel that close to it. Just *imagine*!"

He leaned fully back in his seat, oblivious to my gaping

silence, his eyes lifting to the ceiling where cobwebs swayed in the breeze kicked up by the air conditioning. "New worlds, still unexplored. One of them is a life-bearing planet with similar parameters to Earth. Someday, humans might even get the chance to colonize that planet, and we would have been the first to travel to its system."

I lifted my water glass with a trembling hand, the water inside it rippling as I brought it to my lips, my mouth and throat suddenly bone dry, making me unable to speak. Anxiety speared like a lance through my chest because I *knew*, with the certainty of death and taxes, that this was the "trip" the Lusian had been talking about.

His eyes lowered to meet mine. "*These* are the adventures we're out here in space to have!" He slashed a hand in the vague direction of the resort we weren't at. "Not wasting our time sitting by the pool at some over-priced tourist trap of a resort where you spend more time surrounded by other humans than you do on Earth."

I desperately sucked down water, and nearly choked on it.

He watched me for only a few breathless moments before he snapped, "So, are we going or not?"

I lowered my water glass, using two hands to hold it to keep it from shaking wildly enough that the water splashed out of it. Then I licked the moisture off my lips, covertly studying him through my lashes.

You must claim your destiny. Or you will remain with that male for life.

"Let's do it," I managed to squeak out, noting his broad beaming grin at my answer.

Chapter Two

Khamai (KAH-my)

I was cleaning my day's catch by the evening fire when something monstrous flew overhead with an ear-rending shriek, causing the tree canopy above me to tremble in the wake of its passage.

Certain it was Tytonid himself, the Taker of Souls—or at least one of his avatars—swooping down from the Dark Sprawl above to snatch up unwary spirits, I grabbed my spear from where it leaned against the stone beside me and jumped up from my seat on the ground in front of the flat stone that I'd been using as a work surface. I raced to the tree that held my *sway*—my temporary camping pod.

Tytonid's eyes were supposed to be closed this night, since I saw neither in the sky shining their purple light down upon the Sprawl that would cause a Prdayu's spirit to glow inside his body, like a beacon for the Soul Taker to hunt.

With one hand clutching the spear, I used my other, my feet, and my prehensile tail to swiftly climb up into the tangle of branches from which my *sway* dangled, fitting myself inside the tightest cluster of them, determined to wait out the night in the relative safety of these branches. Though my scales were already darkening to blend into the foliage, I doubted that alone would allow me to hide from the Soul Taker if he was hunting without his eyes.

If Tytonid was on the hunt for Prdayu spirits, then I wanted to be as difficult to catch as possible. I'd force the god of death to claw me out of the dense branches with his huge talons if he intended to consume me. When his ugly face appeared, I would stab at his massive round eyes with my spear.

He was a god, so I wouldn't be able to kill him, but I'd either destroy his physical form or I'd go down fighting. It was said that Tytonid rewarded those who fought against him, when he carried their spirits back up into the Dark Sprawl.

I stared down at the gently rocking dewdrop shape of my woven-vine and pod-stick *sway*, wondering if Tytonid would investigate that first, allowing me a chance to stab at his head from above.

I still heard the roar of wildly rustling leaves from when he'd passed overhead, but it had sounded as if he was heading away from my encampment.

Then a muted booming sound followed the distant cacophony of trees shattering and falling, suddenly silencing every noise in the Sprawl. This time, the trees themselves shook around me, instead of just their leaves, making my sway bounce and rock wildly.

As I crouched in tense silence, waiting for the tree-singers to begin their clicking again before I would dare to relax, the trees slowly ceased their nervous trembling. After a handful of snaps of the campfire burning below like an unintended beacon to draw Tytonid's eyes, the tettigar—the delicious tree-singers—returned to their evening song. The sound swelled back into the typical nightly noise.

My stomach rumbled and my tongue muscles flexed as the sounds of those insects reminded me of my own hunger. I hadn't finished cleaning the dendrobs I'd caught in my slurry traps, much less cooked and eaten them yet. They were down on the ground in their cage by the fire ring, most of them still covered in muck from the mud pond where I'd collected them.

Several of them still writhed in a lively fashion, though most of them had apparently given up trying to escape the confines of their cage. Their vividly colorful, delicately scaled, long bodies lay coiled in the mud soiling the bottom of the leaf-lined cage.

The one I'd been cleaning lay in a heap beside the guts I'd barely had a chance to pull from it before the nightmarish beast had flown overhead. It seemed that Tytonid's avatar had landed somewhere else, possibly pursuing some other prey more accessible than I was. I pitied that other soul but had no intention of trading places with them.

The night still had many fire-sticks left before Urcifa's Scales would reflect the dayglow back to the Sprawl, and I wasn't in a very comfortable position among the branches. I gazed longingly at my sway, wishing I was inside it being rocked to sleep by the gentle night breeze.

The breeze blowing now carried an odd scent to it, something like hot stones wafting past, but not quite. Not like any heated stone I'd ever scented before. I also detected an unusual underlying bitter odor that I couldn't place if my life depended on it.

Which it might.

In all the lore spoken by the village taleteller, I'd heard of many heroes battling Tytonid to save their souls or the souls of others, but the keepers never got into what those heroes scented during their battles. Pity. It might have been useful information to have at this moment. Maybe Tytonid's foul avatars had this scent, and it would be something I could use to track him.

Or avoid him, which would be the wiser course of action.

A tree-singer landed nearby, probably drawn by the firelight glowing from below. Without thought, my tongue shot out and latched onto its carapace. I'd pulled it back to my mouth before the other singers fell silent, and I chewed quickly, enjoying the crunch of its carapace and the weak flutter of its wings before it stopped twitching.

This time, the sudden silence of the tree-singers was more localized to my campsite as they recognized a threat among them, but eventually, they would begin their song again, as they always did, though they might avoid the sway. Or they might not. The tettigar weren't known for intelligence.

This one was only a quick snack. I swallowed it almost as quickly as I'd chewed it, lifting a hand to pick a couple of the legs out of my sharp teeth. I'd come to prefer tettigar roasted over a fire as some of the other villagers liked to do, but when I was away from my fire, it was more expedient to eat them raw as I'd been doing since I was born.

Thoughts of the village brought on the same depression they usually did as I stared glumly down at my dying campfire and the sullenly moving dendrobs in the cage beside it. I had nothing but time to dwell on such things while I waited out the night, knowing Tytonid didn't hunt by day. At least, not according to the tales imparted by the teller.

I wondered how my sister was doing and whether she'd accepted a beaded collar yet, or maybe she'd even climbed the Life Tree already. I didn't know if I had nieces or nephews, and that might be the saddest part of this exile for me.

Our parents had died when she was still a young spawn. Since then, I'd always looked out for her, being ten season-turnings older. I'd hunted for us, spoken up for us in the village, and had even stalked and then slayed the shadow grabber that had crept back around our tree-net, several season-turnings after it had claimed the souls of our parents.

There hadn't even been any remains of my parents to bury beneath the Bone Tree, but we planted their spears at the base of it to guide their souls to Tytonid's Perch so that he might carry them up to the Dark Sprawl. I only hoped my sister continued to make offerings to the god of death for our parents' sake, and that their eternal place among the dark trees was a happy one. Sometimes, I searched the Dark Sprawl at night hoping that some of the glowing lights I saw sparkling among the dark trees were my parents' souls.

At least my sister was still safe in the village.

I would kill for my sister. In fact, I *had* killed for her, and that was why I was in exile now. When our chief had decided he wanted her, but had already given his beaded collar to another, he hadn't accepted her demurral with grace. She'd been too young to defend herself, but fortunately, she'd managed to escape him before he'd completed his assault, and she'd run back to our tree-net, that slurry skink right on her tail.

I flashed teeth as I recalled the satisfying moment of his death at the point of my spear buried in his chest, his body beaten and torn from my fists and claws after our battle. I'd known even then that I would be—at best—exiled for killing him. At worst, I'd be thrown to the snapper grove on the boundary of our village territory. I didn't care then, and despite my depression at being condemned to remain forever alone, I still wouldn't have changed my decision. His position would have let him get away with what he'd done to my sister, and I couldn't allow that.

The chieftain's mate had been the one to plead for mercy for me, and I pitied her, because it was clear she knew exactly what kind of male he'd been. Because of her pleas, I was only exiled, but there were days—and nights—where I'd wondered if it was a mercy to be left alive but forever alone in the Sprawl with nothing but the tree-singers to talk to. They never had much to say, despite how much noise they made.

I'd tried to keep myself busy, building another tree-net in the Dense, where I was the largest predator who could fit through the thick foliage. Over the season-turnings, my tree-net had spread from a single, simple sway to a full net of vine-connected pods, all dangling like ripe fruit from the branches of the largest trees in the Dense.

It was ironic to me that I had the time and resources to build such a massive home when I would be the only one to ever live in it. Adding pods kept me busy, but I had nothing to put in them now. I'd already built all my workshops, not to mention a sleeping pod that would put the chieftain's tree-net to shame.

I'd taken to adding details like balconies and perches because why not? Collecting materials, going through the painstaking process to shape them, and then adding them to my tree-net ate up the time—and I had an abundance of time with no one else to care for but myself.

In a wistful mood, I'd once made a beaded collar, though I'd had no female in mind when I'd crafted it, carving each bead from bone and wood, collecting fibers to make into thread that I'd dyed the same vibrant blues, yellows, and greens as my scales, and then weaving it all together. I'd daydreamed, and sometimes even had sleep visions that guided my choices for color, pattern, and design, and in the end, the collar had been the most beautiful thing I'd ever created. It was a pity no female would ever wear it.

I would never get the chance to climb a Life Tree with a mate. No other Prdayu would agree to living in exile with me. She also wouldn't want to have spawn without having the protection of a village around them.

Not that a village had protected my own parents. It was a bitter thought, but one I'd had often enough.

I'd hidden that beaded collar inside a basket in my weaving pod after I completed it, unable to even look at it anymore, though I'd spent half a season-turning crafting it. It was a painful reminder of what I would never have. It was also a harsh reminder of how lonely I'd become that I would spend so much of my time making something that would never be necessary, for a phantom mate who would never materialize out of my dreams.

Cleaning the dendrobs and smoking them over the fire would have kept me busy enough to avoid all these ponderous thoughts, but hiding in the branches above my sway, waiting and admittedly fearing the talons of Tytonid gave me far too much time to dwell. Enough time that I grew impatient with my rumbling stomach and roiling mind before half the night had even passed.

Feeling fatalistic, I left my hiding spot and climbed down from the tree to return to my campfire.

If Tytonid intended to claim my soul tonight, then I would face him boldly. He would not find me dark-scaled and cowering inside a cluster of branches.

Chapter Three

Vera

THIS WAS OFFICIALLY the *worst* vacation I'd ever been on. The fact that it was also supposed to be my honeymoon only added to the pure misery I was experiencing now. Granted, some of my predicament was my fault, but I laid all the blame for it at Nathan's feet.

If I hadn't caught him tongue-deep in another woman's mouth, I wouldn't have confronted him in a shrieking fury, my temper finally snapping after he'd dragged me on this miserable trip only for him to cheat on me with a woman he'd met literally that morning.

She was the first mate of the ship he'd chartered to bring us to this part of the CivilRim, and it was only *after* we were stuck on a ship with a questionable crew of six that I'd learned that we were traveling to forbidden territory, in violation of probably a hundred different Cosmic Syndicate laws and codes.

Of course, Nathan had insisted that "you didn't get a once-in-a-lifetime experience if you waited until you could wade through all the red-tape of bureaucracy," but I'd still demanded to be taken back to the hotel, telling him he could break the law by himself.

Obviously, the mercenary crew and Nate himself had only laughed at my distress. After that humiliating encounter, I'd hidden in our cramped cabin for hours, but when I'd gone to seek out Nathan later, I'd found him making out with Naja—as she'd introduced herself to us not even six hours earlier.

She'd found my fury amusing, not even bothering to hide her laughter as I'd flown into a rage, calling them both every name in the book. As disgusted as I was by this woman who'd gone after a married man without the slightest bit of hesitation or remorse, the blame really lay with Nathan—the cheating bastard.

He hadn't been nearly so amused by my outrage. He'd turned the accusations back upon me, insisting that I had driven him to seek comfort elsewhere because of my "shitty attitude." Then he'd threatened divorce, and I'd run from the room, blinded by tears.

Since I'd heard him following, I'd found a hiding spot to calm down and really think things through, because I didn't want a divorce, but my heart was breaking, and I wasn't sure I could remain married to someone who thought so little of me that he would cheat on me with a total stranger the minute my back was turned.

Unfortunately, I'd hidden in an escape pod. When I'd heard Nate calling for me, I'd slammed my fist on the big red button on the control panel, thinking I was merely shutting the door to lock him out, but apparently, I'd launched the damned thing.

To make matters worse, the computer in it was an absolute mess, I had no idea how to fly it, it was practically falling apart, and there was no survival pack or even any tools in the pod, because the charter crew was clearly as cheap as Nate was.

So, I ended up landing—sorta crashing—on the life-bearing planet Nate had been so eager about, because that was "the only planet that will support your fragile and woefully inadequate life-form" according to the escape pod's snarky ass computer. It had an attitude. Maybe I shouldn't have called it an outdated piece of crap, but I'd been panicking at the time.

Besides, who knew you had to be polite to a computer?

At least I discovered a survival suit in the pod, complete with heavy duty boots and gloves, and a malfunctioning helmet, with begrudging assistance from the pod-computer. Though the moment I stepped out of the somewhat crashed pod to investigate my immediate surroundings, sans broken helmet because the computer insisted the air was breathable, I stripped off the gloves and tossed them back inside it.

I debated stripping off the entire bulky suit, because it was hot and muggy in the alien jungle that I'd found myself in, even at night. It felt like standing inside a sauna, as sweat soaked my tee shirt and shorts beneath the survival suit.

"I'm dying," I moaned, lifting a hand to tug at the collar of my survival suit as I considered giving up on my plan to check the exterior of the pod to make sure it would hold up for the rest of the night—however long that might end up being.

The survival suit had definitely been misnamed.

"There's this little round thing on the front of your suit called a 'temperature dial,'" the pod computer said from external speakers on the dented-up, rusted, and more than a little scorched side of the downed escape pod. "Perhaps you should turn it to a more comfortable temperature."

I jerked in surprise at the sudden sound in the dead silence of the dark jungle, then realized it was the computer speaking to me as I shifted my glare from the huge rust spots on the side of the pod to the doorway that was still gaping open after I left it. "I totally knew that! I was just testing you to see if you'd actually tell me about it."

Then I patted the front of the suit, searching fruitlessly for said dial.

"The *inside* of the front of your suit," Snarky A.I. finally piped up after letting me flail at the stiff, heavy material of the suit for a couple long, muggy minutes.

"Who puts a dial on the *inside* of a survival suit?" I demanded like I knew anything about proper survival suit design and wore them all the time.

I mean, it seemed like a bad idea to have to open your suit to turn the dial when you were wearing the suit in the first place to protect yourself from the environment.

Then again, this suit was probably as cheap and defective as the escape pod and the computer that controlled it. The helmet was definitely garbage.

"All starship passengers should have been briefed on the difference between a vacuum suit, an environmental suit, and a simple survival suit." Snarky sounded judgmental.

I didn't like judgmental software.

"You'd already be dead if you required airtight suit seals," it said condescendingly.

Was condescension even *allowed* for computers?

Besides, obviously I didn't think it was a sealed suit since I wasn't even wearing the basic survival helmet. And I *had* been briefed on the different safety gear when I'd boarded the shuttle on Earth. I'm not an idiot. I'm just...stressed.

Yeah... stressed.

"Stick your hand inside the chest pouch to access the internal dial." Computers also weren't supposed to sound exasperated. This one was definitely malfunctioning. "The interior of the suit isn't accessible through the control pouch. It's designed to keep the dial safe from external environmental factors so that it continues to function properly."

I slowly slid my hands down the front seam of the suit until I found the split in the material that I hadn't noticed earlier when I'd been pulling it on to check outside the pod for the important things—like food, water, shelter, and getting away from the bargain basement version of an escape pod computer and its constant yammering.

After slipping my hand into the pouch on the inside of the seam, I felt the control dial and turned it until I heard a fan on the back of the suit kick on as the suit puffed out around me from the cool-*ish* air that it circulated when a small compressor also situated on the back of the suit hummed to life.

"Oh good," Snarky said in a sarcastic tone. "You seem to have turned it to cool."

"What?" I shot another angry glare at the escape pod. "Are you saying I could have accidentally made it *hotter* in this suit?"

"It appears you managed not to do so." Snarky didn't have to sound so surprised. "I *did* suggest you listen to the manual prior to donning the suit." I bit my lip as it continued, "And I believe *you* suggested that I 'stuff it, Snarks,' as I recall."

I'd been a little anxious at the time and the computer's constant barking at me had made me a bit...testy in my desire to escape it, and this pod that had nearly killed me by crash-landing me on an alien planet after all, so I already wasn't fond of it.

I grunted a nonresponse, then tromped around the exterior of the escape pod, noting with relief that it was all still in one piece. I didn't go far into the dark jungle before returning to the safety of the escape pod, having spotted not a single grocery store or gas station sign in sight.

"So, about the rescue beacon...." I said as I stepped back into the pod.

I pulled open the suit once the door shut and the climate control hummed in the pod to drift cool air from the vents over my face.

I realized I was not cut out for jungle survival, at all. Even if I did have a suit and heavy boots to protect me from the various and sundry things that could happen to my fragile and woefully inadequate lifeform on a planet where at least I didn't need a helmet.

"I am afraid that is malfunctioning." Snarky didn't sound very afraid at all. It sounded gleeful. "Beacon activation upon landing is standard protocol. However, the beacon appears to be damaged beyond repair."

"Uh... I held up a hand to stop those words I didn't want to hear. "You'd better not be telling me we're *stuck* here, Snarky!"

"I see." It remained silent as I waited for more.

"Well?" I demanded after several long, breathless moments. "*What* are you trying to tell me?"

"You just commanded me not to say we're stuck here, did you not?" it asked smugly.

"Arghhhh!" I clenched my fists above my head. "This can't be happening to me!" My voice rose to a near-hysterical shriek as I gripped the sides of my head.

I'm pretty sure I had a small nervous breakdown after that, but I eventually recovered after I stomped around the interior of the escape pod for a while, calling Nathan every bad name I had ever heard in my life.

Then I collapsed to sit on the floor of the pod, not wanting to squish myself back into one of the dozen uncomfortable seats all crammed in the single cabin of the pod like airline seats. Only the floor by the door of the pod was clear enough for me to fully stretch out and lay down to try to get some sleep until hopefully daylight came, and I could figure out what to do next.

As far as I could tell, I was stuck on an alien planet in a jungle with strange trees, odd giant mushrooms, and flowers that looked big enough to contain human-sized fairies, and I had no way to signal anyone about where I was. Not that I was certain Nate and his new mercenary buddies would even come looking for me.

The oxygen levels were optimal though—even better than the air on Earth. And Snarky claimed not to detect any airborne toxins in the area, according to the pod's scanner. I could survive the environment. In fact, I even felt a bit lighter here, despite the heavy bulk of the suit as I tread nervously along the furrow the pod had made after it had crashed into the trees.

My mood had fluctuated between panicky and depressed and

hopeless, circling back around over and over again throughout the night. By the time the morning broke, I'd awakened still feeling exhausted. I was also very thirsty, and my stomach was growling, reminding me that I hadn't eaten on the charter ship, nor had I drunk any water since I'd boarded it. They'd only offered watered-down booze on that ship.

Snarky had coolly informed me when I'd asked that it had no idea what was edible on this planet, much less where I could find safe drinking water, and since the damned pod had no survival packs—in direct violation of Syndicate Escape Pod Code 37-89, which was *clearly* posted on the wall of the pod by the empty supply cabinet—I had to leave the pod and head out into a terrifying alien jungle with literally nothing to protect me other than an antique survival suit that had probably been too decrepit for the charter crew to pawn.

Given that the cooler in the suit was already sounding like it was about to crap out, I was guessing I would be stripped down to my "Newlywed" oversized sparkly tee shirt and skintight shorts by the end of the day, however long that turned out to be. I *really* wish I hadn't only brought sandals on this trip so I could show off my pedicure. The boots I was now wearing were way too big, even with the adjustable straps.

I'd wasted precious time before I'd started out searching for a sharp stick to bash or poke anything that looked like it was about to eat me, but eventually I had to give up when the thirst grew too strong to ignore. Given how humid the air was, you'd think I could drink water droplets right out of it, but instead, my continuous sweating only dehydrated me more.

I walked cautiously through the jungle, keeping my eyes peeled and my ears open for the sound of running water, though the noise from the alien cicadas was nearly deafening, and I heard plenty of other terrifying scary sounds going on under that constant clicking hum. I felt jumpy, waiting for something to attack me, and I'd already shrieked and leapt away several times from small vines or hanging moss brushing over my head or along my shoulder.

Oh, and those *cicadas* were bigger than my hand, I found out, as I passed a tree where a few of them clung to the bark, nearly giving me a heart attack when one of them fluttered its wings like *I* made *it* nervous.

I hadn't even seen them until it had moved, they were so well camouflaged.

After that lovely sight, I was grateful I had no water left in my body to piss myself, because this jungle only got stranger and more terrifying. I could only wonder what other unseen things were hidden among the thick foliage, huge banana tree-like leaves, massive clusters of colorful capped mushrooms, and brightly petaled flowers.

If a fairy suddenly shoved its way out of one of those tight flower buds and demanded a toll from me, I wouldn't have been surprised.

My fear waned as the morning passed on and the sun rose higher, the light fully piercing the canopy to shine directly on me, I was certain, following me like a spotlight. It just made everything hotter. And me without an ounce of sunscreen, which I'd left in my suitcase on the cruise ship.

I was feeling a little cranky now rather than scared. The heat and mugginess were sapping my strength, and my energy for fear, and the suit felt like it weighed a ton now, even if the fan and compressor inside it was making the temperature mildly more bearable.

By the time I smelled smoke, I felt like I was more likely to die of thirst than from any animal or insect in this jungle. Smoke meant fire, and fire could mean civilization. Surely, someone civilized would have clean water to drink.

Of course, common sense warned me that I was making some heavy assumptions, but I could already taste clear, clean water on my tongue. I shoved through the leaves incautiously as the scent of smoke increased, and suddenly found myself in a small clearing.

Trees towered above me, patches of yellow and blue flowers on long, thick stalks growing around their trunks, and in the center of the clearing, a ring of stones encircled a smoldering campfire. Beside the fire ring sat several large, flat stones—big enough to serve as benches, and next to one of those stones was what looked like a corked gourd the size of a gallon jug.

Close to the smoldering coals, nearly over the fire itself, stood a vertical rack made of sticks that looked like bamboo tied together by some kind of cording. Jerky strips the color of root beer dangled from the horizontal bamboo-like slats of the rack.

"Hello?" I called out, knowing logically that whoever had made that fire likely didn't speak any human language, or even *any* language that the translator devices Nate had bought us would have known. Not that I still had mine, which was no doubt sitting in the cabin on that charter ship.

"Is anyone there?"

The thought of meeting an actual alien might have scared me much more eight years ago, before the Menops invaded Earth. Now, I saw aliens—*extraterrestrials*, I was constantly reminded to say instead—on a daily basis. Still, I was more than a little nervous to meet an extraterrestrial who likely wasn't from a Cosmic Syndicate member species, all of whom spoke English or had computerized translators that spoke it for them.

Despite the jerky rack and the jug, and the still smoking coals, the campsite appeared empty. As I glanced around though, my eyes lifted upwards and widened when I spotted a strange, teardrop-shaped pod dangling among the leaves and branches of the tallest tree. It appeared to be woven of vines and maybe more of those bamboo-like sticks that made up the drying rack.

It was undoubtedly a sign of intelligent life, even if I could have doubted it from the campfire and food. It was also undoubtedly native intelligent life, since whoever had made that pod knew this jungle well enough to build such a shelter.

"Excuse me," I called a little louder, in a trembling voice, my heart thudding away in my chest with my growing terror of meeting some hostile extraterrestrial on their home turf. "Can I have the password to your Wi-Fi?" I chuckled nervously at my own pathetic joke.

I crept a little further into the clearing, too desperate to turn tail and run when I needed food and water so badly that I was certain I wouldn't get far before I collapsed.

Maybe I shouldn't call out. I should probably be stealthy instead. Not that I was cut out for the sneak thief life, but at this point, I would do anything for precious water. And the scents coming from that smoked jerky were pretty heavenly too.

If the extraterrestrial was asleep in their little teardrop home that was way too far up in the trees for me to climb to knock on the door—though I couldn't see from here if it had one—then maybe I could steal some food and hopefully that jug, which I prayed was full of water and not alien booze.

I was shaking with the need for water when I made it to the fire ring without any sounds coming from the tree house. Apparently, the alien hadn't heard me. I needed to move quickly.

I reached the gourd and bent to pluck off the cork, lifting the heavy thing with both hands so I could take a cautious whiff of the contents.

My nose immediately recognized the scent of water, and my entire body ached with the demand that I drink it. Knowing it could contain all kinds of dangerous things, but not having many options and too thirsty to care, I tipped the gourd to my lips right then and there. I couldn't even care that I might be discovered by the alien. I was way too thirsty, and when that familiar liquid splashed against my lips, I moaned in relief and gulped great mouthfuls, until it was spilling down the front of my suit.

I drank so much that my belly ached, but the gourd still had some water in it, and I was *so* stealing it. I felt only a little bad about that, because clearly the alien knew this jungle and could find more.

Me, not so much. It was a matter of survival. Screw ethics and morals at this point.

Then I bent to snag a piece of the jerky, because my stomach, water-soaked as it now was, still grumbled in hunger.

I hissed as I discovered that it was hotter than I expected, and let it drop from my fingers, but desperation had me bracing myself against the heat to grab it again as my mouth watered, allowing me to ignore the sting of it as I brought it up to my nose to sniff it. It smelled a little fishy, but I stuck my tongue out to taste it anyway.

The flavor of some savory spice with a hint of a kick burst over my tongue, and I took a bite, discovering it wasn't as hot as I'd initially thought, then another, finding that the chewy meat had a delicious flavor that was heaven in that moment.

Glancing around, searching the campsite for any sign of the alien, I bent to snake more of the jerky and quickly stuffed it into the front pouch of my suit, before reinforcing my grip on the water gourd. That dial pouch probably wasn't meant to be a pocket, but I didn't exactly bring my jerky-stealing suit on this trip.

I turned to leave, fearing that I was testing my luck with each moment that passed, but I sent one last wistful glance at the campfire and the meat still hanging there, all abandoned and unclaimed by a careless alien who'd just left it out for any ol' animal to come along and steal it.

I guess I was that animal today.

I mean, clearly, the alien didn't need it that badly if they weren't guarding it.

Then I heard a faint sound of rustling leaves coming from the trees nearby, and I decided that I had enough now to get me back to the safety of my escape pod. I could always come back later to see if the meat was still there to take the rest.

Chapter Four

Khamai

The turning of Urcifa's Scales brought on the new day with my soul intact and no sign of the god of death still haunting the jungle. Every creature in the Sprawl was making their usual morning noise, a comforting and familiar refrain that told me all was well, at least as far as the many eyes of the Sprawl could see.

I was still a little tired, having spent most of the night by my fire rather than sleeping in my sway. I'd cleaned and skinned all the dendrobs, and now had several nutshell bowls filled with drying scales to make the pigments for my paints and dyes, as well as plenty of dendrob meat liberally salted and spiced that were now smoking on a rack near the fire. I'd already cleaned and sharpened my stone filleting knife and sheathed it in its leather holder to tuck it back inside my pack.

I left the coals smoldering to dry the dendrob meat but didn't bother to roast the tettigars that grew incautious enough to serve as my breakfast. My tongue was my best weapon when it came to catching a quick meal, and tree-singers were a favorite of mine. There were other insects and small, furred crawlers that also frequently fell victim to my striking tongue, but variety wouldn't be a blessing for me on this day. Despite everything appearing to be normal, I sensed an uneasiness in the hidden life moving around me.

That apprehension didn't come from wariness of a predator in their midst. Something was in the air. It wasn't a smell, or a sound, but rather a feeling of tension, as if the cordage of a pod floor was stretched to its limit and ready to snap.

I debated following the path of Tytonid to see if wherever that booming sound had come from revealed any clues as to the pall now hanging over the very trees. I wouldn't have said I lacked courage, but I also didn't lack intelligence like the foolish tree-singers. I ended up dismissing the idea of stumbling blindly into the talons of a god's avatar.

Let that part of the Sprawl retain its mystery. I would move my camp away from the disturbance—the potential nest of the flying night beast—instead. Once I finished checking the last of my slurry traps.

I packed up all my pouches, bowls, and tools, hanging my packs in the trees near my sway, but left the meat rack by the smoldering coals, along with the large and unwieldy gourd jug of drinking water I'd collected from the basin leaves that stored puddles of morning dew. The setron root I'd added to the fire as I fed small branches to the coals should repel any hungry pests not deterred by the heat of the smoldering coals.

It shouldn't take me too long to collect my traps, and I'd likely have at least a few handfuls more of dendrobs to clean and smoke before breaking camp for good to move on to a location further away from whatever had landed in the Sprawl.

I wasn't eager to return to the Dense, even if I had completed my trapping and gathering trip instead of having only begun. Being back at the tree-net just reminded me of how empty it was, despite all the furnishings I kept adding to it. At least out here in the Open Sprawl, there were dangers to keep my mind occupied. Threats that made my scales shift, though not as many as we'd always been told when we were younger to keep us close to the village.

Shadow grabbers were the worst threat that I knew of, other than Tytonid himself, but they were solitary creatures that claimed large territories. It was rare to come across one, and I'd only ever seen one once in my life.

Once was enough, and I'd slayed the beast, but I wasn't brave enough to seek a repeat of that experience.

The smaller beasts of the Open Sprawl were easy enough for me to kill with my spear or throwing stones, and Prdayu often hunted them, so they were more wary of me than I of them, not that they wouldn't take any chance they got to attack if I had my guard down.

The deadliest creatures in the Sprawl were the venomous ones, but most of them offered colorful warnings, and were usually small and non-aggressive unless I bothered them. Since I'd learned at a very young age not to poke colorful creatures, I knew to avoid disturbing them. Although I occasionally trapped glonuras, the vividly patterned amphibians that proliferated around slurry ponds, so I could harvest their toxin for my blow darts.

That was a delicate procedure, since one wrong move with those creatures would result in my death. I didn't use poison darts often because they were a pain in my tail to work with.

I kept my eyes moving as I walked the Sprawl, heading towards the slurry pond closest to my camp, where I'd sunk some traps after noting that the muddy brown surface of the pond rippled with teeming dendrobs.

It was their mating season, so they were active, making it easier to trap them. They usually remained deep in the muck at the bottom of the slurry, close to where hot water bubbled up from the ground to form the muck-filled ponds, raising the temperature too much for me to fish them out by claw, nor could I spear them when I couldn't see through the mud.

Not only did they move towards the surface during mating

season—and thus into my netted traps—many of the creatures wriggled their way out of the slurry and onto the firmer mud, thrashing around with their partners to leave whorls and ridges in the ground that would harden during the dry season.

Their iridescent, vivid coloring stood out from the muck as obviously as the faceted glitterstones crafted in secret ways by the village stonemaster. Urcifa's scales, the villagers called those stones, formed from the common—but extremely hard—clearstones that were scattered along riverbeds and found in rock crusts in caves and crevices. The faceted versions reflected the dayglow like Urcifa's scales, only even more brilliantly, flashing and glimmering and casting rainbows of color on other surfaces.

A beaded collar made with Urcifa's scales would be a priceless gift for a mate.

The slurry pond was as rippled as it had been the day before, and I was pleased to see that my traps were full when I pulled the netted cages free from the muck. I emptied the dendrobs into my larger muck cage, then hooked all the traps together and tied them to my spear haft, using it as a carrying pole draped over my shoulders to balance the weight of the traps.

I was about to move on to the next slurry pond after wrapping my tail around the handle of the dendrob cage with its writhing prey, when I noted that the Sprawl around me had fallen silent. My scales darkened, my crest bristles rattling softly with tension as I turned my head to search the surrounding trees.

Humid heat caused a waver in the air that mimicked movement, but there was no breeze to cause the leaves to tremble. Everything remained still except for the rippling of the slurry and the plopping and squishing sounds of the dendrobs, who lacked the sense to notice any danger around them.

I unshouldered my spear, pushing the traps off it, then looping the strap around the haft of it as I canted the tip of it forward. My tail coiled tighter around the cage, the three front toe claws of each of my feet digging into the soft ground, while the paired rear toe claws on each foot pushed off from the ground, balancing me in a springing stance.

I didn't scent anything unusual in the air, but my sense of smell wasn't as strong as my vision, not by a long shot. Nor was my hearing, though my ear-flares spread to listen for any unfamiliar sounds in the heavy silence. When I heard nothing other than the slither and slide of dendrobs, I decided that it might be best to return to my campsite and collect my things.

Something most strange was happening in the Sprawl, and I might be better off returning to the Dense to wait out whatever the night wind had brought to this land.

Then again, I wondered if I should worry so much about staying alive, since I had nothing much to live for, and each day was dragging into the next with no real hope of change. In fact, the strangeness of last night had been the first time my interest had been piqued in so long that I realized that I hadn't felt as alive as I did in that moment since I'd fought and then slayed our chief.

It didn't take long to return to my campsite, but as I neared it, I heard a strange cooing sound, unlike anything I'd ever heard in the Sprawl before. It was only a soft sound, and it had come from my campsite clearing. Since I remained in the concealment of the trees, I shifted my scales to fully camouflage myself, moving stealthily through the shadows as I approached my own campfire, edging around the clearing until I crouched below my sway.

My gaze wasn't lifted to my temporary housing though. It was fixed on the odd creature currently stealing the water from my jug, clutching it with pale, clawless hands and gulping it directly from the mouth of the gourd.

The creature stood on two legs like a Prdayu, but instead of scales, it had odd, saggy skin all over its shapeless tube of a body. The creature's body color patch was a vivid orange that was unlike any of the multitude of colors found in the surrounding Sprawl. It appeared to be shorter than me by at least a head, but the bulky body suggested it might still be strong despite its small stature.

The creature also appeared to have a furred tail jutting from the back of its head, and as I studied it from the shadows, I spotted more fur spots above the hollows of its eyes, even though the skin of its pale face and the vivid reddish patches on the cheeks appeared to be lacking fur.

The long head-tail fell almost to the middle of the creature's back and was a light-yellow color that glimmered in the dayglow, reminiscent of the warm rays of light reflected by Urcifa's Scales. The creature's eyes were cast in shadow by the gourd jug, but even from where I stood, they looked to be closed as it clumsily drank my water, allowing half of it to spill down its wrinkly orange skin.

The body color patch turned darker orange when the water spilled over it, causing my brow ridges to pull together as I pondered the strange texture of it. It was almost like it was woven or looped the way our tapestries, rugs, and blankets were. Yet, I'd never seen a weave or loop so fine before, nor fibers so shiny that they reflected the dayglow as the creature's orange body patch did.

I had a brief flash of excitement at the thought that this could be Urcifa, come from the sky to grace my camp, but quickly pushed such a fanciful idea away. If Tytonid had returned to the Sprawl, maybe Urcifa was right on his tail feathers, but the goddess was supposed to be a Prdayu in appearance, with shining scales of every possible color.

Not this ugly orange shade that couldn't be found even in the most garish of Sprawl flowers.

The creature had other color patches on its odd body, in addition to the yellow fur on its head and brow ridges. Its face, neck, and hand color patches were a red-tinged beige, almost creamy in appearance, like the sweet sap harvested from the stem of a dayglow blossom to make fermented vivi drinks. Then there were those brighter red cheek patches.

It also had strange feet that were dark gray, nearly the same shade as some of my bristles. Though those feet were shiny in the dayglow coming through the canopy of trees, they weren't loose and wrinkly like the orange skin on its body. The dark gray skin was pulled tightly around its lower legs, and its feet were smooth with no toes at all.

More like hooves, though not the same as those that the loam rooters had. This creature had odd, flattened hooves that extended forward from the legs at the base of them.

A part of me still wanted to believe that this bizarre creature that was unlike anything I'd ever seen before in the Sprawl was Urcifa's avatar, and so I pictured it as female, though it looked nothing like the females from the village. Even though their crests were smaller than a male's, they at least had them. This creature had only the long fringes of her head-tail fur and that unusual creamy, red-tinged skin instead of scales.

The variations in her coloring didn't seem to be intended for camouflage or even display. In fact, that orange shade was distinctly off-putting to me, as vibrant as it was.

Still, I was beyond curious now, and she didn't look like she posed much of a threat despite the vivid coloration that could indicate toxicity. I watched her set the gourd down and swipe her mouth with one orange arm, then glance around, her gaze sliding right past me without spotting me. I was taken aback by the luminous, striking blue color of her eyes. They were the same shade as some of my bristles.

Their beauty awed me, and again I wondered if this was a goddess standing in my encampment.

Then she quickly removed that notion as she bent and snagged a piece of dendrob meat from the rack between two blunt fingers, and then hissed in obvious pain at the heat of it, nearly dropping it in the dirt. With a clumsy motion, she caught it again and lifted it up to her unusual, beak-like snout—also marked with a red stripe color patch—and sniffed it.

Her face crinkled as she shook her head, but then she touched the meat to her lips, making me wonder if a head shake meant something different to her than it did to a Prdayu.

I could barely see the tiny, round tip of her tongue as she licked the meat with clear caution, then smacked her lips together.

She glanced around again, still not spotting me, then took a bite of the dendrob meat.

She made a humming sound and gobbled it up in three swift bites, barely chewing as she stuffed it into her mouth. Then she sucked the tips of her fingers with smacking sounds. She glanced furtively around again, before crouching by the meat rack to snatch a handful of the smoked dendrob fillets, stuffing them into the front of her orange skin like she had a pouch in the manner of a tree-crawler.

With a final sweep of her gaze over the camp, she grabbed my water jug, carrying it with both hands, and pulled it close against her tube-like body. Then she snuck away, casting a last glance over her shoulder at the campfire, like she wanted to take the rest of the meat on the rack.

She must have thought better of it as she scurried off into the foliage moments later.

Chapter Five

Khamai

I FOLLOWED the mysterious creature as she hoofed her way through the Sprawl with her heavy, flattened feet leaving bizarre tracks in the loam. She seemed unaware that I was there, but that wasn't surprising. I could blend very well into my surroundings when I wanted to, unlike her with her vivid orange skin that didn't appear to shift color at all other than when it got wet, even when she was clearly startled or alarmed at things as harmless as leaves and moss shifting in the breeze.

I noted that we were traveling in the same direction that Tytonid had taken the night before, and my thought that she might be related to the god of death in some way only increased as the Sprawl grew quieter the further we traveled in that direction.

It wasn't nearly long enough before I discovered exactly what she was returning to with my stolen water gourd clutched so tightly against her.

I paused well beyond the scar in the foliage that had obviously been formed by the gleaming, winged monstrosity that nested in the churned-up loam, crushing trees and shrubs beneath its weight. It shone silver in the dayglow, but it was a dirty gleam, pocked and marked with scrapes and reddish spots in varying sizes all along its body.

I wondered if *this* was the mighty Tytonid, his physical avatar slain once again by a great hero.

I returned my skeptical gaze to the orange-skinned female who approached the fallen beast with no sign of fear. If anything, she seemed to speed her steps as she grew closer, and she made more of her odd sounds, adding many noisy exhalations of air to the constant low humming sound she emitted. These new sounds didn't seem quite like she was only breathing.

She didn't strike me as a mighty warrior, despite her bulky frame. But if she *was* the avatar of Urcifa, as I'd initially considered, then perhaps she had great powers I couldn't see at the moment.

I slowly climbed into the tree closest to the scar, finding a safe branch on which to perch to watch her as she walked closer to the beast. I unshouldered my spear and held it ready with both hands as I crouched in the tree, my feet and tail wrapping around the branch supporting me. I wasn't sure whether I was merely intending to protect myself if the monster suddenly came to life, or if I felt protective of the strange orange and dayglow sap-colored creature too.

She exhaled a long, loud breath, her shoulders slumping as she finally set my gourd jug down beside the flank of the fallen beast like an offering. Then she lifted both of her clawless hands to smooth down the furs around her head-tail. As she did so, her wrinkly, saggy skin tightened, revealing odd lumps on her chest.

As I cocked my head and narrowed my eyes, pondering what sort of creature she might be, the beast suddenly made a screeching sound as a maw opened on its flank, instead of at the pointed beak of it as I'd both feared and expected.

It seemed like it would swallow the lumpy orange creature at any moment.

"*Iza boutime,*" the orange thief cawed like a shrill bird, but she seemed more exasperated then alarmed by the suddenly gaping maw. *"Wazeidee ah oflockingme ow teh."*

Surely, the thief, brazen as she clearly was, didn't think she stood a chance against Tytonid, who still appeared to be alive.

Then again, if this was Urcifa, in some bizarre form never described by the tellers, she might be responsible for Tytonid's current grounded condition. Perhaps she even now mocked her eternal rival.

When the fallen beast made an answering call in an odd, echoing hooting, I tensed, gripping my spear more firmly as my tail coiled tighter around the branch supporting me.

"Proto col dik tates a sek ear e t scan." The call of the beast was as eerie as any I'd ever heard, a hollow, ponderous sound that made my bristles rise and rustle. I angled the tip of my spear downwards, scanning the flank around that maw for a weakness.

Those reddish-brown spots that marked the belly of the beast might be a good target. Or they might be its strongest armor.

"Scan shman," the orange thief chittered angrily back at the beast, still showing no signs of fear of that terrifying mouth.

The beast need only lunge to the side to gobble up the defiant creature now standing with her hands on her hips, eyes narrowed on it.

"Yerjusbeein a jerkeh. Iz hawteh outeh heerrre." She suddenly glanced around as she'd done multiple times when I'd been following her, her striking eyes scanning the trees and still passing over my darkened scales without noting me. *"Andere zan ail ee enhere."*

"Dereiz nowdat ulanded," the beast moaned in its hollow echo.

The orange creature threw up her arms. *"Ughhh,"* she suddenly growled, then she clenched her fists and hissed through gritted teeth. *"Zemantix, Snarkee."* She lowered her arms and glanced around again, before bending to snatch up the gourd jug. *"Eyeyam tohawteh todeal wif zisshit."* She clutched the gourd to her lumpy front and lifted a hand to swipe her brow. "*Kikon deair conditchineen.*"

I rose slightly from my crouch as the orange creature stepped right into the maw of the beast without hesitation. I heard the monster rumbling in its hollow echo but didn't catch the bizarre pattern of sounds it made because I was too concerned about it eating my thief.

Then I heard her holler, and before I knew it, I was jumping from the tree, rushing to her defense, despite my fear of the unnatural beast.

"*Dam neh tho zecheep bazterds,*" she squawked in the loudest volume I suspected she could manage. "Noair conditchineen eye can teeliveh wifowteh aircon ditchineen." Her shrieking caws reached a piercing, desperate pitch clearly audible even from within the belly of the beast.

My feet struck the loam, my grip firm on my spear as I charged towards the beast, my bristles fully raised, my lips peeled back from my teeth, my jaws parting as I hissed in fury.

"Release your prey, Tytonid!" I roared, my tongue horn resonating loudly with my demand. "Or I will cut open your belly and free her myself!"

The orange thief screeched even louder as the maw of the beast suddenly slammed shut. Huge, red eyes began to flash all over his body, showing that Tytonid still had plenty of life left in him. For all I knew, he could be fully resurrected now, his physical avatar already healing from any damage that had been inflicted upon it.

I struck him with my spear, hearing a hollow "thunk" as the tip scraped along the hard flank of the beast, scoring a scratch but not appearing to do much damage to the monster.

Curse Tytonid to the Dark Sprawl! How could I possibly cut this beast open when my spear barely made a dent in his unnatural flesh?

The beast was now making a horrendous shriek of alarm, a piercing sound that made my bristles shiver, my crest horns vibrate, and my ear flares bend forward as if they could fully block my ear holes from enduring that noise.

But I still heard the orange creature screeching an alarm from inside the belly of the beast as I again tried to spear its armored flesh. I'd never encountered such a thick, impenetrable hide before, not even with the shadow grabber.

"*EyeyamsorryEyeyamsorryEyeyamsorry youkin haf yerwaterbak.*" The desperate caws and shrieks of the orange thief made me frantic to free her from this monster, even if it might end up eating me in return.

"I will save you, odd, lumpy one," I swore, shouting to be heard over the unrelenting peals of the beast. "I will find a way to get you out of this monster's belly."

I rammed my spear into the seam of the beast's huge, circular maw, attempting to pry it open, but its mouth was clamped too tightly shut. Still, my spear tip pierced that seam, and I felt that it went deep enough into the monster to penetrate the interior of its mouth.

My thief chittered encouragement at me, no doubt beyond grateful to have someone save her, even though the foolish creature had approached the beast so unwarily and then had strolled right into its open mouth. Though, even Prdayu still walked right into snapper groves without realizing it until it was too late, so not every danger was obvious at first.

She had also raided my camp without caution. It was clear she was unaccustomed to considering the dangers in the Sprawl. It would be a shame for her to learn that as her last lesson. She must have been very sheltered in whatever life she'd lived before finding herself wandering alone in the Sprawl.

I had to abandon the notion that she was Urcifa in the flesh, strange as hers was. She was far too terrified to be a goddess, even one that was in physical form. That realization only made me more determined to rescue the poor, frightened creature before Tytonid fully consumed her. She clearly couldn't save herself.

Tytonid was known to be persuasive, to lure unwitting souls

into his waiting beak, summoning them with tricky calls and eerie hoots that drew the incautious to investigate. She wouldn't be the first who had fallen for such calls.

The pealing of the beast made my head ache, and those flashing red eyes on his body would have blinded me if it was nighttime. Still, I persisted, trying to spear the beast's maw again, and again piercing through but unable to pry open the seam of his strange lips.

The orange creature shrieked and squawked and screeched from within the belly of the beast, desperate for rescue. I could hear her rising terror even though I couldn't understand the rapid sounds she was making each time I managed to puncture the beast but failed to force his mouth open.

Tytonid was trying to hoot directly at me now, I was certain, using an unnerving bellowing sound that still rang hollow, but I ignored all his tricky noises. I was no incautious wanderer to be fooled into stepping right into his maw.

Realizing that the mouth wasn't budging even though I was piercing it, I turned my focus to the reddish-brown spots near the bottom of the beast's mouth.

I kept waiting for Tytonid to bring his talons out or turn that pointed beak at the front of his body, in front of his outspread wings, to attack me, but he did neither.

I suspected it was because he had been gravely wounded at some point. I couldn't even see his talons, and though his huge body rocked a little with each thrust of my spear into it, Tytonid made no move to shift away from the tip of my weapon, much less get up and slash at me or even fly away.

He did hoot louder at me when I rammed the stone tip of my spear right through the center of the largest of the reddish-brown spots on the beast's belly, discovering blackened areas beneath their surface that looked like scale rot. I heard another scream from my thief and feared she was already being burned by Tytonid's belly acid.

"*Eyetolu thiswaza hunkofjunk, howitsur vifedtheatmosfearik-burneh zbeyondeme,*" she howled urgently.

"*Sheildingdamage afder atmosfearikentree exposeda rustedun derhull,*" Tytonid intoned with menace.

"Hang on to your branches, little camp thief," I shouted in encouragement. "I'll soon cut you free from this monster."

I followed up my promise by plunging my spear deeper into the spot, noting that the beast's armored hide crumbled around the haft as the tip broke through into the mouth of Tytonid.

"*Wayteh wayteh wayteh!*" The orange creature cawed, her screeches growing louder as they emanated from the hole I'd left in the beast's flank. "*Snarkee yougota translat err?*"

"*Eyeyama escaypeh pawd compud err nota diplo matikprogram,*" Tytonid growled in agony.

"*Oh therez abigser prizeh.*" I could hear the growing confidence in my little thief's squawks now, as she must understand that I was winning against the beast that was trying to eat her. "*U notadiplomat. Udon tehsay.*"

Another successful stab of my spear widened the hole in the beast's belly, and I heard my thief chirp with relief that her freedom was nearly at hand.

"*Thinkeh ifeye gifitz waterbak itellgo ayway.*" Her chittering grew more rapid, and I took that as encouragement to speed up my work, so I stabbed faster at the blackened color patch beneath the reddish brown that crumbled further with each poke of my spear.

After some vigorous stabbing, I'd formed a large enough hole in Tytonid's hard flesh that I felt the thief could crawl through, and I drew my spear back and crouched down by the hole. "Come, little lumpy thief," I said in a soothing tone, "the beast can't move on its own." The fact that it hadn't fought back against my wounding assured me of that. "You can escape now."

Her cries and screeches and squawks had died down during my last few stabs, so I worried that she'd fallen unconscious. That might mean I'd have to crawl into Tytonid's belly to get to her. I sighed, rising to my feet to aim my spear to chip away further at the wound I'd made in the beast's flank so it would fit my body, noting the red of its innards flashing strangely through the opening even though no guts or blood spilled out of it.

To my surprise, my water jug suddenly fell out of the opening instead of the little orange creature.

"Youkin hafit bak," my thief chittered. "eyeyamsorree, eyewonteh steelagin."

I double-blinked as pieces of dendrob flew out of the wound to land on top of the overturned jug, the cork keeping the water inside it.

"Takeeetawl." The orange thief's squawks warbled and were followed by odd snuffling sounds, like she was struggling to smell something. "Eyeyam sosorree."

I wondered if she was trying to scent me through the unnatural, bitter odor coming from the interior of the beast's belly.

Tytonid was still shrieking, but it had ceased its hollow hooting.

"You're safe now, little thief," I said in a gentle voice, returning to crouch beside the hole. I slid my water jug aside, bending to one knee to glance inside the beast's belly.

I spotted the orange thief huddled against the strange interior organs of Tytonid, clutching some of its entrails that dangled from the bizarrely jutting ribs framing its stomach. Her eyes were wide as she stared at me, her scaleless face scrunched up, and her cheeks wet from moisture that was dripping from her eyes.

Those eyes were so beautiful, like polished and faceted skystones formed in the secret ways of a stonemaster.

I held out a hand to her, letting her know it was safe to come out of the wound. Tytonid may still be crying out in agony, but the beast wasn't going anywhere.

This had been a butchery rather than a slaying but given the size of the beast and the threat he would have posed if he'd been fully capable of fighting, I wouldn't feel bad about the advantage I'd had that he was already fallen when I found him.

He wouldn't die. He was a god. This avatar might fail him, but he'd be back. He always returned.

Instead of lunging for the opening, anxious to escape the innards of the beast trying to eat her, my camp thief scooted even deeper into the shadows of Tytonid's gut, as if she was trying to hide from me.

Then it hit me.

She *was* trying to hide from me.

I realized that her terror wasn't because of the monster that had swallowed her, but rather because of me, crouching there blocking her escape.

Chapter Six

Vera

I stood and stared down at the hole in the side of the escape pod's hull, the metal and plastic bent and shattered around it. "So... that happened," I muttered like I hadn't just had a horrifying flashback to the Menops invasion as a strange alien tried to tear apart a door to get at me.

I might have broken down a bit, but I was fine now.

Everything was fine.

I swiped at my sunburned cheeks, my hands shaking even more than my voice as I tried for a nonchalant tone to bely the way I'd screamed and blubbered like a ninny when the alien had tried to get in. I didn't even know what a "ninny" was, but I was certain I would have put one to shame.

"Would you like a damage report?" Snarky asked, somehow making his robotic voice sound accusatory, as if it was all my fault that his precious escape pod had been damaged.

I mean, maybe it was, but still....

Who'd programmed this computer, anyway?

I shivered and rubbed my arms, still unwilling to look away

from that hole lest the reptilian climb through it when my back was turned to stab me with his spear. "Are you sure it's gone?"

"The extraterrestrial life form has retreated from the area and is no longer being detected by my external motion sensors." Snarky sounded a bit huffy to my mind, but I was happy he'd stopped with the klaxon and red alarm lights.

They'd both been giving me a headache.

"But he didn't take the water jug or the food," I mused aloud.

"Perhaps the *intelligent* life form only wished to teach you a lesson about pilfering their supplies." There was no need for the computer to put stress on the word "intelligent"—like the alien was the only one in this scenario who was.

"Hey!" I propped my hands on my hips as outrage let me push down my fear. "If you had *any* supplies in this junk heap of an escape pod, I wouldn't need to steal them from some furious reptilian with red-rimmed eyes and a sharp spear and a roar that nearly stopped my heart."

"You are *currently* wearing a survival suit that was provided by my supply cabinet." Snarky sounded offended.

Good.

I pinched some of the thick material between two fingers and pulled it away from my body. "I can hear the fan in this thing getting ready to kick the bucket, and you don't even have functioning air conditioning in here! Your survival suit is trash, and your supply cabinet is as empty as my dresser on laundry day."

Suddenly, the escape pod door slid open. "Don't like my pod?" Snarky said in a *definitely* offended voice. "You can leave it."

I held up both hands, shaking my head quickly. "Hey, now, let's not be too hasty—"

"I insist," Snarky said ominously.

"Now, Snark—"

"Get. Out. Of. My. Pod. Now." With those very abrupt words, the klaxon again kicked on, along with the flashing red lights, as all the rest of the lights shut down, casting me in garish shadows.

"Can we talk about this?" I pressed my palms together pleadingly. "I'm super sorry! I've been a jerk! I know that. I'm just a little stressed. There's no need to kick me out—"

The alarm grew even louder in volume until my eardrums throbbed in pain, and I had to clap my hands over them. "Okay!" I screamed, backing towards the door. "I'm leaving already, you *asshat*!"

As soon as I stumbled out of the door, it slid shut with a finality I couldn't doubt. The alarm was still audible and loud from outside the pod, so I continued to retreat. That is, until I tripped over the water gourd that the angry reptilian with the eerie, red-rimmed black eyes had left behind.

I went down with a heavy oomph, the gourd rolling out from under me just as my back impacted with such force against the normally soft ground that I felt the climate control fan pack and compressor that was sewn into the suit slam into my spine.

I laid there for a long moment, listening to the fan's whirring growing louder and more erratic as the escape pod's alarm finally stopped pealing. My head still throbbed from the sound, but I finally sat up, reaching behind me to rub at my back.

This is a nightmare!

I'm gonna wake up in our house back in Colorado, where it's nice and cool, and not as muggy as my vision of Hell and no doubt filled with various biting insects that carried unknown diseases.

Oh yeah, and the furious reptilian ready to skewer me on his spear like a kebab.

There was no way any of this was happening because I would already be dead if I found myself in this situation for real. I was a city girl, through and through, and I was not cut out for the wilderness.

I'd only survived the Menops invasion by being rescued at the critical hour by Akrellian soldiers, and the plague by some unknown blessing of fate.

This jungle wilderness? No, I wouldn't have lived this long without getting poisoned, eaten, or stabbed through with a spear by the angry extraterrestrial I'd robbed.

And I certainly wouldn't have been ousted from my only available shelter by some rogue escape pod computer that hadn't been regularly updated to keep it from developing an insufferable attitude.

I climbed clumsily to my feet. Even though the gravity seemed lighter here, the suit itself was both bulky and heavy. I sighed miserably, figuring that if this was a nightmare, I would have to see it through until I woke up.

As unlikely as everything that was happening to me was, though, I knew I wasn't dreaming. I was too thirsty, hungry, tired, hot, and sweaty to doubt that I was very much awake and in the real world. A world that wasn't my own.

At least I still had the water gourd, and I wasted no time snagging that to pull the cork and put it to my lips. I gulped greedily, too thirsty to worry about why the reptilian had left it behind instead of reclaiming it after attacking the pod.

At least he was too afraid to actually enter the pod once he'd punctured a hole in the side of it.

I wasn't certain why I knew the alien was male. It might have something to do with the brief flash of his physique that I'd seen, which had a distinctly masculine appearance to it, beneath colorful yellow, green, red, and blue scales. Or maybe it was that when his eyes had met mine, I'd felt a bizarre connection between us.

Almost like an attraction, though surely that was ridiculous.

It wasn't because he was reptilian that I doubted I could possibly be attracted to him. After all, I'd been around enough Akrellians to grow accustomed to their scaled, spiny appearance, and I even found some of them quite aesthetically pleasing.

It was more that I had never believed in the instant attraction thing before, despite there being rumors that Iriduans felt biologically bound to their mates upon meeting them. Humans didn't though.

Did we?

We certainly shouldn't feel attracted to someone when that someone was trying to kill us. That was just too weird to accept.

I recalled the encounter with the Lusian in the restaurant. The very brief conversation that had caused me to impulsively agree to this trip.

Was the reptilian alien my destiny? The one I was supposed to claim?

I pondered that thought as I polished off the water in the gourd, lowering it with a sigh. I licked my lips, then swiped my arm over them to dry them, glancing around as my stomach growled now that its first and most important need was met.

"Damn you, Snarky," I muttered at the pod as I searched around until I found the jerky lying in the leafy dirt.

"Five second rule has already passed." I shrugged fatalistically and bent to pick up a strip of jerky, blowing off the dirt before scarfing it down.

It tasted as good as before, even if it had an added earthy dirt flavor to it now. I sought the other strips, and quickly spotted them, snatching them up and gobbling them down just as quickly.

I never would have eaten things off the dirty ground before the Menops had invaded. I'd been quite a picky eater back then, not to mention more than a bit of a spoiled princess. Months spent in a refugee facility, and then years spent in an Akrellian help center—a type of orphanage, though filled with adults as well as children traumatized by the invasion—trying to get back on my feet and find gainful employment in a devastated world economy, along with many other orphaned teens, had given me an entirely new perspective on surviving—and what I was willing to do to stay alive.

I pushed those thoughts deep, then buried them, just like my therapist warned me not to do. I had no intention of dwelling on the past. I didn't see how it healed anyone to constantly think about and talk about their tragedies. I needed to be constantly moving forward.

So those memories didn't catch up.

Everyone had problems. Everyone had probably lost something—or someone—dear. Especially everyone from Earth. So, maybe I'd grown a bit timid over the years because of a lingering fear of losing the rare people who came into my life who showed genuine concern for me when there were so many others who needed their help and attention. Younger kids, or teens who were more traumatized—or showed it more.

Maybe the arrival of my Prince Charming had seemed like my life finally getting better as he'd swept me off my feet and out of the Akrellian help center.

And into a miserable marriage that had ended with me crash-landed in an alien jungle.

I didn't suppose any of that mattered now that I was down to a couple stolen jerky strips and an empty water gourd and a pissed-off computer program that refused to let me back into the only shelter I had on this alien planet.

At least the reptilian wasn't lurking around, just waiting for me to stumble out into the light so he could run me through with his spear.

That thought had me quickly spinning around to check the surroundings, just to make sure he wasn't skulking nearby. Though the hair on my neck stood on end and my back prickled with more than just the beads of sweat dripping down it, I didn't feel any awareness of him being around.

I'd definitely felt an awareness of him when he'd crouched by the hole he'd made in the pod and met my eyes, speaking in a deep, vibrating rumble that had been far too sexy for the threat he'd posed to me.

So, what were my options?

I eyed the jungle foliage, from the broad, heart-shaped leaves that cast deep shadows to the vivid flowers that spread massive, fragrant petals, to the stubby mushrooms that had vibrant caps with spots aplenty, signaling that they were probably poisonous.

Head back into the jungle in search of more food and water?

I turned to regard the escape pod, my gaze shifting to the hole in the side of it, next to the firmly shut door. I could fit through that rust hole. The pod should at least keep me safe from the reptilian, who clearly hadn't wanted to enter it.

But when I took a step closer to the pod, the klaxon started up again, and Snarky boomed, "Go away," through the external speakers.

My shoulders slumped, and my head lowered as I turned back to face the jungle.

Clutching the gourd to my chest with both arms, I dragged my feet as I trudged away from the only sign of the civilized galaxy on this world. It might have been just an illusion of safety, since that reptilian had made quite a hole in the pod, but I was willing to buy into any illusion if it allowed me to pretend that I was safe for just a bit longer.

Nothing was harder for me than facing a reality where my whole life would be upheaved again and tossed about.

Chapter Seven

Khamai

To my surprise, though I supposed I shouldn't be, Tytonid still lived.

Despite my retreat when I realized my thief was afraid of me —too afraid to escape the beast's belly—Tytonid made an angry shriek not long after I'd returned to the shadows cast by the thick foliage around the scar the beast had made in the Sprawl.

That shriek was soon followed by the beast spitting my thief out through his maw. She stumbled away from his flank, then tripped over the gourd of water I'd left for her, causing me to tense as if I could catch her before she fell. I forced myself to remain still in my crouch, clinging to a lower branch with my feet and tail, my spear loosely held in my hands.

Since I was certain she still feared me, I didn't rush down there to help her, as much as I wanted to as I watched the bulky orange creature lying on her back staring up at the sky with a scrunched face. It took longer than I liked for her to sit up again and then climb to her strange hooves, reassuring me she wasn't harmed.

I was pleased to see her drink the water and then eat the dendrob meat I'd left, though next time, I would make it easier for her to find, and not leave it in the dirt. I had retreated too quickly this time to collect the dendrob slices and stack them in a neat pile on a leaf.

I would bring her more food and water, since it was clear she needed it. I doubted she would have braved my camp otherwise. She seemed more skittish than one would expect for a brazen thief. For now, she at least had some water, clutching my gourd jug to her lumpy body, her baggy skin wrinkling and crumpling even further. I watched her set off into the trees, her head-tail swinging against her back, the long furs sticking to her shiny, barely textured skin.

Following her was easy. Too easy. If I wasn't the largest predator in this part of the Sprawl, she would be in real danger. A shadow grabber could have quickly hunted her down and snatched her up with its many vine-like limbs to pull her to its circular maw ringed with multiple rows of sharp teeth. She wouldn't stand a chance on her own against a creature like that.

Unless she *had* been the one who'd brought down Tytonid. I saw no sign of any mystical powers in my thief, nor did she have any weapons. She didn't even have claws on her fingers, all of which faced forward, with one shorter, stubbier one jutting from the side of her hand. Her bulky, smooth hooves didn't look like they'd be useful for anything other than supporting her as she walked.

It was more likely that Tytonid had been wounded already, as evidenced by the fact that he'd crashed into the trees instead of perching upon the tallest of them. Though given his size, I didn't think there was a tree in the Sprawl that could hold his current avatar.

My thief had likely wandered unwittingly into the area, then been lured to Tytonid, likely in search of more food and water. Those needs could drive any creature, even a cautious one, into putting itself in danger.

I had more water gourds cached along the path to my campsite, since water was heavy to carry, but I made sure to collect plenty of it while the morning dew was plentiful in the leaves. I had more than enough to share, and I had still had dendrob traps sunk into the slurries that were likely teeming with food by now.

I could fetch those things to bring them back to offer her, but I felt distinctly uncomfortable leaving her while she was wandering around the Sprawl. It was clear she had no idea where she was going, since she looked around constantly, her steps hesitant as she chirped softly to herself. On multiple occasions, she'd strike off in one direction, only to change her mind and turn to another direction. She did this more frequently the longer the day went on.

I leapt nearly soundlessly from one tree to the next, sometimes using the vines to swing to a new tree, and even those rustling sounds didn't draw her attention over the noise of the tree-singers and other beasts in the Sprawl. They were accustomed to me and had apparently decided she posed little threat, so they didn't fall silent when she passed.

This made it easier for me to remain on her trail without giving myself away, but I doubted it would have been that difficult even if the Sprawl was quiet. She appeared to be completely oblivious to all the life around her, passing right by several venomous moving vines coiled among the lower branches that kept catching at her head-tail. I wanted to call out in warning, frustrated at the knowledge that I would likely put her in more danger by frightening her when she was so close to those scaled creatures.

They wouldn't see her as prey, given her size, so they would let her pass without striking unless they decided she was a threat. If she suddenly squawked in alarm at seeing or hearing me and moved too quickly when she was close to them, they would definitely view her as a threat.

When she circled her own path, looking around at the trees with scrunched brow ridges, her head turning back and forth as she made little muttering sounds, I wanted so badly to climb down from the branches above her to show her the way back to my camp. If I believed she would follow me instead of darting off in the other direction, only losing herself further in the Sprawl, I would have.

I wasn't certain if she had a camp of her own that was her destination, but it was clear she had no idea where it was in relation to her current position.

I wondered again, as I had many times since I'd first spotted her, where my thief had come from that she seemed so out of place in the Sprawl. And again, I pondered the idea that she was an avatar of Urcifa, fallen from the sky in Tytonid's wake.

I couldn't picture a less goddess-like avatar though.

A fresh breeze carrying the scent of the river swept through the branches, causing the smaller leaves to ripple and rustle. The tree-singers clicked louder in response. My thief swiped her forehead, her beak snout flaring at the sides as she lifted it in the air.

The river was still a half day's trek from here at the rate she was going—though I could reach it quickly by traveling through the branches—but she still appeared to detect its presence, and it was clear she needed more water. No doubt she'd drunk all that had remained in the gourd she still carried.

When she struck off in the direction of the source of the breeze, I wasn't sure whether this was a good change or not. The river would give her the water she needed, but it was also a good spot to encounter larger predators.

Or even other Prdayu.

I would much prefer to provide her jugs of harvested dew instead, but again, I feared she would crash unheedingly through the Sprawl to escape me if she spotted me. All I could do was remain hidden and on her trail, ready to unshoulder my spear to aid her should she encounter any danger.

I had to admire my thief's fortitude and determination, since it was clear her strength was flagging as the day passed. She kept swiping at her brow, and she'd stopped several times to chirp and caw loudly, then stomp her smooth hoof. She even tossed the gourd into the trees, appearing to be angry, but at what, I couldn't guess, since she remained unaware of my presence.

After that baffling action, she covered her face with both hands, and her shoulders shook as she made guttural sounds.

After a brief time, the sounds died away and she lowered her hands, swiping at wet eyes. Then she gasped and went in search of the gourd, digging around in the leaves and shrubs while I spotted a moving vine colored the same browns and greens as the branch it dangled from right above her head.

I hopped silently down from the higher branches, crouching closer to her than I had dared to come before. While her back was turned, the moving vine's head lifted to regard her warily. It completely missed my presence and wasn't prepared to strike when my tongue shot out, the flared tip of it engulfing the vine's entire head so it couldn't bite before I pulled it back into my mouth.

My thief didn't even hear the rustling of the leaves when the vine's body whipped briefly, even after I bit its head off. She was making too much noise herself as I climbed rapidly back up to the higher branches, then settled again to wrap my tail and feet around my perch. I lifted a hand to catch the twitching length of the moving vine dangling from my mouth.

I held onto the long, limp body as I bit off pieces and chewed, noting when my thief found the gourd. She made a sharp staccato sound, then held it up like she was showing the Sprawl that she'd reclaimed it.

I had a meal to sustain me, but my thief was no doubt starving by now. She certainly appeared to be suffering, and her already hesitant steps were now stumbling as she continued to head in the direction of the river, following the breezes that were increasing in frequency until the leaves rippled like the water in the river itself.

Her beaky snout lifted and flared often as she sniffed out the path, following scent rather than sight.

It was a good decision—in that she was no longer traveling in circles.

Not long after her gourd tossing, my ear flares twitched and spread as I picked up the rushing sound of the river over the constant clicking of the tree-singers. She had also apparently detected the sounds, and her flagging steps sped up suddenly as she screeched in another staccato cry.

Clutching the gourd tightly in one hand, she used her other to push aside vines and leaves, and I was grateful to note that nothing among that foliage could hurt her.

Knowing that she would soon be at the river, I climbed to higher branches to scout out the riverbank, determined to detect and eliminate any potential threats before she came across them. To my relief, I spotted nothing more threatening than a pack of scaled loam rooters, snorting loudly as they churned up the river-bank mud with their hooved feet and dug their long, blunt snouts into the dirt, pushing it aside in search of fungus bulbs. They were more likely to run from her than threaten her, though the males had a rack of antlers that jutted from their head between long, floppy ear flares.

Then my thief burst from the trees, head fur tangled with bits of leaf and branch caught in it, face streaked with the many stripes of dirt that she'd put there as she'd swiped it frequently. As I suspected, the pack of rooters grunted and squealed in surprise, then darted for the safety of the trees, away from the perceived threat, leaving her alone on the riverbank.

She held up the gourd and her empty hand and made a loud whooping sound before rushing to the riverbank.

I wanted to slap my crest in exasperation at how she didn't even take a glance around her to make sure there were no threats before charging to the water. Thirst was clearly making her incau-tious and desperate. She even fell to her knees in the mud and began to scoop water up to her mouth without checking the depths for threats first.

This close to the falls, the river churned too much for the muck lurkers, so I didn't have to worry about one of them bursting from beneath the surface to snap at her vulnerable face. Still, I climbed down from the higher branches, unshouldering my spear as my tail coiled around the new branch that supported me, much closer to the ground so I could jump down to rush to her rescue quickly if need be.

She drank several hand scoops before she uncorked the gourd and sank it into the water, all the while making muttering sounds and occasional chirps and coos.

After she filled the gourd, she set it down at her feet on the firm part of the riverbank. Then she sat down in the mud beside the gourd and lifted her leg to set it on her other knee. To my shock, she then pulled off one of her hooves.

Beneath the hoof shell, she had thick, saggy skin in the same gray as the hoof. As I watched, stunned and vaguely repulsed, she peeled that off too, making a groaning sound like it pained her to shed her hoof and then her skin.

My bristles lifted in alarm as she exposed the innards of her foot, revealing a pale, bony under-foot complete with toes, though they all pointed in the same direction and seemed nearly as useless as her hoof shell.

I'd seen many a shed skin, and had shed my own on multiple occasions, but I had never just taken it off like she'd removed her under-foot skin. That thick skin now dangled from her fingers in one saggy piece like the shed skin of a moving vine.

I wasn't certain whether I wanted to vomit or jump down there and beg her not to shed her other hoof if it pained her to do so. I did neither, forced to watch as she set her nearly white under-foot down in the mud of the riverbank and wriggled the stubby forward toes until mud squished between them.

I wondered if that helped ease the pain of removing her hoof and outer skin. She certainly exhaled as if it felt better, her shoulders relaxing.

She tucked the shed skin into the now-empty hoof shell, then lifted her other foot to follow the same hoof-shedding motions. She made a moaning sound as the hoof slipped free of her under-foot and lower leg, then set it beside the other hoof before peeling off the gray skin to expose her bony under-foot.

When she'd stowed the skin in the second empty hoof shell, she rose to her feet again. I regarded the abandoned hooves with intense curiosity, marveling at what a strange creature my thief was. Then she lifted her hands to her throat, bringing my gaze back to her.

She suddenly dragged them down the front of her orange skin, and it sagged more at her sides.

With both hands, she shrugged the orange flesh from her shoulders, revealing an under-skin of the same dayglow sap color patches that marked her face and hands.

While the baggy orange skin fell away, seeming far heavier than a shed skin should be, she exhaled again as if relieved, her head falling back so her head-tail dangled below her waist.

Beneath the orange outer-skin, she had a light blue patch of skin covering her from her lumpy chest to her waist that was nearly as baggy as the orange skin. To my surprise, the waning dayglow flashed on what looked like shiny scales on the front of her blue torso skin. Those scales formed an odd pattern that sparkled like the morning dew on leaves.

A dark gray skin patch covered her lower body that differed from the colors on her lower legs and arms, all of which matched her face and hands, though her under-feet were paler than the rest of her, nearly as white as stripped bone.

I was barely able to process this odd skin-shedding process when my thief grabbed the edges of her torso color patch and then lifted it upwards, pulling it off her by dragging it over her head, revealing even more skin beneath it that now fully matched her face and hands. Except for where two large lumps of flesh were partially marked by white patches.

She folded the blue color patch and draped it over the hooves, careful with it, unlike the ugly orange skin that she'd left crumpled in the mud.

Though my brow ridges pulled together in complete confusion, I watched with great interest as she shed her lower color patch, dragging it down her legs, revealing another patch of white over her groin slits, and more flesh that matched the rest of her under-skin.

As bizarre as all this skin shedding was, especially given how she folded each color patch neatly to add to the pile on the hooves, I wasn't prepared for her to remove the final white color patches, but when she did, my prods pushed at the seam of my groin slit, suddenly eager to explore the seam she exposed in her own groin, which was barely concealed with a thin strip of fur that matched the fur on her head. I saw no abdominal slit visible above it, but her second slit could be so tightly sealed as to be invisible to the eye unless she was aroused, or it was situated between her legs instead.

Her chest rounds were also most curious to me now that they were freed from their white color patches, but I wasn't aroused by them. More like slightly repulsed. It looked like two pink eyes stared from bulging globes of soft, bouncy flesh nearly as white as her under-feet.

As unappealing as those eye rounds were, they didn't seem to spot me any better than my thief did, and I watched her intriguingly exposed body intently as her soft under-skin shifted and jiggled and flexed with each of her movements.

When she turned her back fully to me, I noted that her tailless behind had two pleasingly plump undertail rounds with a cloacal crevice between them, just like any Prdayu female would have. Unnerving as it was to see such an expanse of back with no sign of a tail yet still possessing the rounds that had been hidden earlier by her orange outer-skin, I still found the sight of those curves arousing.

My prods decided her chest eyes weren't repulsive enough to dissuade my arousal, and they pushed free of my groin slit, vivid red and swollen with readiness to mate with this strange female.

Maybe I had been alone too long, since I found such an unusual creature so appealing, but I couldn't help what my body wanted. Not that I would ever act upon it.

I couldn't even approach her without frightening her off. I wouldn't want to see her reaction to my prods pulsing eagerly at my groin, my prod fins already twitching against my shafts.

I willed my prods to retract back inside me, even as I watched my thief wade into the river.

Chapter Eight

Vera

My nightmare continued, though I knew for a fact it wasn't just a lucid dream no matter how much I'd wanted it to be. I was so focused on just finding water that I didn't have a moment to think about anything else while lost in the jungle, but once I found the river I'd smelled on the humid and heavy breeze, I just wanted to collapse into a heap at the edge of it and cry with relief.

Or scream.

I fell to my knees but did neither, too thirsty to worry about what bacteria or amoebas or snakes or whatever else could kill me that might be in the water to hesitate in drinking it. I scooped it up in my dirty hands and drank it that way, not even thinking of filling the gourd until after those first blissful handfuls.

The water was cool, at least in comparison to the air temperature that made me feel like I was melting as my body constantly dripped sweat, and the river water tasted fresh rather than fishy or brackish. The fact that it had a swift current suggested that it wasn't stagnant enough for life to thrive easily in that spot. Granted, at this point, I didn't care.

After filling the gourd with—hopefully drinkable—water, I sat down to regard my throbbing feet, trapped inside uncomfortable survival boots. At least they'd come with socks, though those hadn't been encased in plastic when I'd pulled them out of the boots before putting them on, so I had no idea if they'd been clean. They definitely weren't now.

I hated this survival suit, even if the thick, nearly impenetrable material protected my skin. I hated these boots, even if they guarded my feet from whatever might puncture my soles. The climate control fan had crapped out not long after I left the escape pod area and struck off into the jungle in search of food and water, and shelter.

I definitely would need some shelter, since I was certain night would be falling soon. I'd wandered in the jungle for what felt like forever. Surely, it would be dark soon. Granted, it didn't get much cooler, even in the shade, as the sun set, but with heat and humidity this intense, a few degrees felt like a huge difference.

Stripping off my survival suit made me a whole lot cooler, and now that I wasn't tromping through the jungle, I was less worried that something would sting or bite me, so I didn't think I needed the protection of the thick material over my skin. Without that fan going to cool me off underneath the bulk of the suit, I didn't think I could put the thing on again. I was pretty sure I would collapse from heat exhaustion in it, and I was honestly surprised I hadn't already.

My tee-shirt and shorts were soaked with sweat, along with my bra and panties, so I wasted no time stripping them off too. I didn't like going all Eve in Paradise but at this point, I would rather wear leaves than put those wet clothes back on. I was chafed in areas I didn't want to mention.

I felt hot, sticky, and in need of a bath like nobody's business.

The river looked nice and cool and refreshing, as long as I stayed near the bank and away from that strong current dragging everything downriver in the center. Once naked, I stepped cautiously into the water, moaning in relief as the cool liquid closed over first my foot, then ankle, then up to my calf.

The current barely tugged against my foot and leg this close to the bank, and I didn't plan on wading too deep. I just wanted enough water to sit in and let it flow over my entire body. Maybe dunk my head under a few times to soak my hair and my sunburned scalp and face.

It was difficult to see the bottom of the river as it grew deeper, despite it being shallow enough for me to stand, because the water was frothing from the rapid motion of it, and the slippery silt that my feet kicked up only made the water murkier.

Once I was up to my mid-thigh in river water, I figured this was as good a place as any to take a seat and let the blissfully cool water wash over my entire body. But as I turned, my foot slid over a particularly slippery rock, then flew out from under me so quickly that my body splashed into the river before I even had a chance to throw my hands out.

Now that I wasn't braced against the current with my feet firmly planted, it grabbed ahold of me, whisking me downstream as I screamed in alarm, my arms flailing desperately to keep my head above water.

River water rushed into my mouth, and I coughed and choked, turning my head to spit it out as I struggled to get my bearings, the current battering me against slippery rocks on all sides. My feet dragged against more rocks, but no matter how much I tried to grip them with my toes to pull me to a stop, the current was too strong and continued to drag me downriver.

The riverbank rushed past me while I struggled to keep my head above water. I had stopped screaming, saving my breath, because every time I opened my mouth, water tried to steal my last gasps of air.

Not that long ago, all I could think about was getting a mouthful of water. Now, the next mouthful might drown me.

I'd been worried about predators, bacteria, amoebas, venomous snakes, stinging insects, but my dumb ass hadn't even considered drowning in the river that had seemed like my salvation just a short time ago.

The current slammed my back against a large boulder with bruising force, causing me to cry out in pain. A gush of water filled my mouth, and I was once again choking, the rushing of the river nearly deafening me to my own desperate sounds as I struggled to remain breathing.

Yet I wasn't deafened enough to miss the growing roar of something up ahead. Something like a large waterfall. The kind that killed people who went over it, even if they were in a barrel.

I'm gonna die, naked and alone and scared beyond all reason!

It might have been better to drown than to go over the falls and crash onto the rocks below, breaking every bone in my body and probably crushing my skull.

Despite my despair, I struggled more desperately now, still holding onto hope that I could possibly survive even as the edge of the river grew closer and closer. My grasping fingers couldn't hold the slimy rocks and boulders while the current dragged me under low hanging branches that I'd barely noticed before as the trees stretched their limbs past the riverbank.

I should have been grabbing for those vines that dangled from some of the trees. Thick, rope-like, Tarzan-traveling vines that could have saved me if I hadn't been flailing uselessly like an idiot instead of looking for a means of salvation.

Changing tactics, I swiped at some of the vines as I neared the drop-off—and failed every time to grab them. They were always just out of reach.

My last hope loomed before me. A huge tree with broad leaves and sprawling, thick branches spread over the river, draped in vines like a rich society lady wearing strings of pearls. With all my might, I lunged against the current, aiming for the closest, thickest vine as I rapidly approached the drop-off.

I grabbed for it, putting the last of my strength into my effort.

And I missed.

I screamed in frustration and hopelessness as the current

towed me to the edge, pulling me away from that precious vine. My arm was still lifted towards it, as if I could think it into my hands.

Suddenly, something thicker than the vine wrapped around my wrist, and my body was jerked to a stop, my lower legs already dangling over the edge of the waterfall.

I stared at my wrist in shock, noting the scaled tail wrapped around it. Then my gaze trailed along the length of that tail, to the reptilian that had nearly speared me earlier in the escape pod. He now clung to the swaying branches of the tree whose vine necklaces had been just out of my reach.

His strange feet were tightly wrapped around the heavy branch that extended out over the edge of the cliff far enough above my head that I wouldn't have been able to reach it myself in a last, desperate grab. His clawed hands dug into the bark of the same branch, which was now bouncing and swaying as his tail kept me from going over the fall.

He coiled his tail towards him, dragging me against the current as I babbled with incoherent gratitude.

I didn't know if he planned on using that spear resting against his back to kill me or not, but I'd rather die that way than to be smashed upon the rocks that were undoubtedly at the base of this waterfall.

His scales were surprisingly yielding in his tail, flexing against my wrist as he tugged me closer to the tree and out of the worst of the river current. As he reeled me in, he crawled along the branch, moving himself towards the bank and out of the danger he'd put himself into just to catch me before I went over the edge.

I got my first really good look at him in those relief-filled moments and noted that he had thick quills on his head, similar to an Akrellian's quills, only these were longer, until they reached his back, then they continued on in a single ridge of short quills along his spine, where an Akrellian male would have a full set of quills from shoulder to shoulder, all the way down to his waist. This reptilian's quills were also far more colorful, being various shades of blue, green, yellow, and gray that were likely natural rather than the dyed quills of an Akrellian.

Those quills were all lifted until his head looked too large for his body, and he had ears that flared out like small crests on either side of his head with green flaps of skin between each of the four bony spines that formed them, as well as two large green horns curving back on the sides of his head, with a smaller green horn between them.

His scaled body was completely naked, but he had a lovely striped variation of greens all along his body, interspersed with splashes of red, blue, and yellow in spots and stripes.

He was vivid, like a chameleon, and made a striking contrast against the dark greens, browns, and grays of the tree to which he clung as he drew me towards him.

Then I was close enough for him to catch my arms with his clawed hands, the five fingers of each strangely split, so three faced forward and two backwards. His feet, which appeared to have the same odd digits, tightly clung to the branch beneath him as he tugged me out of the water in one heave that seemed effortless for him. Given the size of his muscular frame, I wasn't entirely surprised by how strong he was.

I *was* surprised to find myself suddenly wrapped in his arms, his tail releasing my wrist to coil around my legs as he pulled me close against his powerful chest, the scales over his pecs and abs a striking yellow that contrasted with the striped greens that covered most of his body.

My surprise meant I didn't struggle automatically, which was good, because we were still above the river, only now we balanced in a tree. Him holding me close was the only thing keeping me from dropping right back into the water, mere feet before it went over the cliff.

His black eyes were wide in the center of the striped, red scale patches that surrounded them, the yellow marked brow ridges above them lowered like he was angry. His lips peeled back from sharp teeth as he growled something incomprehensible, an odd, deep vibration resonating from his throat with each sound he made. I assumed whatever he said was directed at me. I also assumed it was words, even though it sounded animalistic.

I had no doubt of his sapiency, even though he was unclothed. That spear was a good clue, even if his campsite hadn't been.

So, he was pissed at me still, judging by the way he suddenly hissed in what I didn't think were words.

Now, I'd even lost his gourd so I couldn't return it to him, and I'd sorta eaten the food I'd tried to give back to him. But then again, he'd left it there, so I'd assumed he didn't want it.

He was still hissing as he carried me to a different branch, his tail tightening a bit around my legs when I shifted my own weight, feeling strange being carried like this.

"I know you probably can't understand me," I said hesitantly as I dangled in his powerful, unyielding grip, "but I'm *really* grateful to you for saving my life." My gaze shifted nervously to the spear poking up over his shoulder, and I bit my lip, his black gaze shifting to it as his brow ridges pulled tighter together, "Even if you plan on killing me yourself, at least I'm not dying right now by having every bone in my body broken on the rocks."

Chapter Nine

I WAS SO angry I wanted to bellow with my fury until my crest horns vibrated, but my thief was already trembling with fear and reaction to nearly going over the falls. I'd barely managed to save her, and I felt shaken myself at how close I had come to losing her.

She'd slipped in the shallow part of the river and had been swept up by the current so quickly that I'd struggled to keep up with her as her body was dragged downstream trailing her desperate screams, her pale arms flailing and splashing in the churning water.

I'd moved rapidly through the trees, swinging across the river-bank using vines, then leaping from branch to branch to catch up to her, but I'd seen that she couldn't grab ahold of anything to slow her rush to the edge of the waterfall.

I'd only had one chance to get to her before she went over it, and that meant crawling along the branch that hung over the edge to snag her with my tail.

I still struggled to believe I'd been lucky enough to make that grab successfully. It had been so close! Far too close for me to forget the terror I'd felt in that moment when her legs had poked over the edge.

Now, I clutched her wet, slick body against mine, her under-skin incredibly warm and soft against my scales. I could feel the tremors of her muscles and hear the fear in the warbling of her chirps as her eyes met mine.

She shouldn't have been in the river in the first place! I wanted to yell at her but knew it would likely only make things worse. She probably couldn't understand me any more than I could under-stand the chirp-murmur sounds she was making.

Still, it had been foolish for her to go so far in. I should have stopped her when she'd first waded into the water, but I hadn't expected her to go so deep, nor had I expected her useless under-feet to be so ill-suited to the slippery riverbed.

My arms tightened around her soft body, my tail coiling further around her legs as I finished crossing the branch and then used my feet to climb down from the tree. Once on the ground, I adjusted my position, using both hands to heave my thief up onto my shoulder, ignoring her squawk of alarm. When she struggled, her small fists pounding on my back beside my spine crest, I smacked her soft, tailless backside.

Her shriek was louder than the sharp sound of my palm meeting smooth, jiggling flesh, but she stopped struggling against my arm as it banded around her thighs. My tail had shifted to coil around her lower leg, since I was reluctant to release any part of her. I had a very reasonable fear that if she could escape my hold, she would dart off into some new danger that I might not be in time to save her from.

I could practically feel her debating grabbing for my spear, which was slung over my opposite shoulder. Her body had tensed after that one whack on her backside, and now she lay suspi-ciously still. So were her palms as they rested on my back like two comforting warming stones.

Holding her in my arms wasn't comforting, though. It was

arousing, and though I was angry enough to smack her backside again, I resisted the urge, just like I resisted the urge of my prods to poke free of my groin slit.

She smelled delicious, even after being dunked in the river, and her body put out heat like I'd never felt before. I could pile a hundred warming stones onto my scales and not get the same level of soothing heat that simply holding her against me provided.

It had been so long since I'd held someone close that it was an almost unfamiliar experience, and I'd never held someone so close to me who was so different from me and yet still so appealing.

"I wouldn't," I growled in warning as one of her palms lifted from my back, and I felt the brush of her arm against my bristles as she reached for my spear haft. When she didn't lower her hand, I whacked her bottom again, my anger growing along with my frustration.

Would this reckless female continue to make terrible decisions that put her in danger? She couldn't possibly know that I wouldn't harm her. Not if she kept shying away from me. So why would she try something so stupid as to grab for my weapon like she could wrestle it from me in time to turn it upon me?

She squeaked, her hand returning to join the other on my back in bracing her. I glanced over my shoulder and saw her captivating eyes staring at me from over her own shoulder, her pliable face pulled in what appeared to be a frown.

I'd had enough. I wouldn't rest easy until I had her safe in my camp, tied up in my sway so she couldn't run off into the dangers of the Sprawl again when I went to recover her skins and hooves.

Though I wasn't keen on ground walking, I didn't want to risk carrying her in the trees in case she started struggling again, so I strode along a much slower trail until I reached the log that spanned the narrowest part of the river. I felt her body shuddering as I crossed over the log, carrying her slight weight with ease. She wasn't light, but she wasn't that heavy, either. Her mere slip of a form was smaller than some of the animals I hunted.

After a long silence passed between us while the tree-singers started up their chorus again once they decided I wasn't an immediate threat, I heard her begin to chirp and squawk, and my ear flares perked, though I had little chance of understanding any of her sounds.

Even knowing I couldn't understand her, I still felt anticipation at having her company in my camp. Not only had it been far too long since I'd been around others who were intelligent enough to understand *any* language, but this particular creature, odd as she was, appealed to me in a way I'd never experienced before.

It wasn't just that she caused desire in me, as I'd felt aroused by Prdayu females in the past, on many occasions, and had even acted on them from time to time. There was something more about this alien creature that I couldn't explain that drew me to her and made me eager to be with her, even if I couldn't understand a sound she was making.

My terror at the thought of her going over the falls had been out of proportion to how important she should have been to me given my complete lack of knowledge about who, or even *what*, she was. That she already meant so much to me made little sense, but I couldn't argue with it. I'd felt like losing her would be akin to being exiled all over again, facing a lifetime of emptiness and loneliness and purposelessness.

Maybe I wanted to keep her so badly because she did give me a sense of purpose. First, to follow the thief who'd brazenly stolen food and water from my campsite. Then to save her from Tytonid, then the Sprawl itself, then death at the base of the falls.

Now, her clawless fingers drummed on my back scales, and she braced her elbow against the muscles of my back and propped her chin on her palm, exhaling heavily.

Her thighs shifted, and my arm securing them against my chest tightened to let her know I wouldn't tolerate any more struggling. Even though we were now on solid ground, and if she managed to break free and fall, she wouldn't fall far, I knew she would take off if she could get to the ground, and I had no intention of chasing her.

Although the thought of chasing her caused an unexpected spear of lust to goad my prods into everting from my groin slit. I shifted my tail to block her weird, pale under-feet from brushing them, uncertain whether I was more concerned about her reaction to them, or about whether the touch of those odd feet against my prods would cause me to release spawn rain or afterseed.

It had been too long since I'd done either, and the last few times I'd experienced any kind of release had been at my own hands, my afterseed coming fast, followed by the gush of my spawn rain from my upper prod. That lack of control had been embarrassing, but there'd been no one around to see it, so I supposed it made no difference.

Now, this alien female in my arms might accidentally bump either prod if I didn't get them back under control and force them to withdraw back into my slit where they belonged. All four prod fins on each shaft were twitching with my desire to bury my prods inside her.

My thief chittered and chirped as her delectable body shifted against mine, her tailless, round backside temptingly close to my face. The scent coming off her was heated and compelling. Compelling enough that I wanted to taste the soft skin that kept brushing against my cheek and ear flare. I wanted to drag the broad tip of my tongue along that skin, caressing it as her flavor teased me and begged me to taste more of her.

I thought of probing her upper groin slit with the length of my tongue, driving it deep inside to taste the source of that enchanting scent. Just like I would taste a Prdayu female to see if she was ready for seed.

Of course, I was assuming she had two slits, like a Prdayu female. One to fill with spawn rain, which would cause her body to produce and release mature eggs, and the other to contain my seed.

A Prdayu female's orgasmic contractions opened her egg pouch to drop her eggs into the seed pouch inside her abdomen to fertilize the spawn. Filling a breeding female with spawn rain repeatedly in the days that followed spilling seed inside her would not only spur maturation of her eggs, but also bring on an orgasm to make the most use of that stored seed.

I had to stop thinking about mating, and groin slits, and whether this irate female who again drummed her fingers on my back had another slit besides the fur covered one I'd already seen. My prods were already leaking mating slick, which eased the penetration of both prods into the slits of Prdayu females, and my fins were quivering with readiness.

My prods weren't even close to withdrawing back into my slit. They were closer to spewing their contents all over the legs of this female if I didn't get my thoughts under control.

I had to think again about how close I'd come to losing her, and how much danger she kept putting herself in. She wouldn't like it when I tied her up and left her in my sway, and there was no way to explain to her why I felt it was necessary to do so, because she couldn't understand me. She also feared me, and I'd seen her eye my spear with nervousness, showing again that she was an intelligent creature, like a Prdayu, even if she didn't look like one.

I was certain she'd want her outer skins and hooves back, given how carefully she'd tended to them, so I wanted to retrieve them, but that meant a trek back through the Sprawl to the riverbank where she'd left them, and though it wouldn't take me nearly as long as it had taken her to find the river, it would be long enough that she could get herself into real trouble if I left her unbound.

I didn't like to do things this way, but I wasn't willing to risk her safety just to make her feel safe in my presence.

I ignored her chatter, grateful my prods were finally withdrawing after concentrating on how angry and scared I'd been when she'd put herself in such danger in the river. As long as I didn't focus on how good her warm body felt against my scales and how soft and yielding she was against my hard chest, and how sweet and fragrant she smelled, suggesting she had just as tempting a taste, I would avoid another....

Curse Tytonid for my wayward thoughts!

My prods were fully engorged again.

Think of something repellent!

I thought about her lumpy chest eyes for about half a fire-snap before I realized that those soft rounds now squished against the scales of my back felt remarkably arousing, and my brief closer look at them had allowed me to determine they weren't actually eyes, but simply nubs of skin like some animals had to suckle their young.

I wanted to explore her alien body, beginning with those intriguing chest rounds and those pink, misleading buds of skin that tipped them.

Even as I had that thought, more mating slick leaked from my upper prod, making the tip of it extra slippery just as her foot jerked against the grip of my tail and the bottom of it slapped the head of my prod.

I winced, but not in pain as the female froze, her entire body tensing.

I hoped she didn't fear I would force an unwanted mating upon her. I'd killed a Prdayu for trying to do the same to my sister. I would never be so dishonorable or disgusting. But how could I reassure her of that when my prods were out just because of the feeling of her body against mine?

The end of my tail coiled tighter around her straying foot, and I felt her forward-facing toes wriggling against the tip of it, which caused my prods to jerk with eagerness and more slick to well from the tips to drip down their shafts, spilling over the pulsing fins.

"*Deed eyejusfeel whadeye thinkeyefelteh,*" my thief cooed in an odd sing-song chirping.

I had no idea what that sound said about her thoughts, but her toes continued to wriggle in my tail coil, and she made a soft humming sound that was much more appealing than the incessant hum she'd made before, when she was still in her outer orange skin.

Her fingers no longer drummed against my back scales. Instead, she began to trace them over my stripes and spots, causing my back crest and bristles to twitch in response to the pleasing feeling of her clawless fingers stroking my scales.

That was not helping my embarrassing erections go down at all!

"Sumtinslip perry onmytows." Again, she made a strange cooing song-like pattern of sounds. *"Eyethink eeliikez mee."* She hummed again, then splayed her fingers on the scales of my back, only to stroke her palm down my back towards my waist, where my tail jutted above my cloacal crevice. *"Eyelikeyoutoo hawtstuff. Imma marreedwoomun butnadedidn seemtogivea dam bouthafin aring soweyeshoodeye."*

I tried to focus on the rhythm of her chirping, noting how it rose and fell with each individual sound, able to distinguish differences in them like I could detect differences in the clicking of the tree-singers that let me know where individual ones were in the cacophonous noise of the Sprawl.

Still, I couldn't understand anything she was saying, but she continued to stroke my back, now with both palms, and I felt them growing closer and closer to the base of my tail. If she stroked that too, I would likely lose both spawn rain and afterseed at once given how engorged and eager my prods were at the moment.

I was so grateful to see the clearing of my campsite up ahead that I almost forgot I had to get my body under control before she saw what her foot had bumped.

She was acting in a way that seemed affectionate now, and my body was hoping that meant she would welcome the sight of my prods, and maybe even invite me to put them into her slits, but I still had to retrieve her outer skins and hooves, and I couldn't trust her not to try to escape my sway, which would be the safest place I could leave her alone. That meant I still had to tie her up, and she likely wouldn't be nearly as affectionate after that.

Chapter Ten

Khamai

BY THE TIME we reached my camp, the dayglow was darkening as night crept in and the Dark Sprawl began to sink down to cover the sky. I knew it wouldn't be long before Tytonid's eyes would crack open to peer down from the darkness, looking for the glow of unwary Prdayu souls. I carried my thief up into the trees, noting her nervous yelp and the way she clutched my shoulders with both hands, her thighs tensing under my arm. Still, she wisely didn't struggle.

I climbed to my sway, then gently lowered her from my shoulder so her tailless backside settled on the leaf-softened floor of the sway. I coiled my tail around the door frame to keep the tree pod from doing as it was named so she didn't feel too nervous about falling out of it.

When her wide blue eyes looked up to meet mine in what I took to be a questioning expression, I gestured with one hand into the interior, where the last of the dayglow spilled through the thin leaves that covered the exterior walls of the sway, indicating that she should crawl into it and settle upon the nesting I'd put in there for my own comfort.

She seemed to understand my meaning, even if she was confused by my encouraging words, her brow furs pulling together when I made the sounds. Despite that confusion, she climbed further into the sway. I briefly watched her move into the deep shadows barely illuminated by the weak, failing dayglow shining through the leaf-covered walls.

After I unshouldered my spear and stowed it in the holder I'd formed of vines on the outside of the doorframe, I followed behind her, inhaling her scent as I passed through the door frame, the woven fabric I used to cover it sliding over my back crest.

I regretted my automatic inhale, because my prods responded to her scent with excitement, surging out of my slit as fast as my tongue would dart from my mouth to catch a tree-singer. I cursed aloud, reflexively, causing my thief to turn around to look at me while still on her hands and knees on the bedding of my nest.

Her eyes slid from my face to my groin, widening as she took in the sight of my prods, thick and red and dripping with mating slick. I held up both hands and shook my head in distress at her gasp and swift inhale as she shied back.

Though my bristles were likely standing on end at this point, only making me look more threatening, I needed to make the point clear that I wouldn't force myself upon her. I backed out of the sway, pausing in the doorway as I held one hand in front of my groin and again shook my head in reassurance, murmuring soothing words as I settled my bristles to hopefully set her at ease, even if she didn't understand what I was telling her.

As I backed further out of the sway, the tension in her body seemed to relax, her shoulders sagging as she turned to sit on the bedding, picking up the camp blanket I usually brought on my trips to soften my temporary nests.

She dragged it over her body to conceal her under-skin and chest rounds from me. Despite this obvious sign of discomfort at being so exposed and vulnerable to me, she didn't appear to be panicking, and much to my relief, my prods had responded to her tension and fear by withdrawing almost as quickly as they'd everted.

She aroused me unquestionably, but her fear was enough to bring me back to my senses. I would do whatever it took to avoid scaring her, though some things would be unavoidable.

Like tying her up so I could walk away from this camp without her wandering off.

Before I did anything like that, I fully intended to make sure she was as comfortable as she could be. She'd had a very rough time, and she looked like she might be exhausted, her single set of eyelids sagging low over her intriguing eyes, her entire body slumping forward, and her arms dangling loosely at her sides.

I held up both hands in a staying motion, hoping she understood the gesture, and was rewarded with a quick bob of her head that I took to mean she did. Then I left the sway and climbed quickly to the branches where I'd tied my storage packs, concealed among the leaves, and wrapped with setron leaves to repel predators and insects.

I withdrew a leather-wrapped pack of dried dendrob meat, a smaller gourd of water than the jug she'd stolen, and a pouch of sweet fire drupes. Then I pulled out a coil of strong cordage, looping that over my head to lay across my chest like the strap of my spear usually did.

I returned to the sway, noting that it was moving gently as my thief shifted inside it. When I pushed aside the *woven* concealing the interior, I saw her still sitting on the bedding, now completely wrapped in my blanket, her eyelids nearly closed and her head bobbing forward, then jerking up as if she was fighting sleep. The fact that the light had faded further deepened the shadows until it was nearly dark in the sway, with just enough green-tinged light from the leaf wall for me to see her.

Her eyes popped open as the sway sank a bit with my additional weight, and her gaze appeared wary as I crawled towards her on hands and knees.

The sway wasn't really built for two, but it would hold. The construction was sturdy. It was just a tight fit. I didn't have far to crawl before I sat back on my haunches in front of her. Possibly too close for her comfort, but I didn't have a lot of room to put more space between us.

I handed her the pouches of food and the flask of water, and she made a chirrup sound that I assumed was pleasure given the way her expression opened up, her brow furs lifting and her lips curving upwards in the same way a Prdayu might smile. Her eagerness was confirmed when she held out both hands to take my offerings.

Her hands were shaking as she set the pouches down and then pulled the cork from the flask gourd and brought it to her lips, clutching it with both hands as she gulped down the contents, barely pausing to breathe.

I wanted to warn her not to drink too much at once, but she probably wouldn't have listened at that point even if she could have understood me. It was obvious she was beyond thirsty.

She finished the flask, then lowered it, her small, round-tipped tongue darting out to swipe over her wet lips. She glanced down at the flask in her hands, then up at me as she bit her lower lip with flat white teeth.

"Eyeyamsorry," she cooed, slowly handing the flask back to me. "Eyekeeptakin awl yerwahtur." Her eyes lowered like she was reluctant to meet my admiring gaze, which I struggled to break away from staring at her unusual features, finding them bizarrely appealing even when they were also completely alien to anything I'd ever seen before.

I picked up the meat pouch she'd set beside her and handed it to her, gently urging her to take it in a soft growl that had my tongue horn resonating just enough to vibrate my crest. She regarded it warily, then glanced up to meet my eyes as she reached for it.

This time, she was a little less shaky as she untied the cord and unfolded the soft leather to expose the dried meat. She lifted it to her beak and inhaled, her eyes closing and her lips parting in a way that made my prods pulse against the inside of my slit.

Recalling her tension from before when they'd exposed themselves was enough to keep them where they belonged.

My thief snagged a piece of dried meat and brought it to her lips, her flat-bottomed teeth still apparently sharp enough to tear off pieces that she rapidly chewed, her earlier nervousness disappearing as she satisfied a clear hunger that didn't surprise me. She hadn't eaten anything during her trek through the Sprawl to get to the river, and as far as I knew, she'd only eaten the stolen dendrob strips prior to that.

I would have loved to provide her with a full feast of delights harvested from the Sprawl. There was so much food in this area that she might even be overwhelmed by her options. Dried meat was simply a traveling ration, not a meal worthy of a mate.

A mate? Now, where had that idea come from?

Surely, I wasn't already wishing to present my beaded collar that I'd made in wistful loneliness to this alien creature whose name I didn't even know, much less where she came from, or even *what* she was. I'd never met a female who I'd even *wanted* to make a collar for before, and prior to my exile, I'd expected I would have to know one for many years before desiring such a commitment.

Given how often she chirped and cooed, and considering the beaklike jut of her snout, I was assuming my mysterious thief had bird origins, but she had no feathers and no wings, and she seemed uncomfortable in the trees.

A featherless ground bird then? With a flexible but still stiff beak?

It would take more study to ponder the mystery of what she was but given the way she clung to my blanket to cover her underskin, I suspected she would be more comfortable with her over skins and hooves returned to her.

She finished the dendrob pieces in the pouch while I studied her covertly, lowering my gaze so I wasn't staring fixedly at her like an aggressive predator. She made smacking sounds with her lips that suggested she was pleased with the flavor of the seasoning I used for the dendrob. It helped to diminish the earthiness of the slurry-dwellers that clung to their flesh even after I rinsed them thoroughly.

Once she set the soft leather aside, I handed her the fire drupes pouch, and she took it with more confidence from my hand, this time not hesitating in pulling open the cord. Once she'd exposed the drupes that I'd harvested from the sweet-fire bush, she made a drawn-out cooing sound as she studied the vibrant crimson fruit, tilting the pouch so the last of the light streaming through the leaves gleamed on the glossy skins of the small, ripe rounds. Then she brought the pouch up to her beak and inhaled until her upper body expanded, followed by a humming sound that I took to be approval, because she glanced up at me with a soft upward tilt of her lips.

Another of her cooing sounds confirmed that she was happy with the offering. "Smeellzz lye keh cherreez."

With two clawless fingers, she plucked a drupe from the pouch and brought it to her lips. As they parted around the fruit, her eyes lifted to meet mine, catching me staring at her. A new tension stiffened her body.

It didn't strike me as fear or even uncertainty this time. It felt like a cord stretched between us that was about to snap under intense strain.

Then she quickly lowered her gaze, the pale, red-tinged skin of her face suddenly turning darker in the deepening shadows, making me realize she could alter her coloration, even without her color patches, though it obviously wasn't to the extent that I could alter my scale colors.

Before I could say anything that she wouldn't be able to understand, she popped the fruit into her mouth and then chewed, moaning softly as the sweet, fiery flavor was released.

That sound nearly undid my self-control, and I knew I wouldn't be able to sit there and listen to her eat the entire pouch if she was going to do that with each drupe. My prods already ached to be free from my slit and my fins were wildly fluttering inside my groin pouch. Her sounds were akin to what I would expect from a Prdayu female in the throes of a spawn rain-instigated orgasm.

I could picture my thief's body arching beneath my own, her head thrown back, her tangled head-tail splayed out on the blanket beneath us, her arms clutching mine, and her interesting forward toes curling. Dwelling for too long on that image would cause me to release not only my spawn rain but my afterseed.

My gaze fell to those toes, which peeked from under the colorful weave of my blanket. I cocked my head as I noted that they were also painted on the blunt tips, which was something I hadn't noticed before. Even in the weakening light, I could see that they appeared to be marked with tiny flowers on a pale background of a shade difficult to determine in the shadows.

Fascinating! Painting designs on beads, sways, pod walls—or even just leaves, I could understand, but to paint designs right on one's claws? It was unexpected, and yet such an intriguing idea.

As simplified as the design was, the flowers looked like the dayglow blossom, just like the creamy shade of her under-skin looked like dayglow sap. Perhaps I should call her Dayglow, then, since she was brightening my camp, and she seemed to have come from the sky in Tytonid's wake.

She clearly wasn't Urcifa, turning her brilliant scales to reflect the dayglow. No, my thief was more like a ray of that light itself, which might explain why she was so out of place on the surface of the world. She belonged to the sky. The Sprawl wouldn't be kind to one who didn't understand the world and couldn't predict its dangers.

Dayglow yawned hugely after chewing and swallowing only one drupe, lifting a pale hand to cover her mouth as it gaped open, stretching her pliable features. Her eyes squeezed shut with that yawn, and they were slow to open again as her entire body sagged.

"Sleep, beautiful light," I told her, deciding I wouldn't tie her limbs, but would instead weave a barrier over the doorframe of the sway. It would take longer, but I wanted her to be comfortable as she slept in my nest, and she wouldn't be if she was fighting against even loose knots. It would take a little more time to confine her that way than just tying her up, but it would likely upset her less, and maybe she would sleep long enough that she wouldn't even notice she'd been confined at all, not awakening until after I returned.

She seemed to understand my suggestion, even if she couldn't comprehend the words themselves. She bobbed her head in a nod, her lids barely lifting from her pale blue eyes—which further convinced me she belonged to the day-sky—then she collapsed onto her back on the soft nest of leaves.

I watched her entire body relax under the blanket, and within moments, a soft, rhythmic breathing filled the sway.

I didn't want to leave her now, but my prods ached just by being in her presence, and I still had a trek to retrieve her skins and hooves. The sooner I wove a barrier for the sway opening and then got on my way, the sooner I could return and maybe bring something more interesting for her morning meal.

After I finished weaving the barrier, a swift enough task for me after many years of forming structures from vines and pod-stick stalks, I climbed to a higher branch to stare up at the sky for a bit, before beginning my journey back to the riverbank. Night had fully fallen and the cool violet glow of Tytonid's crescent eyes glared down from the sky where the Dark Sprawl had claimed the day-sky.

Since his eyes weren't fully open, this wasn't the most dangerous time to be out and about at night. Still, I remained in the shadows of the branches so my spirit didn't glow as it would if I was under the light of Tytonid's open gaze.

I hoped nothing had taken off with Dayglow's skins or hooves, because I had a feeling she'd really want them back to cover her under-skin.

Thinking of that soft, yielding, warm under-skin pressed

against my scales caused my prods to fully extend, and this time, I didn't fight the urge. I curled my hands around each prod, shivering at the pressure against my pulsing fins. Then I stroked them both in rhythm as I thought of my thief, my grip growing more slippery with each motion as mating slick spilled from the tips.

It was my turn to moan in pleasure, though I kept those sounds as soft as the wet squelch of my fists passing over my shafts, just in case she might awaken and overhear me, though I highly doubted she would be aware of the world for many fire-sticks yet.

As I suspected, it didn't take long for my spawn rain to spurt from my upper prod, the thin, cloudy fluid arcing upwards from the tip before falling to spatter my thighs and belly. The crisp scent of it rose from my scales, reminiscent of leaves and grass. My second release came right after the first, which wasn't surprising given how long it had been since I'd stroked my prods.

This time, the release was a more viscous, clear fluid, spurting in copious amounts that covered my thighs and even dripped down to splatter on the broad leaf below my branch, emitting the woodsy scent of tree bark and vines.

I sighed in pleasure and relief, my own toes curling tightly around the branch I balanced on from the strength of my climax as I swiped the fluids off my scales, leaving behind those familiar odors that I had almost forgotten after being alone for so long.

It still wasn't as good as I knew it would be if my prods were buried in my thief's impossibly warm body.

Chapter Eleven

Vera

I WOKE up feeling like I'd fallen off a cliff and hit every rock on the way down. Every bone in my body ached and my joints were so stiff they should have squealed in protest when I moved them. I made more than a few grunts and groans as I slowly sat up.

My back ached so badly that I suspected it was one giant bruise, and I vaguely recalled being slammed into a huge boulder by the river current. To make matters worse, I felt the rawness of a bad sunburn on my face, and heat radiated from those damaged portions of my skin. I sure hoped the UV rays here weren't even worse for human skin than those on Earth. They certainly appeared to have the same effect.

I looked around at the tree pod interior that Hot Lizard Guy had brought me to, trying to distract myself from the discomforts of my body. The bamboo-like rods that made up the frame had vines woven through them, and huge leaves covered the loosely woven outer walls. Those exterior leaves glowed a soft green from the sunlight outside the pod, giving me enough illumination to see my surroundings and note that Hot Lizard Guy wasn't in the pod with me.

I needed a better name for my alien than that, but my brain had been pretty much scrambled by stress, thirst, and exhaustion when he'd carried me to this camp and put me in his pod—then showed me two very red reasons why he was being so nice to me now.

Of course, he might just be a nice guy in general, and his anger at me when I was hiding in the escape pod was totally understandable, given that I'd stolen his food and water without so much as a please or thank you. It didn't have to be because he had *two* very large, very vividly red erections jutting from his groin that were clearly eager for introductions.

As initially alarming as the unexpected sight of them had been, I couldn't get the thought of them out of my head now that I was more alert and aware. Even the aches and pains in my body weren't enough to forget about those obvious erections. They were undeniably phallic, despite having some significant differences from human penises.

The head of each had been heart-shaped with the tip being the narrow end of the heart, blunted by curving endpoints that split to reveal a hole, then flaring out to join the shaft in two bulging curves that came together in a crevice on the undersides of the head, and probably the topside too, though I hadn't gotten that good of a look.

Stranger still than the head of each had been the weird, small, triangular flaps of skin one each shaft. They were like thick, vertically oriented fins, and I'd seen three of them near the heads of each shaft in my quick glance, though I supposed there could be more on the sides I didn't see.

His shafts were also impressively long and girthy, certainly larger than any other male I'd ever seen in real life.

From what I knew of other reptilians, namely the Akrellians, they only had one dick, and it was pointier at the tip than a human male's—or this new reptilian—though it was also bisected, with a broad head and thick muscle roping the girth. They called theirs a "mating claw," which raised eyebrows, but apparently, it wasn't actually sharp, even though the tip was pointy.

I'd never actually been with an Akrellian, but porn featuring them had appeared on Earth's entertainment outlets almost as quickly as the Akrellians had appeared in our skies to help us defeat the Menops invasion. I'd been curious, like most humans. I'd watched some. I'll admit that I'd been intrigued, though I'd never acted on my attraction to any Akrellians.

It was a big step to take, dating outside my own species. I knew of other humans who'd leapt at the chance and given how crappy my human husband had turned out to be, I probably should have too.

Although, if I hadn't married Nate, I wouldn't be here now.

Here with a massive bruise on my back, naked in a tree tent, captive to a mysterious alien I couldn't understand, but who had two very intriguing erections that he hadn't tried to force on me.

I might not be able to understand his words, but I was already getting the impression that he was a good guy, alien or not. Not wearing any clothes probably made it more difficult to conceal those moments of sudden arousal, and he'd seemed embarrassed rather than lecherous when he'd covered his groin and backed out of the tent pod.

He hadn't run me through with his spear for stealing his stuff. He'd left his food and water behind at the escape pod for me. He'd saved my life by dragging me from the river, risking his own in the process.

Then he'd carried me here and had let me sleep in the surprisingly soft bedding in his tent, even letting me claim what appeared to be the only blanket in the placc—a gorgeous, colorfully woven length of fabric with soft, clearly plant-based fibers. He'd even given me more food and water, and then had left me alone without trying to scooch into the bedding next to me to introduce me to Happy and Slappy in an expectation of repayment for his kindness.

Although, I couldn't say I wasn't intrigued enough by those two long schlongs to shake hands with them. I grinned at the thought, not in the least bit surprised by how my channel clenched and my core heated to its melting point, leaving me soaking wet.

Maybe he wanted a lady friend, and I just happened to conveniently fall into his lap—or steal into his camp—or maybe, just maybe, we were meant to be together, and he felt the same pull that I did that drew us to each other even though we couldn't understand a word the other said.

I knew he was saying words, because they did have a word-like pattern to them, even if he growled them all the time with that throat-resonating undertone to them that was as alien as his appearance.

I found his growliness surprisingly sexy. I had also been surprised at how my inner muscles had tensed with excitement and anticipation after he'd spanked my ass earlier, startling me but also bizarrely arousing me. If Nate had tried to smack my bare backside, I would have smacked his face.

Well, probably not, given how foolishly cowed I'd been by him, but I certainly wouldn't have appreciated it, especially not as much as I did when Hot Lizard Guy did it to me.

I'd recognized that it was a warning and not a sexual act at all. Nice he might actually be, but my new sexy friend clearly didn't put up with crap, even from a woman he wanted to double dick.

I was making some pretty heavy assumptions that was what he wanted from me. Just because he had that visible arousal didn't mean he wanted *me*, specifically. I was a mess, after all. Sunburned, sweat-stained, covered in river muck, with a knotted mass of a ponytail that would be a nightmare to untangle without conditioner.

I'd long ago sweated off the makeup I'd had on when I'd boarded the charter ship what seemed like so long ago, though it couldn't have been more than a day or two. It just felt like such a distant memory after all that had happened since then.

Point being, I wasn't exactly desirable at the moment.

Then again, he was an alien, and couldn't have any idea what an attractive human female looked like. Maybe I looked sexy for his species. I could only imagine what the females of his species looked like. I wondered if they had the same horned crests jutting from their foreheads or the same vividly colored quills covering their heads.

I wondered if they had the same sexily serious, almost severe, face with low, heavy brow ridges and all-black eyes with patches of red scales surrounding them.

It was getting hot enough in the pod that my body was flushed, and I tossed the blanket aside, exposing my naked form to my own examination.

As I'd feared, I was covered in ugly bruises and scrapes. Maybe he would think them a part of my skin pattern given his own color variations. It was too bad they were so tender to the touch. I sighed and slowly climbed to my feet, pausing nervously in mid-crouch as the tree pod began to rock with my motions.

I barely heard my alien on the tree limb outside the pod before his clawed hand thrust aside the woven fabric that covered the opening, allowing more daylight to spill into the shadowed confines of the tree pod. Then he poked his colorful, quilled head inside the pod, his dark gaze seeking mine.

And snagging on my naked breasts instead of lifting all the way to my eyes.

I noted the way his claws clenched more tightly around the frame of the door as he quickly turned his head, his gaze shifting to the curved wall of the pod. Despite not looking at me directly, he held out his other hand out to me in a gesture that was clearly an invitation.

I carefully crawled forward, not particularly loving the way the tree pod moved back and forth like a ship at sea with each of my hesitant steps. It must be an acquired taste, living in a tree.

His gaze returned to mine once I was close enough to take his proffered hand, and when I cautiously set my palm over his, his fingers closed quickly around it. I didn't fight it as he reeled me closer to his body, drawing me further towards the opening of the pod.

He backed out of the doorframe into the shadow-mottled sunlight, and I followed, sighing in relief as a gentle breeze swept across my perspiring skin, carrying the cooler kiss of morning that I knew would grow a lot muggier as the day went on.

As if he'd done it a thousand times before, his arm slipped around my waist when I knelt in the doorway, noting that his tail was coiled around a vine that was part of the outer frame of the pod, holding it steady for me.

I wrapped my arms around his neck, and lifted my legs to encircle his waist, guessing that he intended to carry me out of the tree, and me clinging to him would be the easiest for him.

Although I suppose I could have ridden on his back, but he had those short but sharp looking quills on his spine, so that might not have been a good idea either.

We both froze as soon as my ankles locked over the base of his tail.

His other hand dropped to grip my butt cheek while the arm around my waist tightened, pulling me more firmly against his body. His eyes were fixed on my face, his colorful quills spreading and lifting with what I suspected was an emotional reaction rather than a threat display.

He stood there holding me just outside the tree pod, balanced on a branch as easily as I would stand on a sidewalk, for a long moment filled with unmistakable tension.

Then I felt the rounded tip of his tail coiling around my calf as the tent pod swayed beside us, no longer held in place as his tail tip continued to slide up to my knee.

My breathing was shaky, my lips parting slightly as his expression turned fierce and unquestionably aroused.

I felt his shafts pushing from his groin opening, the top one blocked by my own mound, the lower one extending so fast that the heart-shaped head of it slid inside my already soaking slit as it extruded.

I didn't pull away as the narrower tip of it parted my entrance, and when he spoke in that growly, vibrating voice of his and made to lift me away from it, I clutched his shoulders, protesting audibly as I used the leverage of my thighs clenched around his waist to push myself a little further down until my seam parted around the thicker base of its head.

We both moaned as his muscles tensed against my chest, his arm banding more tightly around my waist, his other hand sliding further under my butt to support me as he rocked his hips, driving his length deeper inside my tight passage. When he shifted, his upper shaft extruded fully to jut upwards, ending up pinned between us, the girth of it laying right over my clit. The four fin-flaps on his shaft began to move back and forth like flicking tongues, both over my clit and inside me, causing me to gasp with delight.

I shuddered with pleasure, my legs trembling and my lower back arching as he withdrew his length slowly, his upper length dragging along my clit, slippery with some kind of clear lubricant that dripped from the tip of it. One of those fin-flaps teased back and forth over my throbbing clit. Then he thrust his second shaft deep inside me again.

This was way better than just climbing out of the tree!

My head fell back on my shoulders as I cried out for more, one hand lifting to clutch the nape of his neck, my fingers threading through the stiff, shifting quills there as my other hand continued to grip his shoulders. I tightened my thighs around his waist, once again rocking my hips downwards to encourage him to thrust deeper.

Deeper and harder.

That little bit of encouragement seemed to be all it took for his control to snap. His tail left my calf to coil around the heavy branch beside us, bracing him, I guessed, because he then began to drive inside me with abandon, his quills fully extended, his lips pulled back from sharp teeth with his intense expression, his eyes fixed on mine as he pumped into my wet heat, the slick from both of us allowing even his thick length to slide easily into my channel. Those fins were now moving so rapidly they buzzed like a vibrator, causing me to release short, sharp cries as the combined sensations drove me towards my peak.

My breasts jiggled against his powerful pectorals, which shifted beneath his scales with each of his frantic thrusting movements. The tree branch he stood on bounced beneath his feet, causing the shadows of the leaves to dance over his features as the rocking momentum shoved him deeper and deeper inside me with each bounce. Both of his clawed hands now gripped my naked hips and held them in place while he buried himself inside me, filling me to the limit, over and over again as I cried out from the kind of pleasure that I'd never experienced before.

My climax rapidly approached as his upper girth continued to tease my clit, that magical buzzing fin stroking over my throbbing nub with each thrust of his second shaft inside me.

His fingers tightened on me as I went over the edge, my channel convulsing around his length, and he closed both sets of eyelids with a long, low moan as his girth jerked inside me in response to my inner muscles clenching it.

My cries of ecstasy echoed among the trees, making me realize that the monster-sized cicadas had stopped clicking while we were in the throes of passion. The leaves around us trembled like my entire body did as wave after wave of glorious pleasure washed over me.

I felt a rush of warm fluid spurting inside me with each twitch of his shaft. He lowered his head to bump his bony crested forehead to mine, his breaths panting raggedly from parted lips as his upper length also jerked with his climax, spewing translucent cum all over my belly and mound. The scent of it was curiously fresh and grassy.

My toes still curled in the wake of my orgasm, and I was also panting heavily, slowly coming down from the high of that intense climax to face the stunned realization that I had just had sex with an alien, and one whose name I didn't even know.

One who couldn't speak my language any more than I could speak his.

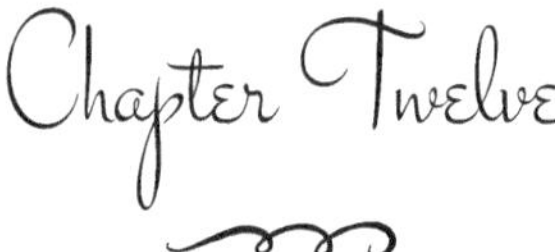

Chapter Twelve

Khamai

I STARED down at the face of the female in my arms in stunned silence, struggling to believe that what I'd been dreaming of the entire night she'd slept in my sway had actually just happened.

It had all happened so quickly that I was still reeling from it, feeling more shaken than I'd ever felt, even on a thin branch in a high wind. My lower prod was still buried deep inside her incredibly warm slit, her inner muscles gripping the slickened length of it as my afterseed slowly dribbled out of her. My spawn rain covered her belly and the fur-striped seam of her groin.

She'd made such beautiful music as I'd pumped into her, and it had sounded even better than I'd imagined, her gasps and cries and moans causing my ear flares to spread to catch every last note as if I could savor it.

But now, I had no idea what to do with the female in my arms. I'd only intended to carry her out of the tree, noting that her clawless hands and stubby forward-facing toes wouldn't be much use for climbing. I supposed I should do that now.

I was having trouble meeting her eyes, and she seemed to also

96

be reluctant to meet mine, the bright red color patches on her cheeks deepening in shade, though the red patches on her beak, forecrest, and the base of her snout remained the same angry red shade rather than the new maroon color of her cheeks.

It was difficult to force my prods back inside my slit, because being inside her felt so good that I could easily go for longer, and my upper prod was still eager to seek her other slit. I had assumed it would be above the one I'd sunk my lower prod into, but instead, my upper prod had only felt a strange little bead of flesh at the apex of the seam beneath her fur strip, that was slightly firmer than the soft petals of flesh below it.

Whatever that part of her was, it seemed to please her to feel my prod fin pulsing against it.

I now considered whether my Dayglow even had a second slit.

I wanted to explore her more thoroughly to find out, but first, I needed to get her out of this tree. Not that I would ever let her fall, or even loosen my hold on her, but she would likely be uncomfortable being dangled so far above the ground when it was clear she wasn't a tree-dwelling female.

A wingless bird of some sort was still my thought, though a magical one that had shifted shape once she'd come down from the sky. Since I'd never seen her like in the Sprawl before, and she didn't seem to know how to survive here, a sky-based origin was the only thing that made sense to me.

It was possible that she actually came from Tytonid's Dark Sprawl instead of Urcifa's brilliant realm. If so, she had to be an escaped soul, not an evil follower of the god of death.

She moaned softly as I withdrew my lower prod from her, and it slowly retreated inside me along with my upper prod, leaving her belly and groin nub wet and slick from my spawn rain as afterseed spilled from her slit. I wondered if my spawn rain would have the same orgasmic effect on her when I released it inside her as it did a Prdayu female.

I really wanted to find out.

Now wasn't the time. She needed food, more water, and no

doubt she'd want to clean off the mess I'd made on her. I settled my bristles against my head again as I uncoiled my tail from the branch beside us, then began moving down the branches, enjoying the way she clutched me tighter whenever I had to take small leaps to get closer to the trunk.

Once we'd reached the ground and stood in the deep shade of the towering tree that held my sway, she made little approving sounds, like she was relieved, reaffirming my certainty that she wasn't entirely comfortable in the tree. Surprisingly, she still clutched me tighter when I bent to set her back on her feet.

I had avoided meeting her eyes during our descent, but my gaze locked with hers now as I glanced down at her face in surprise at her reluctance to be released. I wondered if she felt as stunned as I did, but it was difficult to tell from her unfamiliar features.

Her eyes were so blue and had a depth to them that I really noticed this close to her. The blue wasn't solid but had tiny lines of darker blue and a ring around the edge of the blue color that was also darker blue. The centers of those colored patches of her eyes were as black as my own, but they expanded visibly as she gazed at me, her small tongue darting out to lick her lips.

Then she lifted herself in my arms by flexing her thighs around my waist and tilted her head as she pressed her lips to mine. I froze in surprise at the feeling of her soft lips brushing over mine, her pointy beak bending as it bumped my snout. I stiffened in further shock when her tongue licked along my lips like she was tasting me.

Her tongue was so small and had a tapered tip that slid over the seam of my mouth as if she wanted to taste me further. When my lips parted, she stroked the tip of her tongue along my sharp teeth. Her lips continued to move as she licked at my teeth, then stroked her delicate tongue along the sharp tips of them when I parted them, like she trusted me completely not to bite it off. Not that I ever would, but she couldn't know that unless she already understood that she was mine and I would never hurt her.

The fact that I fully planned to give her my beaded collar was unquestionable now, though perhaps the thought had occurred to me from the moment I'd first laid eyes on her stealing from my campsite. My prods ached for her, and the brief taste they'd had of her only made them eager for more.

She seemed just as eager, her lips caressing mine, her tongue darting between my teeth to stroke over the broad tip of my own. Her delicate flavor teased my senses as the tip of my tongue spread to engulf hers, causing a startled sound from her as she tensed.

Then she hummed in an odd way and snuggled deeper into my arms, pushing her tongue into the hollow of mine as I pulled it further into my mouth to taste more of her. I wanted to taste all of her, to thrust my tongue inside her and taste her slit to see if it was ready for my seed. As soon as I had the chance to explore her body to my contentment, I would also tease the little nub above her seam with my tongue, just to see if she reacted the same way she had to my pulsing fin passing over it.

Her lower back arched forward, rubbing her belly against mine, reminding me that she was still covered in my spawn rain. As much as I would love to cover her some more with it, I had entered the sway to fetch her so I could feed her, not to take advantage of her. Still, she seemed to be enjoying stroking my lips with hers as much as I was enjoying it, though it took concentration not to let my prods evert again.

My hands lifted to her back to press her closer to me, but I froze when she tore her lips from mine to hiss, her body trembling as her eyes scrunched shut.

"Fuuuck thathertz," she cried out, her eyes popping open as she reached back to grab my wrist with one hand and tug at it like she wanted to pull it away from her back.

Her little side stub of a finger worked surprisingly well to clamp around my wrist with the rest of her clawless fingers.

"Allmose forgoddaboutze bruzeez," she cooed after a heavy exhalation of breath.

I might not understand her words, but the fact that she was in pain was immediately evident to me. Her features weren't so far removed from Prdayu that I couldn't recognize the signs of discomfort.

I quickly carried her to the campfire ring, though the coals barely glowed to chase off the chill of morning. I bent to set her down on the sitting stone where I'd piled the fabric I'd fetched from the riverbank, her limbs unwrapping my waist. The orange skin wasn't among that pile, because something had carried it off, leaving only a muddy mess behind where she'd abandoned it.

Though the stone was situated in the shade rather than in the warming dayglow that managed to break through the tall canopy above the clearing, the heat of the fire should help keep my thief warm in the morning chill if she needed it. I could always bring my blanket from my sway if she shivered or trembled from the cooler air. Given how much heat her body put out, it was difficult to imagine she could ever be cold.

She had eyes the color of the day-sky, hair as golden as the light that brightened it, skin the color of the sap from the flower that was named after the dayglow, and emitted warmth that rivaled the heat of it.

She *must* be the dayglow taken form—a beautiful form that had blessed me with her presence.

This time, she didn't resist me releasing her, though her hands were slow to lower from my shoulders as I straightened.

I now knew that the color patches I'd fetched from the riverbank and probably the orange "outer skin" my Dayglow had removed were actually material woven so finely that the fibers were barely visible and had an unnatural sheen to them. The shiny scales on the front of the blue material turned out to be small, clear, faceted stones unlike any I'd ever seen before. Though they sparkled like Urcifa's scales, they lacked the weight and brilliance of those glitterstones and several of them were dulled and scratched in places, like they were easily worn away.

I hadn't taken much time to study her strange fabrics, nor the "hooves" that had turned out to be encasings formed of a leather-like material, though not like any of the leather I tanned and used.

I'd been in too much of a hurry to return to her to really examine them, but as soon as I'd picked up the blue material, I'd recognized it for what it was, despite how impossibly fine the weaving and stitching were or how strange it was to think that she'd covered her body with blankets cut and formed to fit over her limbs.

My thief hadn't shed myriad layers of skin as I'd initially thought. She'd simply been covered in multiple blankets of unnaturally slick wovens, and I'd realized after some consideration that her soft skin might be the cause of that odd desire to don blankets to cover it, even when it was warm in the Sprawl.

She crowed with apparent delight now as she settled on the fabric-softened stone, and clapped her hands together, a broad smile baring her flat teeth. She snatched up one of the smooth leather foot casings sitting next to the stone and held it up in front of her. The inner gray wovens that she'd peeled from her feet after removing the casings were still inside them.

She made a face at the casing, not even checking inside to see if the gray woven was there, but when she turned her gaze to mine, she smiled again.

The corner of one side of her mouth kicked up higher as I handed her a length of cloth from my own pack that was laid out on the stone beside the one where I'd stacked her cloths. As she set the foot casing down to take it, I mimed wiping my belly scales with my other hand, even though I would have preferred to wipe off her delicate skin myself.

And then make a mess on it all over again.

"Thankew hawtstuff," she trilled softly, her smile widening as she used the cloth to sop up the remains of my spawn rain that hadn't yet dried, leaving her belly slightly shiny and rosy from the roughness of the cloth passing over it. "Yewneet abettername." She set the cloth down beside the stone she now sat upon, then tapped a finger to her little, round chin, humming briefly. "Weeshud introdooze owerselvez."

I cocked my head curiously as I moved to the large gourd I'd filled with dew harvested from the basin leaves of the nearby bzul tree when I returned to the camp not long after Urcifa turned her scales to the Sprawl. At this time of day, the dew was plentiful, cupped in small pools in most of the lower leaves of the bzul tree.

As I bent to grab the hand-sized bzul nut shell scoop that sat beside it, I kept my eyes on her, curious as to what she'd do next, since she now seemed relaxed and at ease in my presence. Finally, she understood that I meant her no harm.

I scooped water out of the gourd, then handed the nut shell to her. She took it in both hands, and immediately lifted the edge of it to her lips without my having to mimic drinking from it.

She gulped it down thirstily, exhaling with clear satisfaction when she lowered the empty scoop. I held out my hand for it, and she handed it back for me to refill it.

She drank the second scoop just as eagerly, though she nursed the third as she cradled the scoop between her palms. She was again making those humming sounds as I dug into the pack I'd brought down earlier from the trees and withdrew more meat, fruit, and nuts that I normally used for travel rations.

I hadn't wanted to be away from her too long, so I'd put off hunting for fresher fare until after I'd seen to her needs, uncertain when she'd awaken. I had stopped at the nearest slurry before returning to the campsite this morning to sink my traps again, and I intended to check them after I made sure Dayglow was comfortable. I would prefer to give her fresh dendrob meat and some more drupes, nuts, and seeds for her midday meal.

As I collected the pouches and brought them all to her, setting them down at her feet before settling on the stone beside hers, she lifted a hand and pressed her flattened palm to her chest rounds. "Veeerah."

She patted her chest rounds, repeating her soft coo, the yielding flesh bouncing with her motion, drawing my eyes the way the flutter of a tree-singer's wings would. I watched those pink beads of flesh that tipped her chest rounds harden within their larger pink ring under my curious gaze. It took great effort, but I kept my prods behind my slit and my tongue in my mouth, even though I wanted to let it shoot out to engulf and tug on one of those nubs to taste and feel it.

I couldn't keep my tail from unfurling to coil around her ankle, drawing her foot closer to mine. She made a soft rippling sound, baring her teeth in a smile as she glanced down at her captive ankle, then stretched her foot out to me, her forward toes pointing at me.

Accepting the invitation, I curled one hand around her ankle and lifted it up to settle the back of her foot—which was a hard round surface rather than back toes—on my knee as she leaned back on her seat, resting her weight on her palms on the fabric-covered stone.

I ran my fingers along the sides of her unusual foot, tracing the shape of it as she made that rippling sound again that reminded me of light dancing over the leaves in the grip of playful breezes. It was a happy sound, and it seemed to bubble in the air like the joy that was bubbling inside me in this moment.

As if she was aware of my thoughts and the satisfaction that caused them, she wriggled her stubby toes under my curious gaze, then made her ripple sound again, pressing her foot flat on my knee when I trailed my claws along the skin beneath it that was thicker and coarser than the smooth skin stretched tight over bone and tendon on the top of her foot.

"Itickles," she said in a ripple shriek, her voice breaking into more little sound ripples, spreading like aural rings around the fire. Her little toes wriggled some more, intriguing me so much that my tongue automatically shot out of my mouth to engulf the largest of them.

She yelped in surprise, trying to jerk her foot back, but my tail tightened around her ankle instinctively. I quickly unstuck the tip of my tongue from her toe and drew it back into my mouth, mortified at my reflexive movement.

My own hunger and my prey's sudden movement had a tendency to spur my tongue into striking. My hunger for her was of a different nature than for my prey, but it was a hunger all the same. Still, I quickly released her foot with both my hand and my tail as she stared at me with wide eyes, her mouth hanging open.

She slowly drew her foot back to her stone, then tapped her toes on the ground beside it. Then she sat up straight, her chest rounds jiggling and again drawing my gaze.

Suddenly, she threw her head back and a much louder and more staccato ripple of sound left her, taking on a cawing nature that made me concerned that she was alarmed and afraid of me, until I realized that she was smiling broadly even though her mouth was open, and her teeth were bared.

Chapter Thirteen

Vera

Note to self, *don't tease the chameleon guy by wriggling your toes.*

Maybe they look like bugs when I do that.

I couldn't help my burst of laughter, because my lizard lover was looking horrified at his own actions. His head quills were all spread out and his eyes were wide, and his mouth was still slightly ajar even though that ridiculously long and thick tongue of his was now safely behind his teeth again.

That very long, very *thick* tongue of his....

It had shot out of his mouth like a bullet, so fast that my poor little toe was already engulfed like the tip of his tongue was a flexible suction cup by the time I'd realized he'd even parted his lips. The end of my toe was still a little sticky from whatever he had going on with that tongue that probably gave it that surprisingly delicious taste I'd enjoyed during our earlier kiss. It had a flavor almost like honey.

I'd been amazed at my own daring in boldly kissing him, but

given what we'd just done, it had felt appropriate at the time to steal a kiss from my alien.

I pitied any insect that ended up on his menu, though. Although, with a tongue that size, I doubted insects were the only things that fell prey to it.

Given the look on his face, he hadn't intended for my toe to be on the menu, and he was deeply regretting what was probably an instinctual reaction. Of course, I could be entirely misreading him and maybe he did intend to eat me, but usually, the simplest answer was the correct one, and in this case, he'd already made it clear that food wasn't what he wanted from me.

I glanced down at the fabric he'd given me to clean off his cum, and smiled wickedly, recalling the intense pleasure he'd just given me and already wanting more of it, even though my stomach rumbled with hunger, and my body aches had made themselves known again as soon as he'd pressed his palm on my bruised back.

I looked up to meet his eyes as he watched me, his quills still slightly extended, like he remained nervous, despite my laughter. Maybe it was my cackling guffaw that had him looking so alarmed. To reassure him, I stretched my foot out to him again, and his prehensile tail coiled around my ankle, recapturing it even though I suspected that was a flash of uncertainty that I saw cross his expression.

Before he grasped my foot by the heel again, he bent and picked up one of the leather pouches he'd pulled from the fat pack slumped beside his flat-topped stone. He handed it to me, and I could scent the dried meat inside it as I took it and brought it closer to my nose.

I giggled softly as his hand enclosed my foot so he could trace my toes with his claws, his jaw muscle ticking like he was gritting his teeth tightly to keep his tongue behind them. Instead of looking at the food as I opened the cord on the pouch, I watched him with a sly smile, wriggling my big toe teasingly.

He glanced up from my foot, noted my expression, and

suddenly, a broad smile tilted his lips, baring those sharp teeth. Even though he had alien features, I could tell he was amused and not aggressive by his relaxed body language. His hold on my heel remained gentle, his tail tip still coiled around my ankle loosely.

The way the smile lightened his expression made me realize that his normal demeanor was severe, like he was a serious, intense person who didn't relax often.

Or maybe he *did* smile often, and it was only around me that he looked so forbidding, even if it was a sexy kind of forbidding. I'd always had a weakness for stern men. It was just too bad that some of them really *were* assholes through and through, like Nate.

Recalling that bastard, I suddenly realized that I'd just cheated on my husband with an alien.

I shrugged mentally, not needing the vivid image of his tongue in Naja's mouth to remind me why I hadn't felt the least bit guilty about doing so.

Nate had never respected me, and though he'd been admiring in the beginning of our relationship, telling me often how beautiful I was and how creative and talented he thought me, and how sexy my body was, those compliments he'd initially showered me with had slowly dried up over the four years we'd dated. In fact, the more serious I'd become about him, the less he'd seemed to try to please me, until it turned out that I was the one doing all the pleasing in our relationship by the end of it.

I had also been the one to constantly bury my hurt and anger and frustration to avoid yet another haranguing lecture from Nate about this or that or the other, because they only added to those negative emotions, and near the end, he'd started using threats of leaving me to scare me into silence. By then, I'd been more afraid of being alone than actually losing Nate himself.

Now, I felt...relieved. Despite being crash-landed on an unknown alien planet, ousted by an offended escape pod computer that wouldn't let me near the only possible exit from the planet—if I could even find a way to fix the beacon, and captive—technically—of an unknown reptilian alien, I felt incredibly relaxed.

In fact, I felt pretty damned good! The after-sex rush of hormones probably helped, but the way my chameleon alien was sweetly tending to my needs, seeing to it that I had food and water and a comfortable, if shaky, shelter, without once bitching about the expense of any of it, made me feel wanted and cared for again.

The last time I'd felt that way had been before the Menops invasion, when my parents were still alive.

I quickly pushed those thoughts away. Everyone had lost someone during that invasion. Some of us had lost everyone, and everything. It wasn't worth dwelling on the past when you couldn't change it.

Always keep fighting to move forward, no matter how much the past tries to mire you down, my daddy would say whenever I'd dwell too much on things I couldn't undo.

He'd been a stern man, my father, but a caring and loving one too, despite the severity of his outward demeanor. His serious nature had concealed a secret romantic. He'd spoiled my mother and I, giving us whatever our hearts might desire—while making excuses for why those gifts were good investments—from designer clothes to expensive jewelry to a brand-new car before I'd even had my sixteenth birthday. He'd even been helping me plan my high school graduation trip that he'd intended to fully fund, because the "experience would be good for me" and therefore a worthy investment in my education, according to his justification process that had allowed him to spoil us without conflicting with his pragmatic worldview.

The Menops had put an end to all those plans—and had claimed both my parents in the process.

It didn't escape me that I'd looked for a man like my father to become my husband, one who focused on hard work, discipline, and personal responsibility, and I'd had found Nate, only to discover that he wasn't even half the man my father had been, and he didn't love me nearly as much as my father had loved my mother.

My chameleon was now exploring my foot with great intensity, and I watched him as curiously as he studied my fish-belly white and admittedly bony foot, toe by toe. I grinned ruefully as he lightly traced the sock line that encircled my ankle with one sharp claw, showing that I hadn't deliberately tanned in a long time, and I usually wore socks whenever I went outside in Colorado, despite my love for pedicures. I didn't love cold feet.

Maybe he thought the difference in the color between my foot and calf was like his scale coloration, which was fascinating, as he had light and dark green striping all over his arms and legs, and dark green marks along his lighter green back, with hints of blue, red, and dark gray streaked along his back ridge just like his head quills.

He'd certainly seemed to enjoy it when I'd traced his markings, noting the texture of the sleek and pliable scales under my palms. I wanted to do it again as my gaze roved over him, from the now flattened head quills to the horns and forehead crest to the sexy features of his face, including the alien cheekbones that jutted back from his face in points like two more horns just below his other horns. Then my gaze trailed down to the tail that was slowly coiling up my calf.

I willed it to slide higher, my inner muscles tightening in anticipation as I thought about that tail tip, nearly as thick around as my wrist, slithering along my inner thigh, inching towards my slick entrance, which still had dribbles of his seed welling from it whenever I shifted my hips.

It was a good thing I was on birth control. Double dicks probably meant double trouble. I supposed I could be grateful Nate had wanted to hold off on having children until we were "settled." Whenever that would have been was questionable, as he'd been reluctant to invest in a larger home than the townhome he and his ex-wife had bought together.

I wasn't sure my chameleon could even get me pregnant, but

I'd prefer not to find out the hard way. Judging by his tree house, there weren't many medical facilities around here, and a hybrid alien baby required a lot of prenatal care, from what I'd heard.

The Akrellians were cross-fertile with humans, which had baffled a lot of people who'd assumed that humans could only reproduce with other humans, until aliens appeared on our doorstop and messed up our worldviews royally.

If humans could have babies with one species of lizardman, I saw no reason to assume they couldn't with another.

I had at least six months before I was due to have my birth control implant renewed, and I wasn't trying to worry that far ahead, since I suspected much would change before then. Maybe I'd even be rescued. Maybe Snarky would fix his own damned beacon and bring some folks to take him off this planet. They'd be bound to look for me too, right?

But did I really want to leave?

I snickered as my chameleon tickled the sole of my foot again, tracing it with his claws as he lifted my foot to stare at the bottom of it. I didn't pull away this time, enjoying the feeling of his hands stroking over my sensitive—and ticklish—skin as he murmured in his rumbly voice, clearly talking to himself.

I was a little embarrassed about the dirt on my feet, but then again, he was walking around barefoot too, so it wasn't like he was unfamiliar with such things. My gaze dropped to his strange feet, noting that he had five toes that were all around the same length, each as long as my hand and twice as thick as my fingers. What was most strange about them was that three of them pointed forward, and the other two pointed backwards, so his foot was like his alien hand, only larger.

Or a chameleon's foot, I supposed. Perfect for grasping branches.

I wondered if he'd let me investigate his feet the way he was touching mine. I had to admit to curiosity, though I was far from a foot person. I leaned more towards looking for a nice ass on a guy, and my chameleon had a very sweet tail, if I did say so myself.

I'd gotten a good look at the deliciously round curve of his buttock below the thick base of his tail, and the strong thigh muscles below it when he'd had me over his shoulder.

He was powerfully built all around, with not a visible ounce of fat on him. He didn't look soft anywhere.

But despite his menacing appearance, he was as gentle as a kitten with the way he handled me, and it had been me, not him, who'd instigated sex. Sure, his erection had gotten a little more friendly than he'd intended, but that had clearly been an accident. My choosing to drive it deeper inside me had been all a choice.

A decision I'd recognized even then meant no going back. I wasn't sure what kind of culture my chameleon came from but given the possessive way his tail was wrapped around my leg and the way he cradled my foot like he was examining his new prize, and the fact that he was giving me food, water, and shelter, I suspected I might have just bagged myself an alien mate by giving into my own desire for him.

The gray alien had said I needed to claim my destiny, and from where I was sitting, my destiny was looking pretty freaking good!

Chapter Fourteen

Vera

MY SEXY ALIEN'S investigation of my foot concluded when I began to shift restlessly on my stone seat, becoming more aware as I grew relaxed by his foot massage that I was still completely naked, though it felt heavenly to have the soft morning breezes caressing my bare skin.

As soon as I tugged on my foot, he released it, allowing me to set it back on the dirt beside my stone. Then he looked up at my face, his head cocked curiously. His tail still wrapped around my calf, almost like he forgot it was holding me, but the tip of it slowly stroked over the inside of my knee like an affectionate caress.

I felt surprisingly good despite my bizarre and uncertain circumstances. However, I needed a bath at the very least because his obsession with my feet made me aware of how dirty they were. That reminded me of how dirty the rest of me was. Since I wanted to get a lot more up close and personal with him, I'd rather do it while clean, but I had no idea how to communicate such a concept to my chameleon.

In fact, I still needed to tell him my name and try to get his out of him. Surely that would be simple enough. As growling as the sounds he made were, I figured I could mimic them reasonably enough.

The vibrational throat thing, though? Yeah, that wasn't happening, but I could probably be understood by him and vice versa, if we made an attempt to communicate.

I again patted my chest and said my name slowly, meeting his eyes like I could impart knowledge directly into his brain. Those Lusians had a good gig going with that whole telepathic thing they did. Wish I could figure out how to do it.

His head quills splayed further outwards, his ear flaps expanding like he wanted to catch more of the sound of my voice. His nictating eyelids blinked. Then his gaze lowered to my hand. I patted my chest again.

"Vera," I repeated, noting his gaze fixing on my palm.

"Veeraaah," he rumbled in a rough voice that had my inner muscles clenching in arousal, that vibration of his resonating even louder, like it was spreading from his throat to the top of his head.

"Yes!" I said with excitement, nodding my head rapidly in the hopes that he would understand the gesture as an affirmative.

He lifted his gaze to meet mine again and rewarded me with more blinks of those double eyelids over pitch black eyes. "Yesss," he hissed, his lips pulling back from his teeth. Then he blinked again.

I pointed at him and the sudden movement had him drawing back, staring warily at my finger even as his tail tightened around my calf. "What's your name?"

When he only stared at me with clear confusion, his bony brow ridges drawing together beneath his horned crest, I sighed and again patted my chest. "Vera."

Then I pointed to him, lifting my brows meaningfully as I waited for a silent beat for him to fill in the blank.

I'd imagined this would be so much easier than it actually was. My chameleon was regarding me with absolute bafflement.

"Veeraah, yesss?" he repeated, his alien resonance humming like an undertone to the incessant insect noises.

My shoulders sagged in disappointment as I realized he had no idea what I'd tried to say.

Okay, so introductions didn't work like I'd hoped. I tapped my fingers on my collarbone as I pondered how to proceed. His gaze shifted to my moving fingers, his quills flexing and twitching as his brow ridges continued to pull together, until there was no space between them.

"Veeraah yesss?" he growled with obvious hesitation.

I loved the way his deep voice caressed my name with that vibrational undertone, even if he had no idea what he was saying. I just wished I could get a name in return, but I supposed that was too much to expect for our very first real conversation.

I still needed a bath though, and I wondered if he would understand the concept enough for a pantomime to work. Then I glanced down at the cloth he'd given me earlier to wipe off the mess he'd made on me, and an idea percolated.

I picked up the cloth, noting that it remained damp, which wasn't surprising, seeing as the air itself seemed to drip with humidity. His body instantly tensed in what I took to be expectation as I lifted the loosely woven material, noting the colorful dyed fibers that were obviously natural, like cotton or flax or some other plant-based thread. The dyes were vivid, the pattern free flowing and amorphous but somehow all coming together in a visually pleasing display, like the blanket in his tree nest.

I waved the cloth in front of me, and then noted how intent his expression grew, his hungry gaze shifting from the cloth to me like I'd just waved a red cape in front of a bull. Before he could misinterpret my meaning, though I would absolutely love a replay of earlier and another mess to clean up, I quickly mimed wiping off my skin, not actually touching it with the damp cloth, but making it clear what I intended.

As I moved my hands all over my body, exaggerating my "washing myself" motions, his brows shifted apart again, and his quills smoothed back along his head. Then he suddenly rose to his feet, his tail uncoiling from my leg so he could stride away.

He walked right to the edge of the camp, then paused with his back to me, only to quickly turn around, rush back to the campfire, then hold both hands out to me in a staying motion that must be universal. His expression looked concerned.

At least, I thought it did. I might be making assumptions, but his features were humanoid enough that I was probably correct.

I nodded that I understood, and his stiff stance relaxed as he again turned away, grumbling something I think he meant to be encouraging before striding off until he disappeared into the shadows of the foliage surrounding the clearing.

Suddenly, I was alone in the jungle again, and as I sat there waiting, I became aware of the clicking hum of those giant cicada things starting up again after they'd fallen silent when my chameleon had stood up. They seemed to realize the threat was gone. Then other sounds joined in, caws and cries and howls and the occasional piercing shriek that I'd heard before when I was trekking through the jungle looking for water.

The sounds were unnerving, but I'd already determined them not to be a threat to me, at least not an immediate one, when I was alone in the jungle before.

It was scary, but also exhilarating to be in such a wild, untamed place with no sign of modern civilization around me. Maybe this was what Nate had meant when he'd insisted that he wanted to move away from the tourist haunts and head out into the unexplored parts of the universe. This excitement, the thrill of the unknown, heated my blood and made my heart pound in a way that reminded me I was alive.

Why hadn't I wanted that when I was with Nate, but now it felt good to me?

Probably because Nate had never made me feel safe. Hell, I'd felt safer on my own in the jungle than when I was with my husband. In fact, he'd always made me feel tense, anxious. Fearful. Not that he'd ever physically abused me, but he'd always been so harsh and critical and had used threats of leaving me to keep me on the defensive and too afraid I'd upset him to speak my mind freely.

I realized now that he'd used that constant criticism and condescension to sow self-doubt and feelings of isolation in me, because he'd managed to convince me that he was the only person who would bother to stick around in my life now that my parents were gone.

My chameleon had left me alone in his camp, and yet I still felt like he was protecting me. For one thing, he'd gone off without his spear, which I noticed was lying on the ground next to his pack if I really needed a weapon. That made me think he didn't plan on going far, and that wherever he was going didn't have serious threats that he'd need to arm up for.

It also probably meant that he wouldn't be gone for long.

Just as I had that thought, he came rushing back, his strides quick even as he carried a huge bucket with clear water sloshing inside it.

As he grew closer to the smoldering campfire, I realized that the bucket he carried in both hands was made from some kind of reddish-brown nut shell, round like a coconut, but much, *much* larger. The kind of thing that would brain a person if it dropped on their head from a tree above.

I realized then that the dangers in this jungle didn't only come from the animals and insects. There were apparently trees that could drop bucket-sized nuts on people if they weren't careful.

My chameleon seemed to know how to avoid them though, so I supposed all I had to do was follow his lead. He reached my side, then used his odd feet to push the soft earth between our sitting stones into a pile before bending to set the shell half into it. The weight of it made a dent in the soil that kept it upright, so the water didn't spill out because of the round bottom of the nut rolling.

Then he smiled at me, gestured to the water still rippling inside the shell bucket with his inhuman hand, and turned back to this pack. He withdrew several cloths from it and brought them to me. His brows furrowed as he studied me for a moment, his dark gaze roving over my naked body.

That moment extended as his expression grew hungrier. I wasn't sure how I knew when it shifted from clinical to heated, but I saw a definite change in the arrangement of his features that told me where his mind had gone.

He was so damned sexy that when the slit at his groin pushed outwards and his dual erections poked their heart-shaped heads out, I was more than a little tempted to put off my bath time and give them a welcoming kiss.

Then he hissed and turned away, his free hand lowering to his groin and covering it like he could push Happy and Slappy back inside him. He tossed the cloths onto the stone next to me and then bent stiffly at his pack again with his back turned towards me.

He rifled inside it for far longer than I would think it would take to examine every single item in the overstuffed pack. He pulled things out that were in pouches and packets, some wrapped in vibrant fabric, some in soft leather of many different shades, some even in scaled pouches, though nothing that looked chameleon-like, thank goodness. I would hate to imagine my hot alien was a cannibal or even just used the skins of his own kind for carrying bags.

Finally, he withdrew a leaf-wrapped pouch tied with a rough cord and made a vibrating grunt of discovery, or what I assumed to be discovery. He still set that at his feet by the other pouches and dug into the pack further before withdrawing another pouch, this one made of soft leather.

Then he repacked all the other things and picked up the two pouches to bring them to me. By this time, he had his erections under control, and I spotted no sign of them poking from the slit at his groin. Though, after watching his sexy tail flick back and forth at the base of his powerful back, coiling and uncoiling in the cutest way at the tip with his agitation, I regretted that sexy times were on hold.

Still, I was more than grateful when he bent to set one of the pouches on the stone beside me, then opened the other to pull out a chunky, rounded stone from a collection of them that filled it.

It was my turn to look confused as he lifted it from the pouch to show it to me. Noting my expression, he set the pouch down beside the other while holding onto that green-tinged white stone that looked chalky upon closer examination. Then he picked up a cloth in his free hand, dunked it in the water in the nutshell bucket, and rubbed the cloth over the stone.

To my delight, a lather formed where the wet cloth met the chalky stone, and it released an herby scent.

It was *soap*! Alien jungle soap provided by a chameleon guy with the sexiest curly tail in the galaxy.

I didn't even know his name, and I was already half in love with him!

Chapter Fifteen

Vera

LATHERING up my body with herbal chalk soap was far more luxurious than it had any reason being while standing by a campfire, completely naked in the middle of the jungle. It felt so damned good that I caught myself moaning as I dragged the wet cloth over my dirty skin. Even the bruises that now speckled my entire body from the river incident—that was totally not my fault at all—didn't hurt much, except for the one on my back that I couldn't reach anyway, but that I could feel just by moving my shoulders.

I wasn't sure how I would deal with the tangled mat of my ponytail. With those quills of his, my chameleon didn't look like he had much use for a brush or comb, not to mention shampoo and conditioner. I supposed I would cross that bridge after I finished washing my body.

And speaking of my chameleon, he was alternating between fiddling around with objects he pulled from his pack while pretending not to watch me, and actually openly staring at me, then catching himself doing it, only to return his attention to his pack. Every time I moaned or sighed as I lathered or rinsed my body, his head turned towards me, his head quills lifting like the hair on the back of my neck might lift.

I'll admit, I took those opportunities to tease him, because the closer I got to being fully cleaned by the herbal soap rock, the more eager I was to take up where we left off earlier. I began to caress my naked curves with the rinsing cloth, letting the cool, lathery water slide down my body to drip at my feet. I noted his gaze shifting from my hand gripping the cloth, to my clean skin exposed beneath it, to then trail downwards in the path of that water. His gaze would always snag on something interesting on the way down.

Based on the fact that his crouch beside his pack had turned into more of an uncomfortable hunch, I wasn't in the least bit surprised when he rose to his feet to show that both of his scarlet shafts were extended. My already wet entrance grew slicker with my arousal as he stalked towards me, bending to snag a cloth lying on my pile of soiled clothes that I didn't really want to put back on.

He dipped it into the water bucket, then lifted the dripping cloth to my collarbone, gently touching it there to let the water sluice down the front of my chest.

I gasped when his tongue darted out to stick to my water slickened collarbone, then he dragged it down in the wake of that water, teasing around the swell of my breast. Another squeeze of the cloth had more water streaking my skin, this time enough that it didn't part over the curve of my breast but covered it entirely, wetting my nipple, which was now as hard as the chalk soapstone.

His broad tongue tip again trailed the path of the water, inhumanly long, sticky even against my wet skin. It reached my nipple as his dark gaze fixed on mine, the tip of his tongue curving around my nipple like a suction cup so when he tugged on it, it felt like he was sucking it.

I gasped, my fingers loosening so much that the cloth I'd been holding dropped from my hand. Slick from my arousal soaked my entrance as he shifted his powerful, scaled body closer to mine, his eyes never leaving my face as he continued to tease and torment my nipple with his tongue.

He trailed his cloth lower down my body, curving around the breast he was currently tormenting in the most pleasurable way to slide it over my belly. His free hand cupped my other breast. The scaly pad of his upper thumb stroked over that nipple as he hesitantly massaged my breast. His expression was intent, focused entirely on my face like he was watching to see what pleased me. With each gasp or moan of my pleasure, he continued to tease, stroke, caress in an intimate language that had no words.

Oh, we were definitely communicating clearly now, and I lifted both hands to trail my fingers over the stiff lengths of his shafts, feeling how slippery they both were, like they'd been slicked with lube. It was his turn to groan as I encircled them both in my fists and began to slowly stroke upwards until I reached the dripping heart-shaped heads of them. The finlike flaps beneath the heads of them had begun to flutter and pulse, moving against the skin of my palms.

He switched his tongue to my other nipple, teasing and tugging as his hips rocked forward to drive his shafts through my slippery grip again. Even as he did this, he dropped the cloth and clutched my naked butt cheeks with both hands, his sharp claws denting my soft flesh, growling softly as I again teased my palms over those slippery heads, milking more of that clear slick from their tips.

I stood with my legs slightly parted, my own slick now dripping from my entrance, so I didn't feel his tail tip until it reached the curve of my inner thigh, caressing my sensitive skin there, seeking my slit. My head fell back as a moan escaped my mouth when that tip parted my seam, then slipped inside me, the scaled texture of it rubbing over my inner walls in a surprisingly pleasing way.

His shaft-flaps waved faster, until they buzzed against my palms as he pumped his tail deeper inside me. My entire body trembled with my desire, but I still yelped in surprise when he suddenly withdrew his tongue from my nipple only to jerk me off my feet and pull me against his chest.

Then he took off for the tree that held his tree house. His tail receded from my slick channel only to slide along my crack as if seeking my rosette. He said something in his growly language that I couldn't even begin to comprehend as we reached the tree, that slippery tail now probing my tight back ring.

I was so ready for it to penetrate me, so eager for it that my now empty inner muscles convulsed with my excitement. I ended up disappointed when his tail left me altogether, although his arms tightened around me.

Then I realized it had left me so he could climb the tree, using his feet and his tail to get from branch to branch until we reached his tree house. He moved so quickly, even hindered by me in his arms, that we were at his tree pod before I could even begin to worry about him accidentally dropping me.

As if I needed to worry with my hands still gripping the lengths that were pinned between us, their flaps buzzing away against my palms, more of that slippery substance leaking from the tips. He only loosened his embrace on me once we reached the doorway of his tree house, and that was just to thrust aside the cloth that covered it.

He had to hunch over into a near crouch to carry me inside, but he somehow managed it without releasing me. Then he laid me on my back on the nest of leaves and the blanket inside the tree house.

I still had ahold of Happy and Slappy, and I had no intention of letting go unless it was to put them inside me. He was apparently perfectly okay with me keeping a grip as he crawled over me, the entire tree house bouncing with our movements, but this time I barely noticed. As his face neared mine, I lifted my head from the blanket and pressed my lips to his.

This time, he wasn't as taken by surprise as he'd seemed to be by my first kiss, and his lips quickly parted as mine caressed them, along with those dangerous teeth. It felt a bit like dangling my toes between the jaws of a bear trap, but I found a little thrill in that, just like I thrilled when his sharp claws dug into my skin without ever quite breaking it.

His thick tongue tasted honey sweet and sublime, and he responded to me sucking on it with a hungry groan as he settled his body over mine. I parted my legs around his hips, opening completely for him.

As eager as I could possibly be for him to take me fully.

In fact, I'd never been so excited, but now my pelvis rocked forward, my own hands getting in the way as I wanted to feel Happy rubbing over my clit with those buzzing flaps. I finally released his lower girth but kept stroking the upper one as I rubbed my clit along Happy's shaft. Those vibrating flaps undid me so quickly that I was arching my entire body and breaking our all-consuming kiss to cry out at the strength of my orgasm.

My inner muscles were still convulsing when I angled my pelvis to settle my entrance over that thick tip. My chameleon needed no further urging as my slit closed around it, and he drove his hips forward to thrust it home. His body shuddered as I released Slappy and lifted both my hands to clutch his back, stroking my palms down his sides to the swells of his sexy butt cheeks.

The thick base of his tail jerked between my hands as I gripped his buttocks and pushed on them to urge him to drive into me again. I recaptured his lips as he groaned and obeyed my unspoken desire for him to pump into me.

That tail tempted me, and I curled the fingers of one hand around it, though it was so thick they didn't come close to meeting, noting how his body tensed even further. He growled in that throat resonating way of his, then murmured against my lips like he was urging me to continue. One of his hands lifted to cup my face while the other slid down my bare side, then under me to squeeze my butt, pushing me harder against him.

When I gripped his tail, he thrust faster, panting and grunting and moaning as Slappy's flaps pulsing against my clit brought me back to the peak, then dragged me over it just as he spewed inside me. He broke our lip-lock to hiss, his body trembling as Happy jerked in the grip of my convulsing inner muscles.

Then he quickly withdrew Happy from my still climaxing body and rammed Slappy home, like he needed to bury it inside me before it spewed. My toes curled with the intensity of his flaps pulsing inside me and against my rosette as Happy, still stiff and erect, now stroked along my crack with each pump of Slappy inside me.

The tip of Happy was extra slippery from both his pre-cum and the cum he'd spilled inside me, so it was no surprise that it probed a little inside my back hole with one of his thrusts. I shifted and angled my hips, so it pushed inside a little more with his next thrust.

The feeling of my tight ring squeezing around the tip of Happy caused him to freeze, lifting his head to break our kiss. I captured his face between my hands, begging him softly to keep going, squeezing my inner muscles and rocking my pelvis to drive that tip a little further inside my back entrance.

It wasn't like I'd never had anal sex before. Nate had always insisted on it, saying he liked how tight that back passage was. I'd learned to enjoy it, even with him, but now I *craved* having my sexy, sweet chameleon filling both passages to the limit.

With how lubricated Happy was, the tip slid fully inside my back hole with ease, and I felt that moment when he decided to go for broke. I moaned in intense pleasure as those buzzing flaps followed, driving into my back hole as Slappy filled my channel.

With several quick thrusts of his hips, he buried both lengths fully inside me, filling me to the limit and giving me a stuffed sensation I'd never experienced before, not even when Nate had used a sex toy along with his unimpressive dick to give me the double trouble experience.

It felt so incredible with my chameleon's long, thick lengths pulsing inside me that I nearly came again, even though I'd just had an orgasm. When he began to thrust rhythmically, I couldn't hold off that climax any longer, and once again, my body arched in his embrace and my lips tore from his to cry out with my ecstasy.

Both of his lengths jerked inside me, filling me until his cum leaked from both entrances. His back was arching now, pushing his body more firmly against mine until I was pressed into the soft blanket and the leaves.

His lips pulled back from his sharp teeth in the most menacing and sexiest O-face I'd ever seen, all his quills standing out from his head. He growled in a deep, animalistic sound when I curled my hands around the base of his tail as his body shuddered with his release, the resonance of it vibrating the very air. The agile tip of his tail curled around my wrist to hold my hand there as I made to pull away uncertainly, just in case that sound wasn't from his pleasure.

As the intensity of our climaxes finally faded, I sagged beneath him, exhaling heavily, feeling deliciously exhausted as he slowly withdrew his shafts from me, a rush of his spew following in their wake to drip out of my seam and my puckered hole.

He propped himself on his elbows to cup my face in both hands, staring down at me with his dark gaze, illuminated by the green-tinged sunlight that filtered through the leaf walls of the tree house.

I was no expert on reading alien chameleon-guy facial expressions, but if I had to guess, I'd say his looked as goofily smitten as I felt about him.

I'd definitely passed the point of no return on this one.

Chapter Sixteen

Khamai

I DIDN'T WANT to leave the side of my Dayglow for even a moment, but I still had so much to do to make her as comfortable as possible in this temporary encampment. At least she was sleeping now, quite soundly, her soft, enchanting body curled up in my blanket and nestled on the leaves beneath it.

I still couldn't believe my good fortune or the fact that a beautiful, mysterious female had fallen from the sky to become my mate. I couldn't wait to present my beaded collar to her, and if my home in the Dense wasn't several days' travel away even through the trees, I would have used the time while she was sleeping to fetch it.

I wanted to take her home with me now, to show her the sprawling tree-net I'd built with its many pods and all the furniture and supplies I'd made or collected, but getting to my home meant a lot of climbing in trees, and I wanted to make certain my Dayglow understood me clearly enough that she remained safely in my arms when I carried her from one branch to the next. If she panicked and struggled while I was carrying her, it might be enough to risk that she'd break free and fall.

Travel through the Dense was impossible on the ground, so until I was certain we had an understanding, we must remain here. On the positive side, it gave me time to finish harvesting the dendrobs for this season, and pulling their traps was what I did instead while she was sleeping. Not only would I be able to harvest their scales for the pigments they made when dried and ground to a powder, but their fresh meat would feed my mate, hopefully pleasing her even more than the dried strips had.

Of course, she hadn't actually accepted my collar yet, so I didn't know if I could call her "mate," but after the way she'd eagerly welcomed my prods, I didn't think she would turn aside the offer of my collar.

Would she?

I pushed that concern away, recalling our last mating and how intense it had been. The way she'd gazed into my eyes, her clawless hands clutching and stroking my body, even gripping the base of my tail as she'd opened herself to my prods had to be proof enough of her wish to be my mate.

My Dayglow had some strange desires, but I found them as intriguing as her odd feet and wriggly little toes with their color-fully painted blunt claws. I still had yet to fully explore her body to my contentment, but I'd seen and felt enough of it to know that she didn't have two slits like a Prdayu female, though she did have what I'd taken to be a cloaca for eliminating waste like any Prdayu would from our cloaca.

I'd been more than a little startled when my lower prod had accidentally pierced the opening of her cloaca, and she'd shown excitement about it, and had even shifted her lower body to impale herself further onto it, as if she were begging me to enter her that way. Though it had seemed strange to me, since I'd never heard of a Prdayu female desiring her cloaca to be pierced by a prod, I'd gone with it, realizing that the tightness of that back hole squeezed my prod in the most delicious way, even tighter than a Prdayu female's lower slit would have.

After something like that, surely, she would accept my collar?

I felt so joyful that I practically leaped from tree branch to tree branch on my way back to camp from the slurry, my cage of dendrobs swinging from my coiled tail. My catch wasn't nearly as thrilled by all the movement, but I didn't suppose they had long to worry about it as they writhed and splashed in the bit of muck I left in the leaf-lined base of the cage.

I didn't want to waste too much time away from my camp, though I felt like she would be perfectly safe in my sway. No predator large enough to threaten her would climb into a sway, and even the moving vines usually avoided any area where they scented Prdayu, no doubt aware on some instinctual level that we found them delicious.

I'd debated weaving the barrier over the opening again before I left, but I'd given her food pouches, a gourd of water, and a waste container formed from the shell of a dead-drop nut so she could eliminate without leaving the sway.

As I'd handed her that last, drinking in the sight of her sitting on my leaf nest with her legs crossed and her stubby toes peeping out from my woven blanket, her eye furs had pulled together, and her head had cocked. She'd regarded the large container with apparent uncertainty, so I'd mimed putting it under my tail and crouching, hoping she would understand its purpose.

Her brow furs had lifted, her mouth dropping open in a round shape, then she'd bobbed her head several times and held out a hand for it.

She'd seemed resigned to the waste shell, but she'd been much more interested in the pack of puff leaves I'd handed her afterwards, this time miming crushing one in my hand to release the cleansing sap, then miming swiping it under my tail, before gesturing like I was casting it out of the sway door.

She'd chittered with apparent excitement, a broad smile parting her lips and baring her flat-edged teeth.

After that, she'd been less excited when I'd started to leave the sway again, but when I'd made a staying gesture, she'd bobbed her head and chirped as if in agreement to obey my request. I'd made several more staying gestures as I'd backed out of the sway, until she'd exhaled heavily and her odd blue eyes had rolled upwards, turning her eye openings mostly white for a brief moment as she'd bobbed her head more sharply and cawed at me.

Noting my expression of alarm, she'd released her joyful noise ripple, her lips parted in an expression I took to be happy.

Maybe she felt the same bubbliness I felt after our mating.

After that, she'd waved me towards the door with one hand, lifting the other to her mouth as it stretched wide open. By the time I was climbing onto the branch outside the sway, she had laid down on my nest and tucked the blanket under her chin, her eyelids drifting shut.

When I'd checked on her a short time later, after bathing myself by the cold fire ring with the compressed bubblestone I'd made for journeys like this, she'd been sleeping soundly, giving me the impression that I had some time to collect the dendrobs.

Now, I had checked all the traps and had an excellent harvest of dendrobs to return to our camp so we would both eat well for our evening meal.

Our camp! Just to have another person in my camp would have seemed like a distant dream a few days ago, and now I had a beautiful skyfallen female to keep me company after being alone for many season-turnings.

I again questioned my good fortune and wondered if I was simply dreaming all of this, but then realized I didn't have the imagination to dream of such a lovely but alien female as my Dayglow. I had nothing to compare her to. No beast I'd ever seen was anything like her, though she had fur, and skin, and even spawn-feeding buds on her chest rounds like other creatures in the Sprawl. At least, I assumed that was what those pink nubs were for.

She wasn't anything like them, nor were her fabrics like

anything a Prdayu might weave. Or even *could* weave, the fibers so fine that they were barely visible. It seemed to me like something magically made, ugly as that orange woven had been.

I wondered about Tytonid's avatar that had nearly eaten my Dayglow. Was he still alive, still shrieking in that piercing cry? I hadn't heard it since I'd followed my Dayglow away from his fallen avatar, but I feared the fact that he was so close to my camp, and worried that he would come to steal Dayglow away from me.

I pondered whether I should move my campsite like I'd planned to before I'd discovered her raiding it as I once again approached my campsite with a cage of dendrobs. Though this time, I felt no sense of foreboding, and the Sprawl was filled with the usual sounds that said the many eyes of it weren't warning of danger.

I set the dendrobs by the cold coals of the fire, then rushed towards the tree that held my sway, eager to see my Dayglow again.

Also, more than a little fearful that she wouldn't be there. That maybe she'd never been there, and I'd only imagined it all, even though my prods still throbbed deliciously behind my groin slit at the memory of being buried inside her.

To my relief, the sway rocked gently as I climbed the branches to reach it, and before I could touch the fabric that covered the opening, she pulled it aside and peered out warily with wide blue eyes. Those eyes found mine, and a smile stretched her lips as she chittered in what I assumed was a greeting.

"Myeh hawtlizard geye!" She shifted her entire body closer to the opening of the sway.

Then she held out both arms toward me, like she wanted me to embrace her.

I happily obliged, holding her close as her smooth arms closed around my scales, the heat of her body more comforting than any warming stones. She inhaled deeply as her palms slid down my back to settle on my undertail rounds, and my tail jerked when she squeezed one of my rounds, even though the end was coiled around the branch I stood on.

My prods pulsed against the inside of my slit as my prod fins fluttered eagerly.

But I had dendrobs to skin and clean, and a meal to make for both of us, as much as I wanted to have another mating session with my Dayglow.

I lowered my hands to her tailless backside, gripping her rounds in return, but then sliding my hands lower to urge her legs to wrap around me as they'd done before so I could carry her out of the tree.

She seemed to understand what to do like we'd done this a hundred times before, and before I knew it, her thighs were gripping my waist and her lower legs were crossed above the base of my tail as I held my soft, beautiful female in my arms.

She might not be built for climbing in the trees, but I didn't doubt in that moment that she was made for me. She fit into my arms perfectly and clung to me as if she trusted me completely not to drop her as I moved from branch to branch, my feet and tail doing the climbing and gripping of the tree for me.

Perhaps we would be able to return to the Dense even sooner than I'd hoped.

For now, I still intended to see to her comfort in this meager campsite I'd originally only intended to serve my own paltry needs. I'd had few at the time that I'd set up here, not really concerned with comfort.

Not really concerned with much of anything.

Ever since I'd been exiled from the village, I'd steadily lost the desire to live. Even near-death experiences had left me feeling numb rather than pumped with bloodfire, ready to fight, though I hadn't even had many of those in the season-turnings since I'd left the village for the last time, looking back once to see that only my sister had watched me go, her expression as devastated as my own heart had felt.

Of all the villagers I'd grown up with, it was only my sister I truly missed, though I still had gratitude towards the chief's wife for begging the other elders to spare my life and choose exile instead of the snapper grove for my fate. My sister had also pled for my life, but the elders hadn't been concerned with her pleas, treating her as though she was responsible for the chief's unwanted attentions, which had only infuriated me more.

When I'd first left the village, I'd stayed close to it, looking out for her from a distance, but eventually, a hunter had spotted my tracks and the villagers had formed a hunting party to track me down and confront me with threats and demands that I move further away from the village or die. I'd had no choice but to leave the area after that, and have worried about my sister ever since, but didn't dare to return lest I get a spear in my chest for the trouble.

Now that I had a soft, warm, skyfallen mate in my arms, I could only wonder what my sister would think about the female I hoped would accept my collar. Would she be as transfixed as I was by my Dayglow's beauty? Would she find my female as fascinating and mysterious as I did?

Would she welcome her if we could ever return to the village?

I believed Maika would, though I wasn't certain what the other villagers would do. Perhaps it was for the best that I had been exiled and would likely never see any of them again. Not this far from the village at any rate, and certainly not in the Dense. It was rare for the Prdayu of my village to stray far from its territory.

There were other Prdayu villages, but none near this unclaimed territory. I made certain not to hunt or trap in claimed territory. Prdayu could be hostile to those who didn't belong to their village, especially when they believed the other Prdayu was taking something from their land.

The Dense would be safe for my skyfallen mate, since that was *my* territory, and my territory alone. Even the Prdayu didn't like delving into the shadowed depths of the Dense. That meant they missed out on the clearings, where the thick canopy of the Sprawl thinned out enough for plenty of dayglow to spill through, making a perfect setting for a large tree-net. The Dense required patience to navigate, but those who had that patience could find great rewards by doing so.

My home trees were beautiful, and they received plenty of light, even though the deep shadows of the Dense surrounded them. I had built my many pods to best take advantage of the available light.

I hoped my Dayglow would love my home as much as I did. As lonely as it had been, and as little as I'd cared about anything before she'd stolen into my life, building and furnishing my home had been the only comfort I'd found in my exile.

Now I realized that I'd been building it all along for her.

Chapter Seventeen

Vera

MY CHAMELEON CARRIED me so easily from the tree house that I didn't feel as nervous as I had been before. Not only was his body powerful against mine, but his tail was very muscular, from the thick base of it that lay over his sexy ass to the thinner but no less effective tip of it that coiled around the branches.

He knew what he was doing and moved through the tree branches as easily as I strolled down a street.

I wasn't certain I wanted to be carried everywhere we went for the rest of my life, then realized that I was already thinking long-term with this alien I couldn't even understand. Surprisingly, the thought of being trapped on this planet forever, with no way to get back home to Earth, didn't bother me as much as it should, and that was all due to the lizardman now cradling me in his arms as he made his way out of the tree.

I felt comfortable with him in a way I'd never felt comfortable with Nate. I felt safe, despite our uncivilized surroundings. I felt cared for, even though the male doing the caring knew nothing about me. He'd saved my life without knowing who I was. Heck, even after I'd stolen from him, he'd come to my rescue, risking his own life to catch me before I went over the waterfall.

I couldn't begin to imagine Nate ever doing such a courageous thing, especially not for me. For some reason, he'd treated me like I wasn't that important to him after he'd initially wooed me, and for the longest time, I'd assumed that was just his guarded nature. He wasn't an affectionate person, I kept reminding myself. Surely, he *did* love me, I'd always reassure myself, because he'd asked me to marry him, and then had made it official, willing to commit to a wife again, even after being burned so badly by his ex-wife.

I now realized she had likely been a victim of his infidelity and cruelty like I had and had wisely chosen to escape such a miserable life. He'd said she'd done awful things that had left him scarred emotionally, and I'd assumed them to be true stories, in my own naivety about Nate himself. I'd fallen for his lies and had despised that unseen woman who'd run far from Nate, and according to him, cleaned out his bank account and maxed all his credit cards to their limits. Believing him, I'd painted her out to be the bad guy, and had given my husband far too much credit in the process, forgiving his constant complaining and penny-pinching because of his past emotional trauma.

Now, I understood what a manipulative, miserable bastard he was, and that was all due to comparing him to the male who now carried me in his arms like I was precious to him.

My chameleon didn't release me until he'd carried me to the fire ring, then he allowed my body to slide down his until I stood on my own feet. I was still as naked as the day I was born, and surprisingly comfortable in that state, especially when my bare skin slid over supple scales covering firm, ridged muscles.

The waning day was hot and muggy, so clothing would have only clung wetly to me, uncomfortable and chafing in all the wrong places, whereas the occasional breeze that drifted across my skin felt heavenly. Since the clearing was mostly in the shade of the canopy, the only sunlight that managed to break through the leaves casting mottled shadows around the fire ring, I didn't even need to worry about getting sunburned.

Or aggravating the burn I already had on my scalp and face. They would peel. I was certain of that.

My chameleon had an intent expression on his face after my naked body had rubbed against his, and it looked like he was debating a repeat of our earlier activities, but then he lifted a hand to cup my face, gently stroking his clawed double thumbs over my red cheek, his hungry expression shifting to one that looked—to me—to be more affectionate than heated. His gaze was searching as it roved over my sunburned face, like I was a mystery he was desperate to solve.

I completely understood the feeling.

Then he lowered his hand and turned to the side to gesture to the stone where my clothing still provided padding for my seat. With that gesture, he rumbled something in his language that made me wish I could at least understand it, even if I could never replicate that resonance, before stepping away from me to crouch by the fire ring.

When he turned his back to me, I plucked my tee shirt off the top of the pile, thinking maybe I should put it on before the night fell and the air cooled off, though it hadn't cooled enough to be chilly since I'd been here.

Then I took a seat on the stone, holding onto the tee shirt, but reluctant to pull the dirty material over my head.

I knew he remained very aware of me, because his tail coiled around my calf, the tip of it caressing the top of my foot, like he just couldn't resist touching me.

More signs of affection for me that made me feel special and wanted, unlike when I was with Nate. If I wasn't careful, I could grow addicted to this feeling. I certainly felt hooked on watching my chameleon, his initially alarming appearance now more than merely appealing to me as he began building a fire, the muscles of his back bunching and flexing beneath his colorful scales.

His head quills also flexed and twitched like he was aware of my gaze. Even as I focused on them, it seemed like their colors suddenly grew much more vivid, the shades of blue and yellow and green and gray brightening considerably.

They'd just shifted to brighter shades! The more I stared at them, the more I was certain of it.

I'd be willing to bet my entire outfit, which I honestly never wanted to don again, that he was changing his colors to show off for me. It was totally working, because he was so visually striking that it was difficult to look away from all those hues that should be clashing but somehow came together in a delightfully aesthetic display.

Much like the woven fabrics of his cleaning cloths and blanket. It seemed my chameleon had a good eye for color and pattern, and maybe it was from looking at his own reflection.

I watched as he cleaned out the old coals, then built a tent of fallen branches in the ring, with a nest of dried fibrous material tucked below the wood. Then he used a primitive but apparently effective stick and board method to spark a flame in a small bit of kindling that he cradled between his palms and gently blew on until it began to burn in his hands. Without freaking out the way I would at holding a literal flame as it licked at the fibrous material, he tucked the burning kindling into the rest of the kindling, and the fire quickly took hold.

It was so fascinating watching him build a fire that when he turned, he caught me staring fixedly at him, clutching the fabric of my tee shirt between my hands without realizing it.

He rose from his crouch by the growing fire and approached me, his tail never releasing my leg, like he needed that physical connection to me. He knelt on one knee beside my stone, then touched the crumpled blue material of my shirt. He rumbled something that sounded sexy as hell in my ear, then gently stroked the fingers of his other hand over one of my smaller bruises, which was already beginning to change color.

He lifted his brow ridges as he glanced down at the bruise, then touched another one, then looked at his fingers, which pinched the material between his claws. When he lifted his gaze to meet mine, his brows were drawn together, his quills flexing as he rumbled more alien words in what I took to be a question based on his expression.

I couldn't possibly explain the bruises, or even the tee shirt, but I did open it to show him the sparkly but cheap plastic crystals glued to it that spelled out "Newlywed."

He traced a claw over the crystals as I glared down at them with a frown, recalling how excited I'd been when I'd bought this shirt before the Justice of the Peace wedding that I'd settled for, reminding myself we would have a luxurious honeymoon cruise instead.

I realized now how much I despised this tee shirt. I glanced up at the fire as he continued to trace the line of the crystals, murmuring something in his language when he looked up and caught my expression.

When I suddenly jerked the tee shirt from under his claws and rose abruptly to my feet, so did he, his quills spreading and his body tensed as he watched me, like he was alarmed. His tail slipped away from my calf to coil behind him. I strode to the fire that was just beginning to really crackle and burn as it flickered around the tent of wood. I crumpled the hated shirt into a ball, then dropped it into the center of the flame.

Then I turned on my heel, my chin lifting as I gazed at my chameleon, whose widened eyes were shifting from me to the fire then back to me, his quills now fully extended, and his entire body stiff, his arms dangling at his sides with his claws twitching like he had no idea what to do with them. After a long moment, his tail slowly uncoiled from behind him and returned to hesitantly wrap around my calf again as he growled in a questioning way.

I knew it was a question, without understanding the words. It was his body language that told me, and the way he kept glancing from the burning shirt to me, then back. He even gestured towards it with one hand.

I lifted my chin a little higher, giving him my most sultry smile. "My daddy always said you can't let the past mire you down, my sexy chameleon, and I don't think I've ever wanted to take his advice more than I do now. *Screw* Nate, *screw* the ring he gave me that was a damned lie rather than a genuine promise, and *screw* that stupid tee shirt that I'd been so *stupid* to buy with any hope for our marriage and future!"

I dusted my palms together in dismissal, wishing I had the ring Nate had given me that was probably cubic zirconia knowing him, so I could toss that into the flames too. Too bad I'd yanked it off my hand as I'd run away from him and Naja and had blindly thrown it somewhere on the ship.

Can't say I didn't wish I had Nate to throw into the fire too, but then again, that would require he be here right now, and I preferred this place without him fouling it up with his presence.

Of course, my chameleon had no idea what was going on, and my words didn't help clear anything up for him, but as I closed the distance between us, his confused expression shifted to one of anticipation, and his tail traveled higher up my leg, until the tip teased my inner thigh.

When I lifted my hands to his shoulders, he lowered his head so I could reach his lips with mine. His arms slipped around my naked waist, his scaly palms settling on the top curve of my butt. My hands threaded through his quills as they flexed then settled when he deepened our kiss, his lips parting so his thick tongue could slide between my lips.

I felt his body tense against me as I sucked on that honey sweet tongue tip, and he growled in a panty-wetting way that made me as slick as a waterslide. Things were just getting interesting as I hungrily sucked his tongue, and his tail traced along my seam, when a sudden wet, splatting sound made itself known over the ubiquitous cadence of the monster cicadas that surrounded our campsite.

My chameleon lifted his head with an exhale, his tail slipping away from its interesting exploration, leaving me wanting as he released me hesitantly, like he was also disappointed. I added my own sigh of disappointment as he turned away from me to stalk to one of the other flat stones by the fire.

Then I watched him curiously, my arousal fading to a manageable level as he picked up a cage of sorts in one hand, with a leaf covered base. He lifted it to chest height as his gaze shifted from it to me, like he was showing it to me.

It was around the size of a large cat carrier, formed with bamboo-like stalks that served as the bars, with additional smaller sticks woven between them so I could barely see the slimy, colorful scales that whipped past the bars, but the slopping sound was unmistakable now. I realized I'd been so distracted by my chameleon and my own issues that I hadn't even noticed the cage sitting by the other stone.

He set the cage down by the stone again and moved to his pack. He withdrew what looked like a sheathed knife then made his staying gesture to me. I propped one hand on my hip, cocking my other leg in a relaxed stance, and nodded in understanding. That seemed to reassure him because he turned and headed towards the line of trees nearby.

I worried that he would leave me alone with the mystery scaled creature—or creatures—in the cage that were now slopping around more loudly, as if they'd just awakened and were growing agitated. He paused at the nearest tree and lifted the end of his tail to catch the lowest branch, which he tugged down so he could cut off one of the broad leaves.

He returned with it in hand, his knife in his other hand, now unsheathed so I could see that it looked like some kind of translucent stone that was chipped into a sharp-edged blade. He bent to set the leaf on his flat sitting rock, and the leaf was large enough to cover the top of it. Then he set the knife beside it.

I decided he wouldn't be holding me in his arms anytime soon, so I settled back on my stone to watch him as he fetched another of those huge shell halves, like the one that held the washing water near the stones. Also, like the one he'd given me to use as a chamber pot. At least they had a primitive version of toilet paper, which was actually softer and felt cleaner than real toilet paper, come to think of it.

The shell half he had now was empty, but he used the smaller cup-sized shell by the water bucket to scoop water into it until it was half full. After he set that by the leaf-covered stone, he collected a couple of bowls from his pack and a handful of small pouches.

Then he sat on the dirt in front of the flat stone, his tail seeking my leg again as he set the bowls and pouches beside it. He pulled the cage closer to him, and I watched with a queasy tightness in my gut as he opened the top of it and withdrew a wriggling eel-like creature covered in slimy muck. It had two legs near the front of its body, with webbed feet like a frog. Its head was rounded like a fish head, and as it thrashed in his unyielding grip, I spotted sharp teeth in a large, gaping mouth that took up half its eyeless head.

He dunked the writhing creature into the water bucket he'd filled and used his other hand to rinse off the muck as he held it under. Then he plopped that bad boy onto the leaf and chopped off its head so fast that the water in the bucket was still settling when he flicked the head to the dirt beside his stone with a casual motion of his knife hand.

My jaw gaped at how rapidly that thing had gone from alive to dead under the knife of my chameleon. I recalled him spearing a hole in the escape pod, going after something he likely had no comparison for with a ferocity I'd never witnessed before. I'd been so scared he would kill me when he broke through that pod, but now, considering how he treated me, I wondered if I'd misinterpreted his determination to get me out of that pod.

Regardless of his intent then, he'd clearly decided he wanted to keep me. Given how sweet and gentle he was with me, I'd forgotten how dangerous he actually was until his efficient slaughtering of the eel-fish-frog thing reminded me what he was capable of.

I didn't have much time to notice how vibrant and beautiful the purple scales of the eel thing were before he'd skinned them off it, then gutted it and pulled out its innards.

I gulped and swallowed, keeping my eyes away from that eel head on the dirt, but also away from my chameleon's skillful work.

He knew what he was doing, I'd give him that, and after two more heads joined the first, I managed to overcome my queasiness so I could watch him work, realizing that he was humming softly and not just with his throat vibration, but actually a tune, his focus intent on the eel thing beneath his knife, though he would glance up to meet my eyes from time to time, like he was checking on me. His tail was now firmly coiled around my calf again, holding on like he never wanted to let go.

I realized that it was fascinating to watch his swift, economical movements as he cleaned and gutted the eel things, stripping their scaled skin to lay it on one side of the stone like he intended to use it for some purpose. The cleaned eels he stacked to the other side, and he scraped the guts of each one into one of the empty bowls.

As I watched his knife blade move, my mind began to wander, and I imagined myself sitting at a modern kitchen island watching my reptilian master-chef prepare a meal for us. I imagined what outfit I would wear, then considered how I would do my hair for the occasion.

Then I remembered that my hair was in a hopeless, tangled mat of knots that were so bad that I couldn't even get the ponytail holder out of it. That ponytail holder and the filthy matted mess my waist-length hair had become was like the last vestige of my previous life. A reminder of the kind of burden that civilization settled upon a person.

Granted, in a civilized world, I could buy my fish-eel things from the supermarket, already neatly filleted and nicely bundled and not looking at all like the creepy, slimy, writhing things my chameleon was currently cleaning, but I still had to maintain a civilized appearance and demeanor. I had to cover up my naked body, and keep my hair nice and neat and untangled, and wear makeup to conceal the natural flaws in my features so that I was pleasing in appearance to others.

My long hair was my best feature, Nate had always said. Thick, silky, slightly wavy, and golden blonde like the hair of a Nordic princess. It took so much work to maintain it at this length that I didn't want to count the hours of my life spent in the endless tasks to keep it clean, and conditioned, and brushed, and also, to keep it out of my way but still looking loose and flow-ing, for Nate's sake.

Suddenly, I rose from my seat and approached my chameleon, my hand thrusting out in a demanding gesture I didn't intend to be so abrupt. But my stomach was churning, and my chest was burning, and my scalp itched like I had fleas crawling in that nest of tangled hair.

I needed his knife.

His quills lifted as he glanced up at me, then his head tilted to the side, his ear flaps extending and expanding as if he listened for an explanation of my behavior that wouldn't mean anything to him.

I gave it anyway. "Burning the shirt wasn't enough. I need something more freeing. Something truly transformative." I pointed to the knife. "Please let me borrow that."

He looked from me to the knife, then lifted it a bit like he was asking if that was what I wanted. I nodded, then reached for it.

He handed it over hesitantly, his expression wary as he regarded me with his dark eyes. With his other hand he swept aside the eel he'd been working on and reached inside the cage to pluck out another. I took the knife in a shaking grip as he dunked the eel and rinsed it, then slapped it on the leaf, its body only wriggling slightly.

Then he looked at me like he thought I wanted to do the honors.

I shook my head just as abruptly as I'd demanded the knife, my entire body tense with nerves that felt like they would all snap from the strain of what I was about to do.

It was only hair, right? It would grow back if I hated the cut—the jagged, blind cut I was about to give myself.

When I lifted the knife to my head, gripping the tangled ponytail in my other hand just behind the tie, my chameleon jumped to his feet, sending the eel thing to the dirt to wriggle and writhe, its slimy body quickly turning dirt into mud.

His tail wrapped around my wrist, stopping my hand that held the knife as he growled in a sharp way that I took to be alarm or concern.

Or warning?

I jerked on my hand to pull it away from his grip, but his tail only tightened. Not hurting me, but not yielding either. His tail grip was as strong—maybe even stronger—than his hands would be. Those hands that were now covered in muck and eel guts. That might be why he was using his tail to stop me.

"I need to do this!" I insisted desperately. "Don't make me hesitate for too long, or I might chicken out."

It was *only* hair. Sure, I'd worn it long my entire life, and it *was* the feature most people complimented me for, even more than my blue eyes.

Still, it was holding me back now. It was hot, heavy, tangled, matted, and hopeless. Hopeless like I had been with Nate.

My chameleon wasn't budging as he grumbled and rumbled a whole lot of sounds so rapidly that I couldn't even begin to detect a pattern to them that might be words.

I released my ponytail with my other hand and poked him in the chest with one finger. "Let me go, hot stuff. I love ya, but I'm not gonna to keep my hair in this tangled mess even for you."

I froze, my jaw dropping as I realized what I'd just said.

Did I just use the L-word towards someone whose name I didn't even know?

Now wasn't the time to think about that. I again jerked on my hand, poking him in the chest with my other hand, my finger tip bending upwards at the hardness of his pectoral muscles. "Let me go, bucko!" I snapped, my voice quivering.

His tail loosened slightly around my wrist, but it didn't fully release me. He stared at me with a deep and obvious frown that pulled his lips so far downwards that some of his sharp teeth were showing in a scowl. His brow ridges were pressed tightly together beneath his horned crest, and his black eyes were narrowed, the red-striped outer lids vibrant in contrast to the slits of his shiny black eyes.

With enough play in my arm, I could do what I'd intended, though now both hands were shaking as I again gripped my ponytail under his watchful glare.

I brought the blade behind me, pulling his tail along with it, though he gave me just enough slack to do what I needed to do.

I began to slice, feeling the give in the hair in my grip as the sharp edge of the stone blade sliced through the matted strands. At first, I was fighting the urge to give up on this wild idea and leave my hair long. I'd find a way to detangle it, surely. My chameleon had cleansing toilet leaves, right? I mean, he'd figured out a solution to that hygiene need. Surely, the jungle would provide, and he could rustle up a comb and some conditioner from somewhere. Or make it, like I suspected he'd made the soap-rock.

But as I cut away the hair, feeling the weight of it growing in my hand as it no longer had my scalp to support it, I experienced a strange sense of lightness. Like I was cutting away ropes that had bound me for so long that they felt like a part of me.

My chameleon's gaze was searching as he watched me slice off my ponytail, though his frown had lightened. It seemed that he wasn't upset I was cutting off my hair, though I knew Nate would probably have an apoplectic fit if he was witnessing this. I guessed that my chameleon had been worried I would harm myself with his knife. Maybe he thought I wanted to kill myself.

I wondered then if his kind was even familiar with the concept, and then suspected my chameleon was more than familiar with it as the tension in his body slowly relaxed while I finished severing my ponytail, probably because he was reassured that I didn't want to do any harm to myself.

It felt so good to be free of it that I sighed in satisfaction as I finally cut the last strands loose, lowering the knife to hand it back to him, aware that I'd just left some eel guts in my dirty hair, but since it was already a mess anyway, who cared at this point?

He took the knife from my slack grip, his tail finally uncoiling from my wrist, but his eyes fixed on my face as my own gaze settled on the hank of hair in my hand.

So, there it was. A lifetime's worth of hair, kept carefully trimmed and excruciatingly maintained, and cleaned and conditioned and brushed. The length of it looked so small and insignificant in my hand now. I couldn't believe how much of my life had been invested in this.

I wanted to cast it into the flames, but the stench of burning hair wasn't anything I wanted to subject myself or my chameleon to. So instead, I threw it to the dirt and stomped on it. Then I drove my heel into it, digging it into the dirt like I intended to bury it.

Maybe my laughter grew a little hysterical in that moment. Maybe I was losing it. Maybe those were tears streaking down my cheeks as I suddenly screamed at the top of my lungs at the offending hair. Shouted at it. Called it a cheating bastard and a liar and a verbally abusive asshole who deserved nothing less than to be jettisoned into space without a suit.

When arms pinned me to a powerful chest, I struggled at first. I fought like it was Nate grabbing me, but the hold on me was relentless against my wild writhing.

And gentle, despite how unyielding it was. Far too gentle to be that piece of garbage that dared to pretend he was my husband while all the while looking for another woman to take my place in his meager affections.

I sagged in my chameleon's soothing hold, sobbing as the strain and stress and trauma of the last... how long had it even been since I'd boarded the transport shuttle to go to the Relativity space-cruise ship with so much hope in my heart that this honeymoon would be the happiest time of my life?

Chapter Eighteen

Khamai

I FELT deep fear for my Dayglow as I remained firm against her struggles to break free from my hold. I suspected that she might hurt herself if I let her go. She might even cast herself into the fire the way she'd thrown her blue woven into the flames.

I was still stunned from what she'd just done to her head-tail, and also completely baffled about why she'd done it. Obviously, it had caused her some pain, but she'd only reacted to the pain of severing it after she held it in her hand. Then she'd gone wild, throwing it to the ground to trample on it with the strange and bony back part of her foot where toes should be.

I wondered if this was some ritual of her people, but I had no way of asking. The things I said to her in the hopes of soothing her were completely lost on her as her cackles turned to caws, then rose to peals of sound that rivaled the pitch of Tytonid's piercing shrieking.

I'd only embraced her when I realized how close she was moving to the fire. In her sudden bout of madness, I worried that she would fall into the flames even if she didn't intend to throw herself into them.

After too many tense moments of her wriggling in my hold as fiercely as a newly trapped dendrob, her body lost all tension and she sagged against me. Then she shook with loud, heaving roars that seemed too deep to have come from her. Her eyes leaked so much that her red cheeks were slick and shiny, and the skin around those eyes had puffed up and turned almost as bright a red as her cheeks.

I would have been entranced by this color change if I wasn't certain that it was a bad sign for my Dayglow. Just like I'd come to suspect that the dark patches all over her pale skin were not good signs, even though they were changing color, albeit slowly and subtly.

Considering her obvious pain, I felt intense guilt that I'd given her the tool to harm herself. I'd been afraid she would do so when she'd lifted it towards her head, but her body had stiffened, and her expression had scrunched up in a glare. Then she'd stabbed at me with her clawless finger like she was angry when I wouldn't release her wrist.

I'd made a compromise by slackening my hold on it, but when she'd cut at the tail that jutted from the back of her head, she hadn't seemed like it was hurting her, so I'd let her do it, assuming she was just cutting the long furs that tangled in her head-tail. Now, I regretted it.

I didn't know what to do for her as she sagged further in my hold, until it was only my arms holding her up. Her body still trembled, and her shoulders shook with each heaving cry, though they were coming less frequently now, and a new sniffling sound was replacing those other terrible wounded sounds.

Finally, she fell silent in my arms, save for the occasional sniff, but her body tensed against mine when she lifted her head to meet my eyes. She also lifted her hand to swipe away some of the slickness on her cheeks.

I wasn't certain how she would react to being held by me now, given that she'd fought against my embrace so fiercely. When she lifted her other hand to trail her fingers along my cheek, a small upward tilt touching her lips. I hoped that meant she understood why I'd had to restrain her.

"Yer tooperfic tobereel." Her murmured croon was much gentler than her earlier caws, and though it sounded almost defeated, it didn't sound angry. Coupled with her expression no longer being pulled together in a hard, narrow-eyed glare, I took it as a positive.

"Tankeww hawtstuf." She exhaled after her soft chirrup, then slipped her hand behind my neck, her fingers seeming to thread through my bristles automatically.

Like she knew my body well, even though I hadn't yet told her my name.

The pressure she exerted on my neck was an invitation that I didn't resist, lowering my head to catch her lips with mine, enjoying the way she caressed them, and enjoying even more when she sucked my tongue tip into her mouth.

She broke the lip touching contact when she settled back on the flat bottoms of her feet, and though her lips still tilted upwards at the corners, she exhaled heavily as if she labored under a great burden. When she pressed her palm against my chest and pushed, I released her, though I didn't let her go far since we were still too close to the fire, and her actions were unpredictable, even if she seemed calm now. I lifted my tail to coil loosely around her waist. If I had to, I would toss her away from the flames rather than let her leap into them.

I understood the kind of despair that made one consider it, even if they ultimately rejected the idea.

At least I now stood between her and my knife, so she couldn't grab that to harm herself again, though she did lift her hand to the severed stub of her head-tail. Then she pinched something on it and tugged. Her wince of what I assumed to be pain made my tail tighten around her waist as I debated pulling her against me again to catch her wrists with my hands, even if they were still soiled with dendrob muck and guts. I'd avoided touching her directly with them so far, clasping my own wrists when I'd held her, not having had a chance to rinse them off before I had to grab her.

She pulled something off her head-tail stub, and suddenly, her head furs came loose and fell around her face in jagged lengths. As alarming as it was to see that sudden change in her appearance, her next exhale sounded like one a Prdayu might release in relief. Then she lifted both hands to run her fingers through the loose head furs. She dragged them away from her face, looking up at me with a broad smile.

"Iyamfree hawtstuf!" Her caw sounded triumphant, then she cocked her head, releasing her head furs with one hand so they fell forward to frame her face. "Ulyke eet?" Her short chirrup followed by an expectant pause made me think she was asking a question.

I pondered how to react when she exhaled again, then lifted her shoulders only to drop them again in a quick motion that seemed practiced. She lowered her other hand, letting her head furs fall over her face, then she shook her head back and forth.

The head furs concealing her mouth billowed outwards from her breath as she let it gust out of her in a burst. To my surprise after her recent expression of pain, a happy sound ripple left her that didn't sound like her earlier tense cackle. She tossed her head until her head furs parted so one blue eye peered from between them, and I spotted her teeth flashing in another smile behind the curtain of them. "Gottacut sumbangeez soeyekinsee."

After her chirping, she again pulled her head furs away from her face, her gaze searching the stone behind me. I tensed when it alighted on the knife sitting beside the pile of skinned dendrobs.

"No," I growled, shaking my head as my bristles rustled. "No more hurting yourself, my Dayglow."

Her gaze shifted back to me, and her eyes narrowed as her jaw jutted. She tapped her odd foot. "Needeet." Then she pointed to my knife, which I had already suspected was her aim.

I shook my head again and held up a hand in a staying gesture. "No. I won't make the same mistake twice, Dayglow. I won't let you cause yourself any more pain." I didn't know why she'd suddenly severed her head-tail, but it was more than clear that it had wounded her.

I could tell that she was frustrated when she stomped her foot, the bony back round denting the soft dirt, and made a growling sound closer to my language than any other sound she'd made thus far, but I took it to be progress, because it seemed like she understood my meaning, even if she didn't know my words.

She knew that I wouldn't let her use my knife again.

That progress in communicating excited me even though her brows were lowering as she used both hands to part her head furs and loop them behind her bizarre, rounded ear flares. Then her arms crossed over her chest rounds. Her foot tapped even faster. "Gunnahgeevme ahardeetimeh bouthenifeethingeh arenteya."

I was certain that I should be grateful I didn't understand that low-pitched clucking coming from her, but I mirrored her pose, crossing my own arms over my chest to see if that got my message across. Then I shook my head again.

Her body sagged, her shoulders bowing forward as she exhaled. Some of her head furs slipped from behind her ear to cover one side of her face, and she released a gust of breath that sent them flying outwards. Then she pointed with one hand at the loose furs as she met my eyes, her brows lifted.

"See," she cawed. Then she pointed to my knife again. "Eyeneedeet."

Again, I suspected we were successfully communicating without understanding each other's words, because I was certain she was insisting again on getting ahold of my knife.

I was also certain I intended to say no, and I tightened my tail around her waist to add weight to that message. I wouldn't let her near it, even if I had to restrain her again.

She suddenly threw her head back and made an odd noise that sounded a lot like a growl mixed with a caw. Then she stomped her foot again, her little fists clenching at her sides. "Sooofruztrateeen." This time her vocalization sounded more like a growl than a caw or coo.

I pointed in a commanding gesture to her wovens softening the sitting stone.

I still needed to complete the preparation of our evening meal, and the dayglow was swiftly fading. Soon, Tytonid's purple-eyed gaze would be upon us. I was hungry, and I was certain she would be also.

She glanced at my pointing finger, then at the stone, then back at me, her eyes narrowing further. Then she made that lifted shoulder motion again with another heavy exhale, raising a hand to tuck her head furs back behind her ear flare.

I wondered what those head furs felt like, watching how they slid through her fingers like the finest threads of the rare singer's lure blossoms. I'd already noticed how they'd shined in the dayglow, but now that they had been severed from her head-tail, they seemed to be even glossier.

She turned towards the stone like she intended to obey, then suddenly shrieked in a piercing sound and began to hop, her knees lifting high in a stomping dance as she flailed her arms, her hands spread wide and flapping back and forth.

"Eetbiteemeee," she squealed, doing that strange, rapid knee-lifting dance as her chest rounds bounced wildly. Her head furs flopped in her face, breaking free from the restraint of her ear flares.

I wondered if this dance was another part of a ritual involving the head-tail severing.

The screeches that followed her squeal sounded alarmed, like the warning calls of some of the birds in the Sprawl, but a swift glance around the clearing showed no sign of predators, and the tree-singers had only fallen silent after her first squeal, so they'd detected nothing to concern them other than my Dayglow herself.

"Grohzz!" She squealed again, then pointed with one hand while the other continued to flap. "Awlll thoseteetheh."

I glanced down at where she was pointing and noted that the dendrob I'd dropped earlier had wriggled its way towards her and had possibly mouthed her foot.

Dendrobs had what appeared to be sharp teeth, but they were only for straining the muck for their food. Those apparent teeth were very flexible and would bend on scales, or even skin, rather than cutting into it.

"Geteet aywaay frumee." My Dayglow continued to squeal and screech and dance, knee-lifting her way closer to me and away from the dendrob that was writhing its body towards the fire, probably sensing the warmth and wrongly assuming it was a slurry, because those muddy pools were warmer than the air due to the water that bubbled up from the ground to form them.

"Keeleet," she cawed as she clutched at my arm with both hands and squeezed, pulling her soft body closer to mine. "Keeleet wid fyerr."

Now it was clear to me that the dendrob had startled her, probably even frightened her as she pressed herself against me like she wanted me to protect her.

I liked that. I liked that very much.

As much as I would love to pretend it was a dangerous creature that I was rescuing her from, I knew it was unwise to let her remain afraid of it. There were many things that could hurt my Dayglow in the Sprawl, but this creature wasn't one of them. She needed to learn the differences between food and threat just in case I wasn't there to help her.

Though I didn't like to think of that happening.

I struck at it with my tongue, catching hold of it just before it writhed itself into the fire to pull it back to me. I caught it in my teeth, and its body slapped against my snout as it wriggled frantically to break the grasp of my tongue.

My Dayglow was now shying away from me as I lifted a hand

to pluck the dendrob out of my mouth after snapping off its head in one quick bite.

I showed her the body of the dendrob, then cast the muddy thing onto my cutting leaf. Then I spat out the head, dragging my teeth gently over my tongue to get all the gritty dirt off the sticky end of it.

As I swiped the dirt off my teeth, I turned the dendrob head towards her even as she retreated from me. I used the first forward claw of my other hand to pull open its mouth, then press on the flexible muck strainers she probably believed were sharp teeth. I demonstrated that it was harmless by then closing the mouth over my arm so she could see that it couldn't break the skin.

When she still stared at it with wide eyes, looking appalled, I tossed the head into the fire and motioned to her stone. This time she didn't hesitate to take a seat, lifting her foot to examine it like she feared there would be a great wound there.

She'd just severed her own head-tail, and she was more worried about a dendrob's "bite?"

My Dayglow was a strange one, but I realized I wouldn't have it any other way as I looked over at her affectionately, smiling at her murmurs and coos as she cradled her foot with one hand and rubbed the fingers of the other over her toes like she didn't trust her eyes that there was no wound.

I rinsed my hands and then used a shell full of water to rinse out my mouth, spitting the muddy water on the ground near my stone before returning to kneel in front of her so we were eye level.

She lifted her eyes from her examination of her foot and regarded my fond expression. A slow smile tilted her lips, baring her flat teeth. Then she released a happy sound ripple, followed by another. She said something so quickly that I couldn't even detect the pattern of sounds as she pointed to her toes.

I took her foot in hand, and she let me without hesitation, showing great trust in me, even after I'd had to restrain her earlier.

I caressed her stubby toes, noting that the skin of them

remained unmarked, as I'd expected it would be. She seemed to enjoy when I rubbed her bony foot, even letting me press my palm against her back foot round that she'd stomped repeatedly against the ground as I checked to see if she'd caused any damage to it. Not that the ground was that hard around the campfire.

She released a soft moan as I rubbed her foot, teasing my claws between her alien toes, then tracing the tip of my first forward claw over the little flowers painted on the hard but blunt tip of the largest one.

I wasn't sure what it was that intrigued me so much about her feet, except for simply the alienness of them, but I enjoyed touching them and examining them. What I enjoyed even more was her response when I caressed them, like it felt good to her to have me rub and stroke them.

It seemed to relax her entire body as she slumped on the stone, exhaling in a long cooing sound. Her knees parted as I settled her foot on my thigh, then reached for the other one.

And that was the first time I got a good look at the slit that had gripped my prods so deliciously earlier. It glistened in the fire-light, the skin around it looking soft and plump as it cradled that seam. The way her breathing hitched when she realized I was staring so fixedly at that slit had me tearing my gaze away from the intriguing sight of it to glance up at her face.

Her lips had parted, her breaths growing short, and her chest rounds heaved with each one. The black center rounds of her eyes had expanded, and her red cheeks had deepened in color.

I'd seen this color change before, and I knew what it meant.

My Dayglow was feeling the same desire I was. The desire that was even now causing my own colors to shift.

Chapter Nineteen

Khamai

My Dayglow's knees spread further, her toes curling on my thigh as she opened for my gaze. I felt the intensity of her eyes watching me but couldn't break my own gaze away from that tempting slit. My tail coiled around her calf, and while it normally comforted me to hold onto her like that, this time, the brush of her soft, yielding skin against my scales made my prods ache to evert from my own slit.

I settled my hands on her knees, leaning forward on my own as her foot slid up my thigh. The feeling of her toes walking their way towards my groin was all it took for my prods to push free, their heads already throbbing and leaking mating slick.

I shuddered with desire when she teased the length of my lower prod with the top of her foot, stroking the smooth skin of it along the underside of my prod. I slid my palms up her inner thighs towards that seam that called to me to explore it, and my Dayglow shifted her lower body on the stone so I could get a better look at it.

And the small, puckered cloaca beneath it.

The sight of both intrigued me and begged for further exploration, even as my prods begged for a chance to be inside her again. But I wouldn't rush this. Not this time.

No matter how much I still had left to do to prepare our night's meal, nor the fact that the evening was coming and Tytonid's light would soon shine upon the Sprawl, I wouldn't hurry this moment, my gaze entranced by the sight of her glistening entrance, highlighted by the light from the fire that crackled behind me.

She gasped and rubbed the top of her foot harder against my lower prod when I trailed my claw gently over the plump petals of flesh that framed her slit. They were slick from what I suspected was her own arousal, but not near as slippery as my prods were becoming as her foot teased the lower one, and the sight of her being fully open to me teased them both.

It was driving me so wild that I was already aching with my desire, but I was almost paralyzed with indecision, because I wanted to touch, taste, and penetrate both of those openings all at once. I also wanted her foot to keep stroking my prod.

My tail released her leg and switched to her other calf to lift that onto my other thigh, hoping she would tease my upper prod the way her other foot was toying with my lower one.

She appeared to understand exactly what I wanted, and again, I was excited by the fact that we were able to communicate without words. We seemed to be in tune with each other, like instruments that were carved by the same songmaster.

Her second foot teased its way up my thigh, then she was dragging the silky, fragile skin on the top of it along the shaft of my upper prod as I moaned softly, glancing up from her delightful slit to meet her eyes, which were nearly as black as my own now, the blue only a small rim around the dark centers. Her lips were parted, her breaths still coming in short gasps, and the nubs tipping her chest rounds had stiffened into tight, tempting beads.

But my gaze was drawn back to the juncture between her

thighs. I caressed those plump petals, trailing my thumbs upwards to the top of her seam, careful not to scratch her with my claws. I spread the petals, exposing a fascinating display of darker pink coloration shaped like a petal of the firelick flower. A small nub had been hidden under the outer skin and was now displayed for me.

Without forethought, my tongue darted out, though not at a speed to capture prey. Instead, I wanted to taste and tease that nub, and my Dayglow's reaction to the sticky tip of my tongue closing over it was far better than I could have hoped.

Her lower back arched on the stone, her hands clutching the edge of it behind her as her elbows buckled, rocking her upper body backwards and thrusting her lower body towards me.

Her feet settled on my thighs so her toes could dig into them, which felt almost as intriguing as the tops of them caressing my prod shafts. Her head fell back so I could no longer see her face as her chest rounds jutted upwards.

But it was the delicious cooing, gasping sounds she made as I tugged and teased on that nub with the broad tip of my tongue that made so much mating slick well from my prods that the shafts were thickly coated with it, and my slit was soaked from it dripping down them.

Her own slit below the nub I toyed with had grown shinier with slick too, and I shifted my thumbs lower to stroke over those soft petals that were now slippery from her excitement as I splayed my fingers over her upper thighs, holding her legs apart. Not that she made any effort to close them as her feet braced on my thighs, her toes still curling and flexing on my scales.

When I parted those lower folds, I spotted two openings. One was clearly too small to be for a prod, though I pondered the mystery of its purpose. The other though.... My prods seemed to recognize it immediately, jerking forward like they could reach it as I released her nub with my tongue and trailed it lower to probe at that opening.

A long moan left my Dayglow as her legs trembled beneath

my palms. Her hips shifted further forward, exposing more of her puckered cloaca to my view as I slid my tongue over the slick flesh that guarded her slit.

She rocked her hips, urging me on, her head once again lifted so her eyes could fix on me. When I glanced up at her, she nodded, gasping. Then she grasped one of my crest horns with her hand and tugged on it to further goad me on.

I didn't need any more convincing that she wanted me to taste her readiness for breeding. I'd already felt the low ache in my groin that told me my body was producing seed now, no doubt because I desired this female, and I was ready to mate her.

My tongue darted inside her, and her inner muscles clenched around the length of it as it delved deep, drawing a soft cry from her followed by a long, low moan. The flavor of her slick was sweet on my tongue, but her coos and soft gasps were even sweeter as she pulsed her hips forward, rocking them in a rhythm so my tongue was moving inside her like a prod.

The tip of it brushed her womb just as she sped up her rocking, and I tasted her fertility and knew she was ready for my seed. That taste was all it would take for my body to release it. Then her gasps and soft moans became loud, ecstatic cries as her inner muscles convulsed around my tongue, her entire body shivering as her toes dug deep into my thighs.

I nearly lost my seed and rain both, right then and there, barely holding on with the force of will because I wanted to fill her with my seed so she would bear my spawn someday.

I withdrew my tongue as I grasped her calves with my hands and reluctantly removed her feet from my thighs so I could straighten and position my body above hers. I settled my hips between her thighs, my lower prod jerking against her stiff nub as my prod fins buzzed with my eagerness.

This only seemed to drive her wilder as she straightened on her stone to grab my other horn, gripping them both now to tug my head down so she could press her lips to mine as the tip of my lower prod probed her slick entrance. Her tongue licked over my lips until they parted as I shifted my hips to bury my prod inside her, my upper prod rubbing over her nub, the fins fluttering rapidly against that clearly sensitive skin.

As soon as my lips parted and the tip of my tongue slipped between her teeth, she sucked it into her mouth, her hands tightening on my horns, clutching me like she was afraid I would stop if she let go.

As if I could at this point, the fins on both my prods moving so fast they were buzzing while I thrust the lower prod inside her, teasing out my seed, which came so quickly I was almost embarrassed.

Or would be if I could think straight.

I remembered that she should have my spawn rain inside her, before I ended up spilling it all over her soft belly, so I quickly pulled out of her slit and switched prods, only getting a few thrusts in before my upper prod spent inside her too.

Almost immediately after it filled her, her body convulsed again around my upper prod in a climactic response, telling me my spawn rain was working as my lower prod slipped up her cloacal crevice, the fins of it teasing over her puckered cloaca.

She broke her mouth away from mine, releasing my tongue long enough to cry out in a sound of ecstasy that echoed from the trees, silencing the tree-singers completely. Then she opened her eyes, which had been clenched shut when she'd been sucking on my tongue.

Suddenly, she gasped, her eyes widening as they fixed on my face.

Chapter Twenty

Vera

"You're so beautiful!" I blurted to my chameleon as my body tingled and buzzed even more than those crazy flaps on his shafts.

The intensity of the orgasm I'd just had blew away any other sexual experience I could ever recall—and I wouldn't have forgotten something as powerful as this.

I was in awe of him. I'd already found him aesthetically pleasing in his colorful daytime appearance, but that was in the sunlight.

Now, the surreal, purple-tinged moonlight coming from two —freakin *two*—crescent moons that had risen overhead while we'd been...*occupied* caused his face and body to fluoresce, so he glowed a beautiful bioluminescent blue wherever the bone lay close to the surface beneath his scales. It gave him a dangerous, alien skull-like, demonic appearance, complete with glowing horns, that was surprisingly hot as hell to me. All his quills were glowing in the dark too, like a spiky mane splaying out atop and behind his head.

This gorgeous male had just rocked my world, blowing my mind with how much pleasure I was capable of feeling, and now, he knelt over me glowing like some primitive alien death god, and I was so willing to embrace the darkness of the Underworld if it meant he'd keep those lengths moving inside me. He was handsome in a way he shouldn't be, like some monster from a nightmare world who turned out to be sexy as well as scary.

If it had been dark when he'd attacked the escape pod and he'd looked like this, I would have probably had a heart attack from fright.

Or I'd have thrown myself at him because this terrifying look was really doing it for me in a way that made me ask uncomfortable questions about myself.

Eh, I'd already admitted my feelings for my alien aloud, so what the hell? My hair was chopped off, and I was walking around naked like I'd lived in a nudist colony all my life. I'd already embraced my new circumstances. Why not embrace that secret inner part of me that made me happy here, in my chameleon's arms?

Impaled on his monstrous red erection, while the other one teased along my crack with its vibrating flaps.

Unfortunately, my shock at his unexpectedly luminescent appearance must have made him think I was upset rather than in awe, because he quickly withdrew his length from me, then rose to his feet to back away, holding his hands up in front of him and murmuring softly like he was trying to soothe a frightened animal.

Ugh, sometimes, this inability to speak to him frankly drove me crazy!

I sighed and sat up straight on the stone, pulling my shorts out from under me to swipe away the fluid spilling out of my slit in the wake of his withdrawal.

That second shot of his had caused a tingling, blissful sensation inside me from the moment it spurted into me. I still felt the aftereffects of it as it seemed to cause pulses of pleasure to tighten my internal muscles.

I'd noticed this before when he'd come inside me with that upper length, but it seemed even more intense this time, and it made me wonder if what he was spewing inside me was actually safe for my body.

Safe or not, it felt damned good, and I wasn't complaining.

Which was why I held up my free hand to wave him closer to me again, lifting my gaze from my wet shorts and slick flesh to meet his eyes. When he still seemed hesitant, like he wasn't entirely certain I was asking him to return to me, I rose on legs that were still shaky from multiple orgasms—something I'd never experienced before—and stepped closer to him. I tossed aside the soiled shorts, even though more fluid gushed from me to drip down my inner thighs as I stood.

Didn't care. Needed my glowing lizardman back in my arms. This instant!

He didn't back away as I approached him, which was progress, but he still hesitated, his luminescent quills standing out from his head as he watched me with what I assumed was wariness, but it was difficult to tell with his face lit up like it was.

The firelight had died down along with the fire itself. We'd been too busy to feed it more wood, so now it was only a small flame. Fortunately, the moonlight was plentiful, even though the two crescents had a very blacklight quality to them, which was probably why my guy was glowing the way he was.

Damn, why was that so sexy? I stared up at his skull-like features and wanted to leap on him and take him to the ground to ride those rods of his until the moonlight faded, and the sun was high overhead.

Oh yeah. I had it bad! What we'd already done didn't feel like nearly enough to satiate me. Though my body was still pulsing with pleasure, I craved more. I felt wild with need. My limbs trembled with it.

When his tail curled hesitantly around my calf as I moved

even closer to him, I murmured in encouragement, running my palms down my sides in a teasing display of my body to him.

My words, he might not understand, but as his tail tightened more confidently around my calf, and he closed that last bit of distance between us, I realized that he understood what I wanted.

His erections had withdrawn inside his body, but that tail was sliding through the slickness soaking my inner thighs, the tip moving unerringly towards my slit, which was throbbing with need, just like my clit. I moaned when it probed my entrance as his hands lifted to massage my breasts. Then he lowered his head, bringing his glowing face closer to mine, and I wasted no time grabbing his horns to pull him down for my kiss.

His tail pushed inside me, satisfying my need to be filled by him, but only just. Still, I was grateful for it as it thrust inside me while he caressed my breasts and teased my stiff nipples, his tongue darting between my lips so I could suck that deliciously sweet flavor from it.

I was hungry for food, my stomach growling to let me know it had been hours since I'd polished off everything in those food pouches earlier, but I barely focused on that as he fulfilled another hunger inside me. Literally filling that empty need inside me, his tail pumped until I rocketed to another peak and then went over it, breaking our kiss and releasing his tongue to cry out with my pleasure.

He cradled me close against his hard body as I snuggled in his arms in the aftermath, one of his hands lifting to slide his claws through my short, loose hair. His hands lingered in my hair, his fingers stroking it like it was enjoyable for him to caress it.

I loved the way he explored me like I was a wonder to behold. The same way I found him to be a wonder. I wanted to explore his body too. I wanted to touch every hard scaly surface of him and stroke his body until I had him moaning the way he made me moan.

Again, I barely felt satiated as his tail slowly slipped out of me, but it had to be enough for now because my stomach chose that moment to growl in an imperious reminder that I hadn't eaten yet.

My chameleon's brow ridges lifted as he glanced down at the source of that noise, but I merely responded to his obvious confusion by lifting on my toes to kiss him. Then I gestured with one hand to the leaf and the gross eel-frog things sitting on top of it that I was guessing tasted much better than they looked.

He seemed to understand, because he released me, though he appeared as reluctant to let me go as I was to be set free. Still, he turned to pick up a stick to stoke the fire, and when he had it burning nicely again, he fed some wood to it before returning to his work with the eels.

I walked to the clean water bucket, noting that it was running low on water and hoping my chameleon had a solution to refill it. Of course, he would. This jungle wasn't exactly a dry place, and I suspected he knew how to get moisture out of the very air if he had to. For now, there was enough water to use the shell scoop and get some to drink.

He glanced my way as the firelight limned his features, dimming the fluorescent glow of them as it competed with the moonlight. The effect gave him a half-glowing, half normal—for him—appearance that I wished I had the skill to paint.

I'd only really mastered painting tiny flowers, lines, swoops, and diamonds. Anything that could fit on a nail I could probably do with some practice but capturing my gorgeous chameleon on canvas would likely always be beyond me. Still, I wished I could preserve this image of him, because he was strikingly beautiful with both day and night aspects of his appearance coming together like this.

I suddenly realized that I'd had to lose everything to find someone this precious to me, and now I understand why the Lusian had urged me to take this journey.

Though I still didn't know why such a creature would even concern itself with my destiny. That was a mystery I would likely never solve, but I was eternally grateful to that small gray alien that had approached me in the restaurant.

Not only was I with this captivating alien male, but I'd also broken free. Not just of Nate, but of a civilized modern life on Earth that I realized now had been restrictive to me. The comforts of modernity were nice, but in a jungle like this, where it seemed that any delight could be found or made from the plentiful resources surrounding me, I suspected I could figure out how to have those comforts again with a little time and exploration and experimentation.

What I wouldn't have were all the expectations of a modern world that I could never seem to meet, a husband who didn't care about me, a society that was even more rapidly determined to modernize with expensive alien technology and move away from more primitive things, like handmade arts and crafts, after Earth's apocalyptic invasion by Menops, and staggering bills to pay when I never seemed to have enough money of my own, nor could I wheedle any more out of Nate.

Even small things had begun to weigh on me back on Earth, making me feel confined by a growing sense of hopelessness that I'd ever feel truly free and happy. Things like customers who wanted to haggle me down from my already cheap nail prices because my flowers were a little crooked or the gemstones I'd glued onto their nails weren't the more expensive crystals. Things like that had made me feel worthless, as if my time and effort had little to no value to others. They'd made me believe that what Nate always said about me was right.

Now, stripped of all vestiges of civilization—quite literally— shorn of my long hair, helpless and inexperienced in surviving this new environment, and wholly dependent on the good graces of an alien I couldn't understand, I somehow felt happier and more liberated than I had ever felt in my life.

If only I had a better name for my new lover than "hot lizard guy." Though that *was* on the nose, I thought as I settled on my stone to watch him finish preparing our meal.

Chapter Twenty-One

Khamai

I KEPT STEALING furtive glances at my Dayglow while I finished cooking our meal. The firelight traced her beautiful body, teasing me by outlining her gentle and alien curves, as if I could desire her any more than I already did. It was difficult not to stare fixedly at her to drink in her beauty and think about how good it felt to hold her, taste her, feel her, and bury my prods inside her.

I'd spent my seed in her this night. I was certain of it, since thick, white fluid smelling of rain on warm stone had still dripped from my lower prod when I'd withdrawn it from her, instead of the thinner, clear fluid of my afterseed. It would be many days before my lower prod would produce more, but I was hoping I wouldn't have to wait that long for my Dayglow to carry my spawn.

She was fertile. I'd tasted that when my tongue had touched the opening of her womb. Though she didn't have a seed pouch inside her like a Prdayu female, I'd also tasted some of my previous spill when my tongue had delved into her, letting me know that some of it was retained by her body, at least for a time.

Maybe long enough to find a place to grow in her womb.

I could still please her with both my prods until my seed replenished, and I would be certain to fill her with spawn rain as frequently as possible until then in the hopes that would speed her fertile eggs to what amount of my seed remained inside her. If nothing else, we both enjoyed the process.

Even if no spawn issued from my mating with my Dayglow, I didn't care. I was so happy to have her that I couldn't care less if we ever had offspring, as nice as it would be if we could. I wasn't entirely certain we could, but she was skyfallen, so possibly she'd been touched by the goddess Urcifa, even if she was not a goddess herself. She might even be Urcifa's gift to me after I had suffered for so long in the wake of punishing my sister's defiler.

I had many things to think about now that I had my Dayglow. Things I hadn't needed to consider for many openings of Tytonid's predatory eyes. Tytonid himself was one of those concerns I still needed to put to rest.

Had his avatar been slain successfully, or did it still cling to life in that wound in the Sprawl? I hadn't heard his shrill shrieking since my Dayglow had escaped him after he spat her out, but that didn't mean he wasn't lying in wait, gathering his strength for another attack.

I needed to return to that place and verify for myself that Tytonid's avatar wouldn't regain its strength and come for my Dayglow. I wouldn't let anything take her from me. She was *mine*, and I would slay a thousand skygods to keep her if I had to. Many great Prdayu heroes had slain Tytonid's avatars for far less than the precious prize of a skyfallen female like my Dayglow. I wasn't afraid to face him, even if he were to heal and regain his full strength and mobility.

I would fear no threat, not where my Dayglow was concerned.

That she was connected to Tytonid's avatar in some way was undoubtable to me now. He had eaten her, then had spit her out as if he didn't like her taste.

Or maybe I'd wounded him badly enough that he'd expelled

her because of the pain of the hole in his flank. Whatever the case might be, I knew that if Tytonid still lived, he threatened to take my Dayglow away from me.

After she fell into slumber this night, safe in my sway, I would make the journey to the scar in the trees to ensure that Tytonid was truly gone from the Sprawl.

For now, I wanted to see to my mate, as I was already considering her in my mind, though it would be many days before I felt confident enough to carry her through the trees to my home in the Dense, where I could then present her with my collar.

She was probably as hungry as I was, though I'd staved off my hunger earlier with munching on tree-singers I'd caught with my tongue as I'd checked the slurry traps.

The dendrobs would be nicely seasoned to have a firebite to their flavor, and they were even better fresh than dried.

By the time I had the first sticks of fresh meat cooked, I was salivating as hungrily as my Dayglow looked as she stared at those sizzling chunks of dendrob impaled on sticks by the crackling fire.

She'd been mostly silent as I'd worked, watching me with curious eyes, studying my movements and occasionally cooing or chirping, though she'd only smile and make her abrupt shoulder lifting motion whenever I'd glance at her at those sounds, apparently not wanting to distract me by attempting to communicate.

We were already communicating well in other ways. Her body welcomed mine, just as mine yearned for hers. When it came to mating, we didn't need words to speak the same language. What was even more important to me than our successful mating was the fact that my Dayglow appeared calm and relaxed now as she sat on her stone.

The severing of her head-tail no longer appeared to bother her, though she frequently lifted her hand to run her fingers through her loose head furs like she was checking to see if it was really gone. The severed tail lay abandoned in the dirt between her stone and the fire, and I was planning to collect it if she forgot about it, but I didn't want to do so in front of her for fear of reminding her of how upset cutting it off had made her.

I would hold onto it for her in case she wished to see it again when she was less bothered by the sight of the cut length, though I didn't think it could be reattached. Maybe another would grow in its place, like a lost Prdayu tail would regrow over time.

I wished I knew why she'd cut it off. Hopefully, someday my Dayglow would learn to speak my language instead of constantly cawing and chirping. Some of the birds in the Sprawl could mimic the words of a Prdayu to the point where they lured the unwary into dangerous situations, like snapper groves or even grabber nests. The mimic-birds even managed to fake the resonance of a Prdayu tongue-horn, but even if my Dayglow couldn't do that, she might still be able to learn the words of our language.

If those birds could learn Prdayu words, then so too could my flightless skyfallen bird with her adorable little flexible beak that crinkled between her eyes sometimes when she made her chirp sounds or flashed her teeth just before releasing a happy sound ripple.

Even if we never fully understood each other's sounds, I suspected we already understood each other on a deeper level than words. She'd opened her body to me, bared her slit for my prods, and even gripped a horn of my crest in demand that I taste her fertile readiness so that I would be encouraged to spill my seed inside her.

She'd eagerly offered to bear my spawn before I'd even had a chance to offer her my collar. Most Prdayu females would play coy, encouraging a male to play a long game of pursuit, complete with offering many gifts while revealing beads intended for her collar that were carved just for her.

My collar had been woven with beads I'd found or carved with vague dreams and hopes for the kind of female who would wear it. I realized now that many of those beads had birds carved into them, and one wooden bead had two purple spots on it that I'd left uncarved, thinking they looked like Tytonid's eyes. Scary as those were, they'd seemed appropriate for my mating collar, though I'd never understood why until now.

Even though a lot of the beads on that collar now seemed to be too perfect a fit for my Dayglow not to be a sign from the gods, I would like to carve her new beads that I would show her to gain her approval for a second collar, once she'd accepted the first. I wouldn't just use carved beads either. Skin as soft and graceful as my Dayglow's should be adorned with the colorful sparkle of Urcifa's glittering scales.

I would brave entering the territory of a Prdayu village if I had to—though not my own—in order to find some of those scales, at least one or two, to put into her second collar. She was worth the effort.

She was worth so much more than such a paltry effort. I gazed at her with all my affection in my eyes, wondering if she could tell how much she meant to me when she looked up from the sticks of meat to catch me watching her. The way her lips parted to flash her teeth in a smile suggested she just might know.

When our food was ready, I laid the first choice slices of seasoned dendrob on a small leaf I'd prepared for her. She reached for it with both hands, then her eyes widened in surprise, the fire-light reflected in the blue curves of them, as I knelt beside her sitting stone instead of handing the leaf to her.

She watched me with a slightly cocked head as I plucked a piece of meat from the pile, surrounded by the seed and nut paste I'd also made for our meal from my stored rations. I dipped the freshly cooked meat in the paste, which enhanced the seasoning on it, then held it out to her, caught between two of my claws.

She lifted a hand to take it, but I shook my head and pulled it away. When her hand lowered, I shifted the meat closer to her lips. Her mouth had fallen open in a gasp when I'd withdrawn the food, but now her lips tilted upwards as she lifted her eyes to meet mine. Then she leaned forward and parted her lips to let me feed her.

The way she moaned after her warm mouth claimed the meat

from my claws made my prods jerk inside me, but I pushed away that arousal, determined to see that my Dayglow was fed in our official "intention meal."

I hadn't wanted to waste this ritual earlier when she was hungry and tired and seemed miserable, but now, I felt like it was the right time, though we'd already mated. The ritual that declared my intention to provide for her might be a little behind the pace of our courtship at this point, but I'd never hoped to have this chance to woo my mate after being exiled, so I didn't want to miss out on this important gesture, nor did I want to disrespect my Dayglow by not showing her the same courtesy I would show any Prdayu female I wanted to court to accept my collar.

She seemed to accept the ritual, though I couldn't know if she understood its significance. She claimed each morsel I fed her with hunger, licking her lips after she took it from my claws and chewed it. I hadn't expected it to be this arousing when I'd decided to do this, but in retrospect, I should have. Even though we'd just mated recently, I still wanted her.

I didn't think I'd ever stop wanting her. The slightest bit of encouragement had my prods pushing against my slit to break free. My spawn rain was eager to spill inside her to spur her womb to accept my seed.

This ritual didn't involve mating, because it was supposed to take place very early in a courtship, and mating was supposed to come *after* a climb into the Life Tree, well after a Prdayu female accepted the beaded collar.

Not that some of us didn't sneak in an early mating from time to time, even with those females who had no intention of accepting any male's collar yet. Traditions were important, but all Prdayu had needs and the more modern ones of my generation fulfilled those needs more openly than our parents had in the past. As long as a male didn't spill actual seed inside a female's lower slit, no spawn would issue from such casual liaisons.

It was difficult to make it through feeding her the entire leaf's worth of food without tossing it aside to pull her into my arms and give her another reason to moan with pleasure than the flavor of the dendrob meat. I managed, just barely, though the more she licked her lips, the more intent her gaze grew as it roved over my body.

Without understanding a sound she was making, I knew she felt the same desire I did.

When I fed her the last morsel from the leaf I held, I rose back to my feet, unwinding my tail from her calf, where it seemed to coil reflexively whenever I was close enough to her for it to reach. She held out a hand to grab my forearm to stop me, and I immediately froze as my eyes lifted from the empty leaf to meet hers.

Then she patted her chest rounds with the palm of her other hand.

"Veraaahhh," she crooned, patting her chest rounds again so they bounced, the buds on the tips of them stiff.

I dropped back to my knees in front of her, the leaf falling from my slack grip as my mouth watered, my tongue growing thick with the urge to capture one of those pink buds.

Her hand on my forearm lifted to cup my chin, then pushed upwards on it, until I realized she wanted me to look at her eyes again, even though she'd patted her chest rounds to draw my attention there.

"Veeeraaahh," she said, again patting her chest rounds.

Again, my gaze shifted to them.

She'd made that sound before, touching herself in exactly the same way, and I'd mimicked it, much to her apparent excitement. I wasn't sure why she wanted me to know what her chest rounds were called in her chirping language, but I focused on them intently and repeated the sounds, my tongue-horn vibrating reflexively at my effort to mimic her again.

Her hand tightened on my chin, and she tugged on it to lift it again, my gaze following. Then she leaned forward until her beak poked my snout, her sky-tinted gaze fixed on my eyes.

"Eyez upheer hawtstuff," she said in a sharper chirp. Then she repeated the cooing sound, though this time, it had a sharper edge to it too. "Veeraah."

She was trying to communicate something that was important to her. Something that had to do with her chest rounds.

My shoulders straightened as I gasped in understanding.

She was letting me know she was fertile! Those chest rounds were how her kind fed spawn. She was telling me she was fertile... or veeraahh, as she called it.

I nodded with great excitement, careful not to bump her bendy beak. "Grzetgar!" *I know,* I explained in my language, happy that she acknowledged her readiness and hoping it meant she was eager for spawn, especially after I'd spent all my seed inside her.

Not that I would regret that even if she wasn't fertile yet.

She straightened, lowering her hand from my chin. "Ger-rzetgaar?" she mimicked, her throat sounding like she was choking as she attempted the vibrational undertone to the word, her eyes blinking rapidly.

Then she cocked her head, her gaze searching as she studied me. "Gerzetgar." This time, it was easier to understand the actual word since she gave up on trying to add the tongue-horn's song to it. Something she clearly wasn't equipped to do. "Nyeeztomeetu Gerzetgar."

As I struggled to determine the meaning behind the first sounds before the word I recognized, she released a happy sound ripple. "Feyenelly," she cawed, throwing her hands up in the air. Then she lowered them to settle on my shoulders, her smile wide as she gazed at my face. "Gerzetgar," she murmured, butchering the word like I slaughtered dendrobs.

I smiled too, experiencing that bubbly feeling inside at her adorably terrible mimicry and the fact that she was chirping "I know" repeatedly now.

"Veeraaahh," I growled, my gaze lowering to her belly as I thought about my spawn growing inside her. More happy bubbles filled my chest at the thought.

"Yezzz!" she cawed, suddenly slapping her palms together in front of her. "Veraaahhh, yezz!" Then she pointed at me. "Gerzetgar!"

I nodded at her pronouncement, pleased that her mimicry had already gotten better.

Then she pressed her lips to mine, and all other thoughts fled my mind.

⌒

ONCE I HAD my Dayglow tucked up in my blanket, sleeping soundly in my sway, I crawled out of it and wove a vine barrier in front of the entrance to keep her from climbing out of it before I returned. Then I grabbed my spear, my happy mood of earlier fading as a more somber and determined one replaced it.

Dayglow had access to my knife, which I'd hidden inside the sway for her to cut her own way through the barrier if I didn't return, knowing she would be clever enough to find it and know what to do with it if too much time passed without my reappearance. I hoped she would never need to use it, and that I would be back before she even knew I was gone.

I didn't think she'd harm herself with it again. She'd recovered from her strange mood, and now she wanted to create life, not take it. Her actions had convinced me of that, just as her telling me she was fertile in her own strange language had let me know she wouldn't turn the knife upon herself.

It was time for me to face Tytonid again, and this time, I would make certain his avatar was destroyed.

Nothing would ever take my Dayglow from me, because I was willing to climb up into the Dark Sprawl itself to get her back if I ever had to.

I made swift progress to the scar in the trees, goaded on by my desire to be done with this and return to my mate. She was veeraahh. Fertile and ready to bear spawn, and I wanted to spill more spawn rain inside her to take advantage of her veeraahh time before it passed. I had no idea how long such things lasted for my Dayglow, but saw no reason to waste the opportunity, since I also happened to really enjoy it.

Only this creature stood in the way of my happiness, so when I saw the glimmer of its carcass lying among the trees, in the exact same place that I'd left it, soundless and motionless, I felt a sense of great relief that it showed no signs of life.

Still, I dropped from the trees and approached it after a careful survey of the area, just to make sure it wasn't pretending to be dead. There was a sense of emptiness to the creature, and not just because of the hole I'd left in its flank.

It made no sound as I walked right up to it, and I sensed no life stirring around it.

More importantly, the tree-singers started up their song again after their initial silence had fallen only when I'd appeared in the clearing. They didn't fear Tytonid's avatar, and they most certainly would if he remained alive.

I sucked in a deep breath, my chest expanding as my eyes closed in gratitude. I exhaled on a fervent prayer of thanks to Urcifa, determined to make an offering to her shrine as soon as I returned to my home in the Dense with my Dayglow.

Tytonid had dropped this nightmarish avatar upon the Sprawl on one fateful night, but with him had come my Dayglow, and I felt like, in some ways, I had the god of death to thank as well as Urcifa.

Perhaps I would even make a journey to his darkest of shrines to leave an offering of thanks after seeing my Dayglow safely ensconced in the Dense.

No sense in tempting fate by angering Tytonid through my neglect.

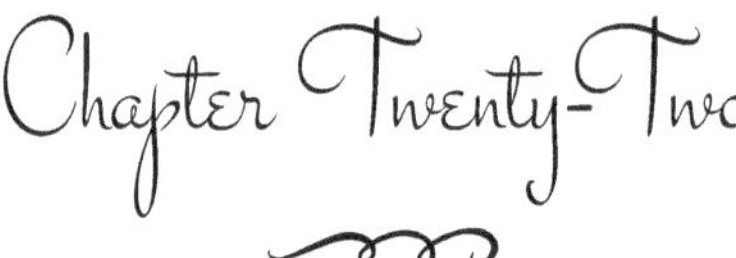

Chapter Twenty-Two

Vera

I WAS LIVING in a primitive paradise and despite the lack of indoor plumbing—or much of an "indoors" for that matter—I felt happier than I could ever recall being in my life.

When I'd first crash-landed on this planet, time had seemed to crawl, each moment taking an eternity to pass while I struggled to get my bearings and then survive on an alien world.

Then my beloved chameleon had come to my rescue, and suddenly, time raced past us as we came to know each other in ways I'd never known, or trusted, another person. Despite how alien we were to each other physically, I felt such a sense of connection to my chameleon that I wondered how I'd ever lived without this feeling of being complete that I now had.

Granted, even after what had to be several months of spending every waking moment together, we still didn't speak much of each other's language, and what we did speak, or attempt to speak, seemed to cause more confusion at times than anything.

I knew about a dozen words of his growling language, and I

couldn't create the vibrational sound in my throat that he used when he formed his words, so that likely only added more confusion to our attempts at spoken communication.

He was better at mimicking my language in his deep resonating growl, but he also only knew a dozen or so words, mostly for things around our home clearing, like treehouse, or campfire, or very simple sounds, like "yes" and "no." Words we both used frequently.

I knew his name, Gerzetgar, though he seemed amused most of the time when I said his full name, grinning with those sharp teeth in a way I'd come to know as his affectionate, happy expression. Usually that meant he thought I was doing something cute but also funny.

I'd taken to calling him Gar for short, and at first, that had confused him even more, but eventually, he seemed to understand it was a shortened name that was easier for me to say, and he now responded to it with alacrity.

He had also given me a nickname, calling me Darcifa now. Initially, I'd tried to remind him to call me Vera, since he now knew my name, but whenever I repeated my name, it seemed to spur Happy and Slappy into action and next thing I'd know, I would be under him as he buried them inside me.

Though I loved making love to him, a girl could only take so much double penetration before she needed to call a timeout. I'd decided that my real name was too arousing to him for some reason and started answering to Darcifa.

Occasionally, he would still say my real name, and his gaze would grow intent and hungry as his eyes lowered to my breasts, eyeing my nipples thoughtfully.

If he wasn't ogling my naked breasts or darting that tongue of his out to capture a nipple and tug on it in a way that brought me to my knees, then he was gazing at my feet like he wanted to pull them into his lap and rub them or tickle my toes with his claws.

Or let me stroke his erections with them, because my pervy

hot lizard guy had a foot fetish like you wouldn't believe! I found it more than a little adorable how intrigued he was by my feet.

Despite our difficulty in verbal communication, we'd managed to develop our own language of pantomimes, hand signals, and color shifts.

Well, the color shifts were only on his side, but once he'd realized that I would respond to rapid color changes in his scales, he started using them to signal things to me. Things like his mood at any point, darker colors when he was feeling contemplative and serious. Bright, vivid colors when he was feeling joyful. Warmer mid-tone shades when he was aroused.

His colors were often mid-toned around me. They were also often bright.

He also shifted some of his color patches to warn me of dangers, knowing that I would look to him, no matter how far apart we were physically, before I attempted to touch, smell, or taste anything new, and also whenever I reached for a vine.

Oh, those *vines*, and the heart attack I'd nearly had about a week or so after my Gar had rescued me!

I'd lifted my arm to sweep a vine out of my way as he'd carried me through the branches, and his tongue had suddenly darted out at a blinding speed to capture the vine as his scales shifted color in a pattern I'd come to know as a signal of his alarm.

He'd snapped off the head of the snake I'd almost brushed aside with my forearm before I could blink, though I'd shrieked when its body writhed against me, causing him to spit it out along with the fanged head so he could get a better hold of me.

Then he'd had a little meltdown, scolding me profusely, I think, though I still didn't understand the flurry of rapid growls he'd released immediately after that incident as he'd tightened his arms around me to keep me from wriggling right out of his grip in my panic.

His scales had been dark all over his body then, save for all the normally subtle red scales turning vivid until he looked like a black and red, horned demon, though up close it was actually a very dark green and red.

We'd been about four stories off the ground at the time, so I supposed I'd earned the sharp slaps on my naked butt that had followed what I took to be an angry tirade.

Anger and more than a little fear, I suspected, because the rare times that he'd shown fear—always for my sake—his scales had darkened until they were that almost black color so that even the striping and spots on his body were barely visible up close.

After that, Gar had woven a harness of sorts for me, and though I felt a bit like a toy poodle going for walksies while wearing it, I kept it on when we were in the trees for my own safety. It leashed me to him so if I fell out of his arms, or as I learned to walk along the branches myself with his encouragement and assistance, I wouldn't plummet to the ground.

Since I had to wear the harness, I also wore my shorts at times, though when I wasn't wearing that fibrous contraption, I stripped down to my naked skin without hesitation.

The heat and humidity remained punishing, though I'd grown accustomed to them both fairly quickly, my body acclimating now that I didn't often have wet clothing on to chafe me. I felt an unexpected freedom in being naked most of the time, and Gar certainly appeared to appreciate the view. We didn't go a single day without those *other* vivid red *signals* of his that told me he was definitely aroused and ready for another round of hot lovemaking.

The days passed rapidly as he taught me how to live in the jungle, through a variety of different means of communicating. Before long, I was traveling with him on the ground to harvest food, water, and the raw materials to add onto our treehouse, and learning to make my way through the trees, balancing on swaying branches with growing ease.

He'd built a second, larger pod for us to live in together and had anchored this one to the branches so it didn't swing with every movement, which I greatly appreciated. He'd also shown me that I could roll up the leaves on the sides during the day so fresh breezes would cool off the interior of our new home.

Then he'd constructed a ladder from ropes woven of fibers collected in a variety of ways so I could climb in and out of the pod myself.

No more chamber pots, thank goodness.

My new tree castle was surprisingly luxurious, especially once Gar started adding nesting.

I'd sat by his side near the campfire while he'd ground the dried scales from the eel things into a fine powder, then added water and various combinations of harvested saps and plant juices for which I had no name. Then he'd dipped hanks of yarn into the dye. Those hanks of long, yarn-like fibers he'd made himself by stripping the stems of a wildflower plant to make thin lengths then twisting them together into a much longer length of yarn.

He'd turned those dyed fibers into a crocheted blanket in many vivid colors. I'd watched him make it using a wooden needle and a looping motion with his clawed fingers that was so fast I couldn't begin to learn how to do it unless he'd slow down. Since he'd been in a hurry to make the blanket, which I'd soon discovered was meant to soften our bed, he hadn't taken the time to show me, but I did learn, eventually, how to make paints and dyes from the various sources of pigments found in the jungle.

I'd also made brushes from my newly created fibers, experimenting with different fiber sources, that I was ridiculously proud of, and Gar had praised me profusely. Then he'd tapped a claw gently on my big toenail to draw my attention to the sunflowers that had almost all chipped off it by that time.

I'd thought for a moment he was eager to claim my foot again, but instead, he'd lifted his own foot to then tap a claw tip on his toe claws.

He'd watched me expectantly after that, until what he wanted had dawned on me.

Next thing I knew, I was painting designs onto the long claws of my sexy lizard guy. He loved the painted colors, and though I worried some of the combinations he picked out of my selection of pigments would clash, he always seemed to know which ones went together the best.

He already took good care of his claws, even filing them to sharp points to help him in the trees, but he was thrilled by my pedicures and manicures that made his claws look spectacular. After the paint would dry on a new mani-pedi, he would stand up and strut around like he was a male peacock showing off his tail.

Refreshing his mani-pedis along with my own became a regular pastime as I experimented with different materials, like some of the saps that hardened like resin, to make the most chip-resistant natural paints.

I was so proud of all I was learning, and of what I managed to accomplish on my own once Gar taught me. Despite knowing only dozen English words, he was an excellent teacher. It was amazing how much information could be imparted with hand gestures and demonstrations alone.

One word he'd learned in English was "awesome," and he used it often when he praised me, sounding like a California surfer dude from the eighties with how often he resorted to that expression and how excited he sounded when he'd say it. The alien vibration of his voice even made it sound like he was warbling the word at times.

I loved Gar so much that I couldn't believe I'd once been willing to spend the rest of my life with Nate, foolishly thinking that pale infatuation I'd had for him had been anything like real love.

Whenever Gar would cradle my face between his hands and say the nickname Darcifa to me in a certain purring way, I pretended he was saying he loved me back.

He was building us a beautiful home here with each passing day, expanding on his own treehouse and campfire, filling out the clearing with everything from a bathing basin to waste facilities. Despite our primitive surroundings, my chameleon was surprisingly hygienic, and I wondered if he kept his scales so clean to retain the vividness of their colors. He did love color, the brighter, the better. And he especially loved showing it off when that color was on him.

Or he might just like being clean. I still hadn't figured out that mystery, but I wasn't complaining about his proclivities.

He washed himself daily with his soaprock and cloths and often washed me as well, though we did tend to get distracted whenever he helped me bathe, and it took longer to finish.

A *lot* longer.

He'd also added a ground shelter to our campsite to give me shade when the sun sat high enough in the sky that sunlight flooded the clearing. I was careful not to expose myself to direct sunlight now that my sunburn had healed.

Gar had been very curious about my peeling skin, studying my face frequently during the process and murmuring commentary I wished I could understand, his scales dimming to darker shades as he did so, but not entirely losing their joyful vibrancy. I had realized that state of his coloration was his "curious but concerned" shades.

He was also growing even more protective of me lately, I'd noticed, to the point where he was insisting on carrying me again most of the time when we were in the trees, instead of letting me clamber around on the branches as I was learning to do with more ease each day.

I wondered if he suspected what I was beginning to suspect.

I'd been dreading the arrival of my monthly visitor since I'd landed here, knowing that dealing with the mess and the cramps and the hassle would be a real pain in the ass while I ran around in the jungle with no grocery store in sight to pop in and pick up pads or tampons. Since I was usually naked, I would have had to start wearing panties if I wore cloth pads, and I only had one pair, or I'd have to stick some of those plant fibers up inside me.

All of which had made me regret getting the implant over one of the newer birth control methods that eradicated periods along with the possibility of pregnancy, but Nate had wanted the cheapest option besides pills I might forget to take.

But Aunt Flo had never arrived, as days passed into weeks, then into months. Now that at least three months had passed since Gar and I had first started having sex, I wasn't oblivious to the changes in my body that suggested I'd miscalculated on my birth control.

Having a hybrid alien baby in a primitive jungle with no medical care around—not even any other *people* around, human or reptilian—was a terrifying thought, but I'd also felt instantly and fiercely protective of the life potentially growing inside me.

And excited, despite my fears. I wanted to have Gar's baby, and I had the rising suspicion that he wanted it to, with the way he'd begun to stroke his palm over my stomach at random moments, his colors brightening to almost neon shades as he'd brush a hand over my bare skin in a caress that wasn't sexual like most of his others.

I wasn't sure how I would deal with a pregnancy if that was what this was, but I was so in love and happy in my new life that not even those concerns dampened my mood for long.

The more comfortable I grew in the jungle, the more comfortable Gar was with leaving me alone for long enough to range farther for materials. He was constantly improving our home, so he harvested a lot to build and expand.

He'd left me a spear, just in case a larger predator came around, but I got the impression he didn't expect that to happen, since we'd encountered nothing in the jungle near our home that was a threat to Gar. It was more like he thought I needed the reassurance in his absence. It was a thoughtful gesture, showing that he was concerned about my feelings and sense of security.

That was why I trusted him to always return to me as soon as he could whenever he had to leave the clearing.

This morning, Gar had made it clear through gestures that he was going to leave me alone for a bit to check the mud ponds he'd shown me one day, for the eel things that not only made good food—among a vast variety of other foods he'd introduced me to —but also provided the best pigments, which was why I think he caught so many of them when there were many other sources of food in the jungle.

I suspected those eel things he gathered today would be the last for a while, as he'd brought home less and less with each harvest. I wasn't certain if it was overfishing of the mud ponds, or if was just that their *writhing* season was over. I called it that because those things crawled and thrashed in the mud on the banks of the ponds in pairs that told me they were likely mating. Surely, they had a season for that.

Comfortable now in the jungle with the alien cicadas constantly singing in a way that let me know they sensed no danger, I hummed a tune I often heard Gar hum in his throat-vibrating growl as I shelled nuts for our lunch, tossing the nutmeat into a bowl beside me on the sitting stone by the cold fire coals.

I was feeling so relaxed and at ease with my world that I wasn't prepared for the cicadas to suddenly fall dead silent, even as a piercing caw from one of the colorful jungle birds caused me to jump as it cried a warning to its flock.

I rose to my feet, dropping the bowl of nuts still in their shells that I'd held in my lap, my gaze shifting to the spear leaning against the other stone.

Before I could move to grab it, a shiny orb flew out of the jungle, heading right towards me.

"See," Snarky's voice echoed from the orb, "I told you I could find her. Now, about that new hardware you promised...."

I blinked in stupefied confusion at the orb that seemed so out of place in my jungle home. "*Snarky?*"

"Vera?" a familiar and unexpected voice said, coming from the trees rather than the orb that paused to hover in front of me. That other voice sounded utterly shocked—and disgusted.

I turned my head towards the trees, my eyes widening as I spotted a man stepping out of the tree line, his hard gaze trailing from the top of my head down to the colorfully painted toes of my feet.

"*Nate*?" My tone was probably as welcoming as I felt at seeing him, but there was nothing I wanted more than to grab my spear and jab its tip into his smug, sneering face.

Chapter Twenty-Three

Vera

WE STARED at each other in stunned silence, my husband and I, for a long, tense moment. Then he broke that silence by holding his hands out at his sides like he wanted a hug.

"Vera!" he crowed, striding further into the clearing. "I found you! After all these months!" He continued to hold his arms out like he expected me to walk right into them with no encouragement other than that.

In the past, I would have, being grateful for any scrap of affection he'd show me. Now, I held my ground, shooting a glare at the shiny curve of the orb that hovered near me. "Thanks a lot, Snarky," I muttered before returning my full focus to my husband.

He looked as blandly handsome as always, tall, dark haired, and healthy, with just a slight paunch at his belly. The smile on his face was insincere to my eyes, but there were shadows under his chilly brown eyes that hadn't been there before. Almost like he might have worried, and maybe his cheeks had grown a little gaunter since I'd last seen him.

"Vera, my beloved wife," he said as he stopped halfway between me and the trees, lowering his arms slowly, like he was still struggling to acknowledge that I wasn't leaping into them. Then he thrust out an impatient hand, moving his fingers in a demanding "come here" gesture.

I hesitated, shooting another glare at Snarky before sighing and stepping towards Nate.

As angry as I still was at him for cheating on me with that woman, he *had* come looking for me, and it was clear that he'd suffered some stress in my absence. Though it was more than likely guilt than any true grief at losing me.

I had no intention of hugging him, but the least I could do was send him on his way with a polite pat on the shoulder, letting him know he was free to be with whichever woman struck his fancy next, because I had no desire to return to him. Nor even to Earth.

This had become my home, and I wasn't about to leave it, or my beloved Gar, who made this feel like the exactly right place to be.

"You're looking," Nate's gaze trailed down my naked body, then back up to fix on the jagged cut of my hair, "different." The way his eyes narrowed, and his brows pulled together in a disapproving frown had my shoulders lifting defensively—before I reminded myself that I no longer needed Nate's approval.

Gar had finally let me use his knife to cut some bangs, and I'd ended up hacking my hair even shorter under his watchful eye, so now it looked like a pixie cut done with a weedwhacker.

I smiled broadly and lifted a hand to run my fingers through my short and wild cut. "That I am, Nate." I chuckled as his eyes shifted from my hair to the bouncing of my breasts with my movement. "I'm *feeling* different too." I cocked my head as I lowered my hand, smirking at him. "I'm feeling like I don't need you around anymore. In fact," I propped one hand on my hip as I gestured towards him with the other hand, "I think you were only ever holding me back from true happiness."

His expression darkened, his lips tightening into a slash on a tense face as he lifted his eyes from my chest to meet mine in an angry glare. "Vera," he said through gritted teeth, "don't you talk to me like that." He took a few steps closer to me, and I shied back, but then squared my shoulders and lifted my chin, meeting his eyes defiantly. "After all I've done for you—"

"Cheating on me on our fucking honeymoon, you mean?" I snapped, cutting him off with great satisfaction.

His tense expression softened. "Oh, darling, is that what this is all about? You ran away from me because I had a moment—just a mere moment—of weakness that didn't mean anything at all?"

"She didn't mean anything to you?" I crossed my arms defensively in front of my breasts, my skin feeling chilled even in the ubiquitous heat.

"Not even a little bit." He smiled with straight, artificially whitened teeth as he settled his hands on my shoulders. "You're the only woman for me, Veer."

I jerked away from him sharply, his touch making my skin crawl. "You risked our marriage for a woman who 'didn't mean a thing to you,' and that's supposed to *reassure* me?"

"Vera," he snarled, reaching for me again, a flash of impatience crossing his face as I stepped around him to dodge his grasp, "you're making a big deal out of nothing. It was one fucking kiss, for crying out loud!"

"On our *honeymoon*!" I screamed, clenching my fists at my sides, though I'd love to put one through his smug, sanctimonious face.

"Look at you," he said, gesturing with one hand at my body, "running around in the jungle in the fucking nude like you're a neanderthal." His eyes again lifted to fix on my hair. "And your beautiful hair! It was your best feature, Veer, and you hacked it off! What were you *thinking*?" He again swept his hand towards me like he was gesturing at a prize on a game show, only his expression looked like he was catching a whiff of a rancid trash heap. "Do you *know* how long it will take for your hair to grow out again? You'll look like a little boy until it reaches your shoulders!" His eyes roved over my face, which was sweating with my growing rage at his contemptuous tone and expression. "Your face isn't all that feminine, you know. You can't pull off a short haircut."

That was it. We were done here.

"Listen, you bastard," I snarled, poking a finger in his direction, "I'm not putting up with your shit anymore. You've treated me like garbage ever since I accepted your proposal, like you thought you had me all tied down, and then you cheated on me, at least once," I raked his body with my own contemptuous glare, "and no doubt more than that." I waved a dismissive hand in his direction, then crossed my arms, turning my body away from him. "And it wasn't until I found myself completely alone on an alien planet that I realized I didn't need you in my life."

"Oh, but you *aren't* alone, are you?" Nate said in a vicious tone. He suddenly grabbed my upper arm, jerking me closer to him as his fingers tightened on my bicep. "You think the pod computer didn't tell me about the reptilian native that attacked you? After we had a talk with the computer when we located the escape pod, I was expecting, *hoping* even, to find some of your remains to take back to the Syndicate Enforcers who want to *imprison* me because they think I jettisoned you from the charter ship." His grip tightened to the point that I yelped in pain, but I wasn't so distracted by it that I didn't see the two large men step from the trees to stalk towards us.

His voice brought my gaze back to meet his. "But instead of finding some ragged remains of your clothes that I could take back along with this escape pod computer, I find you alive and well, and living like a cavewoman." His eyes narrowed on me. "No doubt *fucking* that creature in exchange for your *comfortable* accommodations." His tone dripped with sarcasm and repulsion. "Why else wouldn't he kill you?"

"Maybe because he's not a bastard like you," I shouted, trying to break his hold on my arm by jerking my body to the side.

To no avail.

The other two men were now standing close enough to us that when Nate thrust me towards the larger one, I had no way of escaping before he caught me in a hard grip, his huge hands clamping down on my shoulders. I only glanced up at his craggy face long enough to see that his expression was lascivious as his eyes roved over my naked body.

"I won't kill you," Nate said without much of a reassuring tone as he glanced meaningfully at Snarky's floating orb, letting me know I had a witness, even if the crappy AI hated me.

It had to record everything, I suspected, whether it wanted to serve as witness to my murder or not.

"But you'll be returning with me, Vera," Nate continued, cupping my cheek as the big bruiser held me still, despite my attempts to struggle.

"Let me go!" I turned my head to escape his hand, his touch more repellent to me than the mercenary holding me so tightly. "I'll give you a damned divorce, Nate. Just send someone with the papers to have me sign them." I shifted my gaze to Snarky. "Or I'll verbally grant my permission to file them to that computer so you can do all the freaking paperwork yourself."

"Divorce?" Nate laughed aloud. "You think I plan on letting you divorce me, Vera?" He lowered his head to whisper in my ear. "When your trust fund doesn't come into your full control until your twenty-fifth birthday? Oh *no*, we'll be staying married until that all that beautiful money drops into our shared bank account."

"*What* trust fund?" I said in shock, completely taken aback at this unexpected turn in the conversation.

Nate chuckled, glancing up at the mercenary who held me so tightly. "You thought all your father's money was lost in the invasion? Well, the bank recovered their databases with the help of our Akrellian overlords, and lo and behold, they discovered that he'd set up a trust fund for you, though he didn't trust *you* to be mature enough to receive the full payout until you were older.

They sent the message to you through the Akrellian Administration office." He grinned, patting my cheek. "But I figured hearing the news would only renew your grief over your parents' untimely deaths," he said with plainly false sympathy, "so, I kept it to myself." Again, he leaned closer to me to whisper, "along with the monthly stipend payments."

I trembled now with rage, seeing red as my eyes lifted to the trees while I struggled in the mercenary's unforgiving hold. "Damn you, Nathan!" I shrieked.

I'd believed for so long that everything my father had worked for had been lost in the destruction of the Menops invasion. To hear that a trust fund he'd set up for me had been recovered and that Nate had been robbing me of my inheritance this whole time, no doubt through some corrupt deal with the trustee, made me sick with fury.

"Let's go," he said abruptly to the other mercenary as he stepped around me. "I don't know where that primitive lizard freak is, but if he's hanging around, I'd rather not deal with—"

His words were cut off by the whistle of a spear speeding through the air to fly right past his head. It thudded into the chest of the mercenary who wasn't holding me. The force of the throw sent him staggering back, his mouth gaping open in shock as he stared at the haft of it sticking out of his chest. He collapsed to his knees, then toppled over.

While Nate and the other merc stared in frozen shock, I brought up my foot and kicked my husband in the balls, then rocked my head back as hard as I could to slam the back of it into the big mercenary's face as he leaned forward reflexively like he needed to get a better look at what was happening in front of him from around my struggling body.

He yelped as I heard a crunching sound when my head hit his face, my skull aching from the impact, but when his grip loosened, I tore out of it and raced towards the second spear.

By the time I had it in hand, Gar's tail was wrapped around the big mercenary's neck, and the brute's face was turning purple as he fell to his knees, blood pouring from his broken nose, both of his hands scrabbling at the thick tail that cut off his air supply.

Gar's head quills were fully extended, along with his ear flaps, making him look even larger than he actually was as he towered over the kneeling mercenary and Nate. His lips had peeled back in a terrifying scowl, and his claws lifted to strike at Nate.

But Nate had somehow recovered enough from my direct hit to his babymakers to pull a gun that now pointed at my beloved chameleon's chest.

It was clear Gar didn't know what that weapon could do to him, so he didn't hesitate to swipe at Nate.

My bastard husband pulled the trigger just as I ran him through with my spear.

Chapter Twenty-Four

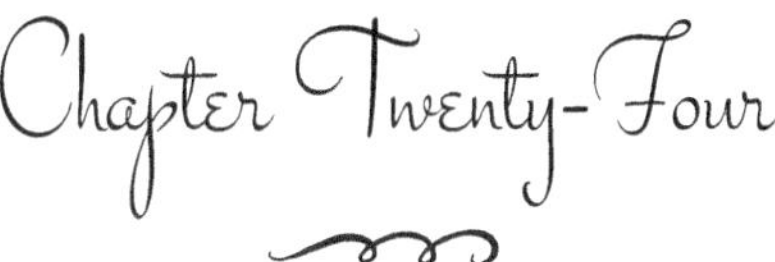

Khamai

"THAT DIDN'T QUITE GO ACCORDING to plan," a strange voice said, but it wasn't speaking aloud. "Humans continue to surprise us with their unpredictability, even when the flux appears to show a clear path."

I lifted a hand to my crest, because the sound was coming from inside my head as I opened my eyes to discover that I laid upon something hard, in an unnerving void of a space.

Was I in the Dark Sprawl? Was this odd voice speaking to me now that of the god of death? I'd expected it to be deeper. More intimidating. Triumphant.

Not vaguely exasperated.

"Tytonid?" I asked hesitantly, glancing around me to notice that the void remained featureless. Gray walls with no sign of trees or shrubs or sky. Even the dirt below was gone, replaced by smooth gray floors. "Have I died then?" I stiffened, my bristles lifting along with my head. "My Darcifa! My Dayglow! Is she okay? Have those monsters harmed her?"

"Be calm, Khamai," the voice spoke again from inside my

head, like a thought, but not my own. An intrusive one that I might expect from a god.

But the wave of serenity that suddenly spread through me made me wonder if I had not actually found myself in the world of a different god. A kinder one.

"Urcifa?" There was little light in this new world, but perhaps the goddess had dulled the reflectiveness of her scales for the sake of mortal eyes.

"Cupid, actually," the voice said. "Though that is merely an affectation, since no such immortal ever truly existed."

Was this a new god that I had never been made aware of before? Would a god tolerate his name being unknown?

I sat up on the hard surface, noting that it was an impossibly smooth slab of some material I'd never seen before.

I was definitely in the world of some god, but I still felt strangely calm, despite my anxiety over the fate of my Dayglow.

And our spawn that I was certain grew inside her.

Suddenly, a figure appeared before me where none had stood before. It simply appeared out of thin air, though it was a strange figure indeed, looking nothing like a Prdayu.

Instead, it was a creature with long limbs and a thin body covered by skin as gray as the walls and floor, but the oddest thing about this god was his large, smooth head that seemed out of proportion with the rest of his body, and the uptilted, egg-shaped, black eyes that appeared much like those of an insect as they stared at me like they could see under my scales and into my spirit.

The god named Cupid appeared to be as tall as I was, though he had no tail in sight, nor any sign of claws, or even teeth in a small, thin-lipped mouth. Not that I could see anything in his mouth, since it didn't move even as the god spoke again, directly into my mind. "Your mate and her developing child are safe. You need no longer concern yourself on that account."

As strange as it was to have the god talking to me in this manner, I still felt that sense of calmness. That feeling was enhanced by an overwhelming sense of genuine relief that my

Dayglow was safe, followed by an ecstatic feeling of celebration that she truly did carry our spawn, as I'd suspected.

"Yes, that part *did* go according to plan," Cupid mind-said like he was aware of the direction of my thoughts.

Of course, being a god, he would be.

"Indeed, I know your thoughts," he confirmed with a brief dip of a pointed chin, "though I am not an actual god. Merely a… facilitator, if you will. Someone who wishes to ensure that certain events come to pass, with a bit of…*minor* intervention."

I glanced around the space again, recalling how Cupid had appeared in front of me out of the very air. "How can you be anything other than a god, with such powers at your disposal."

The thin lips of Cupid's narrow mouth tilted upwards at both edges in a slight expression I took to be amusement. "To your understanding, I suppose the designation of 'god' for my kind would seem appropriate."

"Your kind?" I asked, though what I really wanted to know was when I could see my Dayglow again to verify for myself that she was safe after those creatures had tried to steal her from me.

My spirit would never fully recover from the terror I'd felt when I'd heard her cawing in alarm as I'd returned to our camp and saw those three creatures similar in appearance to my beloved Dayglow—only they were ugly where she was beautiful. The sight of them clearly attacking her had enraged me to a point I'd never been before. Not even when the chief had attacked my sister had I been so filled with fury that my world had narrowed to a simple desire to kill to protect what had become more important to me than my own soul.

I'd known right then and there as I'd grabbed my spear from beside our newly built sway that they were there to steal her back from me. I'd had no intention of allowing that to happen, but I hadn't expected the ugliest of the three to wield a weapon that had struck my chest as fast as my tongue caught prey.

My Dayglow's shrieking was the last sound I'd heard before I woke up here.

I needed to see her for myself, even if Cupid insisted that she was safe. Still, one didn't rush a god or make demands upon them without showing a little courtesy first. Even the god of death deserved respect before he gobbled a spirit up in his beak. "There are more gods like you?"

The narrow shoulders of Cupid lifted in a brief gesture I'd seen my Dayglow make many times. "Many more, though we are not all of like mind—or purpose." The ridged brows above those large, uptilted black eyes pulled together very slightly. "Indeed, we are often at cross-purposes." That shoulder shift happened again as his small mouth tilted upwards. "But few bother to interfere with the activities of the Arrow's crew. Our kind consider us...*eccentric*. A lost cause, but essentially harmless when our machinations make only small shifts in the flux."

I slowly shook my head, completely baffled by many of his words, though I suspected some of them weren't even meant for me so much as him speaking to himself. "I don't mean to be disrespectful, but...."

I needed to see her. The serenity I was currently feeling was simply not enough to fully comfort me without visual proof that Darcifa was unharmed. Safe.

Cupid clasped the three long fingers of each of his two hands together, his lips tilting upwards just a bit more, until I would almost call the expression a Prdayu smile—albeit a toothless one. "Your devotion is *very* romantic." Though the voice spoke inside my head, I still detected a pleased tone to those words.

Then he lifted a hand in front of him, palm facing me. "She will be finished with her exam soon. I'll awaken you then so that you can be reunited."

"I couldn't possibly sleep now!" I pushed myself forward on my palms, scooting to the edge of the slab. "Not until I see her."

"I must insist," Cupid said calmly.

I suddenly felt very sleepy. Even though I struggled against the feeling, my anxiety for my Dayglow powerful, I couldn't resist it for long. I slowly laid back, my bristles settling against my head. My breaths grew more even as my eyes closed.

SOMEONE RUBBED MY CHEST SCALES, and a familiar, beloved chirping fell upon my ear flares like the most beautiful music I'd ever heard.

"I know! Are you okay, my chameleon? They promised me you'd be okay, but you're not waking up!"

It was my Dayglow's voice, making the same sounds she'd always make, with the only familiar word being Gerzetgar, since she repeated it often. I strongly suspected she thought it was my name, but when I'd tried to give her my real one, she'd been confused about my intent and hadn't caught on. It was easier to let her keep calling me "I know."

And it made me smile, I had to admit.

But now, despite hearing her chirping sounds, I also *understood* them like she was speaking in my language. I just... *knew* what they meant in my head. Like magic.

My eyes popped open as my tail swept off the hard surface I was again lying upon and coiled around her calf. Her face hovered above me, her eyes wide and shiny with moisture, her expression drawn with worry.

"My beautiful Dayglow," I said, lifting a hand to cup her cheek.

"I understood that!" Her smile brightened her face until she truly resembled the name I'd given her. "You're calling me *sunlight*!"

Then she lowered her lips to mine, and it wasn't long before she was sucking on my tongue in that caressing of lips and tongue that she'd taught me that made my prods ache to be inside her.

Though, to be fair, they always ached to be inside her.

Her hand slid down my chest and belly to find that they were already pushing free of my slit, and I felt her lips tilt in a smile against mine. Then her fingers curled around my upper prod as she climbed onto the hard bedding to join me.

I used both hands and my tail to help her climb over me, sliding her body down until she'd settled her slit against my upper prod, my mating slick already wetting the shaft of it as her firm grip around it stroked it from me.

She broke our lip lock to moan as she sat upon my prod, and it sank deep inside her slit, my lower prod, already growing slippery with slick, sliding along the crevice between her back rounds.

"There's so much to say to you," she gasped as she began to pump her body up and down on my prod her thighs flexing under my palms, while my fingers gripped the soft uppers of them. "but seeing you whole and unharmed, after I saw that bullet go into your chest...."

Despite the pleasure I was certain she was feeling, some of the moisture in her eyes dripped down onto my chest scales, which I knew was a sign of her sadness.

"Don't you ever scare me like that again," she said in what I'd come to recognize as her berating caw.

Then she moaned again as I thrust my hips upwards to drive my prod deep inside her delicious heat.

She was definitely better than any warming stone could ever be. I could bask in her heat all day, for the rest of my days, until Tytonid finally did come for me, and then it would be a mighty battle for him to defeat me before I'd ever let him take me from her side.

It was a wonder to understand her words, and there was so much I wanted to say to her, and ask her in return, but I completely understood why this needed to come first in our reunion. It wasn't just our bodies rejoining, as they had done many times since our first blissful mating. It was the connection between us that went beyond physical intimacy that our mating translated for us. This intimacy was one language we'd both understood from the beginning.

She braced herself on her knees, my upper prod nearly

completely out of her sheath as my prod fins buzzed. Then she reached to grasp my lower prod to adjust its position, settling the slick head of it against her puckered cloaca.

It was my turn to moan loudly, both sets of my eyelids closing as she pushed downwards, causing both my prods to penetrate her at once. The tight ring of her cloaca closed around the head of my lower prod, then sank down my shaft to engulf my prod fins.

My Dayglow's legs trembled from her eagerness, and her small cries, gasps and moans filled the air along with my own low moans as I clutched her thighs with both hands, careful not to pierce her soft skin with my painted claws, though it took real effort to restrain myself in my excitement.

Once both prods were buried to my slit inside her, she began to pump her body again, more slowly this time at first, but steadily increasing her speed as I moved my hips upwards in a harmonious rhythm.

Her upper body bent over mine, her palms bracing her on my chest, their slight weight only heightening my pleasure. "Those flaps of yours, I know! Oh *god*, they're going to make me come already, and we just started!"

"Khamai," I gasped out, approaching my own climax and completely understanding her despair that this would be over too soon.

I could do this forever, dangling at the very edge of an orgasm as my prods moved inside her. "My name is Khamai."

She paused, cocking her head as she studied me, and I was grateful that momentary break allowed me to draw away from that blissful edge for just a moment before I toppled over it and spilled both afterseed and spawn rain inside her. "You mean, your name isn't Gerzetgar?" She blinked, her gaze shifting upwards in thought. "Come to think of it, that means 'I know,' doesn't it?"

Then she suddenly released her happy ripple sound, and her inner muscles clenched my prods with each peal. "I've been saying 'I know' to you this whole time, when I had *no* idea!" she said through eddies of happy sound, her eyes leaking moisture now for a different reason than sadness.

Though the momentary distraction had initially allowed me to move away from climax, her body clenching around my prods as she expressed her amusement in her way was too much for me and swiftly brought on my orgasm. Both of my prods jerked inside her as fluid pumped from their tips, filling both her openings until it leaked from them, making my shafts even more slippery as it pooled around them.

Her head fell back on her shoulders, the happy sound cutting off abruptly as she moaned, rocking her hips forward several times as my prods pulsed inside her. Then I felt her inner muscle convulsions as her body shuddered in her own climax. My prods jerked again, shooting more fluid when I'd thought I'd spilled it all already as her toes curled against my knees.

She sagged atop my chest, my prods still inside her as she planted her lips on mine. This time, it was only a brief touch of lips before she lifted her head to gaze down at me. "Khamai," she said experimentally. "Guardian."

I knew the word she said in her language translated to my name, because of this magic Cupid had given me so that I could understand my Dayglow.

"It fits." She cradled my face with both her hands. "It definitely fits, my beloved chameleon." Then she grinned, flashing teeth. "My name is Vera. Pleased to meet you, hot stuff." Her smile turned wicked, crinkling the skin covering her flexible beak between her eyes. "Very, *very* nice to meet you." Her inner muscles clenched around my still stiff prods to prove her point.

I couldn't agree more.

I blinked, startled as understanding dawned. "You were saying your *name*? I thought you were telling me you were fertile!"

This time, my Dayglow straightened to throw back her head with a much louder caw than her happy ripple of sound from earlier.

I had learned that was also a sound of her amusement, and in fact, it meant even greater amusement than her softer joyous sound ripples.

"That explains *so* much!" she said once she finally stopped making those amused squawks.

Then her expression suddenly sobered as she settled a hand on her stomach, her gaze meeting mine with an intensity that I'd come to know as her being serious, but not sad. "I suppose I *was* fertile this whole time, Khamai. I'm pregnant with your child."

She watched me as if she was awaiting my reaction with nervousness. I pushed myself up onto my elbows, both of us groaning a bit as her weight shifted on my prods. It nearly distracted me, and likely would have if this topic wasn't so important.

"I know, my Dayglow. My... Vera." I tested the name now that I understood what it meant. My prods still twitched eagerly inside her at the sound of it. It would take a while to untrain them from that response to what I'd thought was her letting me know she was fertile and ready for spawn rain.

Her eyes were searching as they studied my face. "Are-are you okay with this?" She lowered her hand to my wrist, and I shifted my weight to my other elbow so she could wrap her fingers around it and draw my palm to her warm belly. "Are you... okay with us having this child? The Lusians say it's healthy and viable —that *he* is healthy and viable, and they implanted a sensor that would teleport me to the ship when it's time to give birth so I'll have the most advanced medical care possible."

I caressed her smooth skin, not needing her urging to want to touch the place where my spawn was growing. I shivered with my happiness, unable to believe how much my fortunes had changed when my Dayglow had snuck into my camp and stole my heart. "I can't even express how joyful I am at the thought of welcoming our spawn into the world. Not with words."

Her reassurance that Cupid would help her give birth to the spawn was a welcome relief, as I hadn't been certain what I would do when it neared her time. Without a healer or Life Tree, I had no idea what to do for a birth to make sure the mother was safe, and that the spawn was born healthy. It had become a growing worry in my mind as time had passed and the subtle changes in her body had grown more apparent.

I'd even considered returning to my own village or braving another village to seek a healer and Life Tree in the hopes that I could barter for the birth of our spawn with them. I'd struggled with which decision would be most effective—and least likely to leave me dead and my Dayglow alone in the Dense.

Her eyes had shifted to my scales, and her lips were already spreading in a wide smile as the tension left her body. "You're so beautiful when you're happy," she said in what sounded like awe, her fingers stroking over the vivid patches of my scales that had turned as bright as they could get in response to my joy.

Then her gaze returned to mine. "You're so beautiful all the time, my chameleon."

I couldn't help but feel the exact same way about her, and I made sure to tell her so.

As did my prods.

Chapter Twenty-Five

Vera

WHEN THE GRAY calling himself Cupid—unironically, I now realized—said he would send us back to Khamai's home now that we'd been given translators and both of us had been medically examined, treated, and pronounced healthy and well, I'd expected him to teleport us back to our lovely little clearing with the new tree-pod Khamai had built me.

Khamai. I was still getting used to that, but Guardian definitely fit my chameleon mate, so I would probably still call him Gar for short.

Instead of appearing in familiar surroundings, we materialized in a freaking tree-mansion, with huge tree pods attached to massive, towering trees all around us. I gaped as I looked around in wonder.

We stood on a balcony, firm and steady, despite being made of the bamboo stuff—which was actually from the stalks of huge wildflowers—overlooking a stunning view of the tree pods. Khamai put his arm around my shoulders, his chest expanding as he sucked in a deep breath, then exhaled heavily.

"It's good to be home," he said, then he looked down to meet my eyes, which had been pulled back to him despite the fantastical housing around me. "It's even better to be able to bring you home." He cocked his head, lifting a hand to smooth my hair away from my brow. "You look good here," he murmured. "Just right for my home. You're the best thing I've ever found in the jungle and brought to this place."

"*This* is your home!" My entire body warmed from his loving words as I swept my hand out to my side in a gesture at the surrounding trees.

It was wonderful to be able to understand all the sweet things Khamai said to me, though we hadn't actually spoken about much yet. There was so much to say, and yet the brief time we'd spent together on the flying saucer before being teleported back here had been spent communicating through gestures, touches, and the colors that shifted on his body.

Some things seemed too profound to put to words, and others too miniscule and unimportant.

I still had to explain to him about Nate. My life back on Earth. Heck, I had to explain to him what a spaceship was, and what Cupid was, since he still insisted Cupid was a god and we were in some mystical, magical world while on the ship.

Yet here I stood in a truly magical place that seemed more alive and fascinating than the cold sterility of Cupid's Arrow—which was actually a saucer-shape, but I admired Cupid's commitment to the bit.

"Do you like it?" he asked as if I could possibly not appreciate the beautifully constructed pods that somehow blended with the trees. "I will anchor the sways and make walkways between them so you can get around more easily. You won't have to always have your harness on." His tone seemed uncertain about that last part, like he wouldn't mind always having me tied to him to protect me from falling.

He also sounded anxious about presenting this place to me, like he needed to sell the idea of this being our home.

I'd have been content to live with him in a single, small—in comparison to these pods—tree pod for the rest of our lives, and this amazing reptilian was giving me a dozen huge pods in a sun-mottled clearing in a shadowy forest with glorious thick foliage—and he was asking if I *liked* it?

"It's almost as perfect as you are, Khamai," I said sincerely, wrapping my arms around his waist as I looked up at his striking features, wondering when his alien appearance had become as familiar to me as my own face.

Heck, I hadn't even seen my own face in a while. Cupid had asked if I wanted a better haircut before he teleported us back to the planet, and I'd declined. I liked this look even though I hadn't seen the end results of it in a reflection. My weedwhacker haircut had great meaning for me, and Khamai told me I was beautiful just as I was.

Not that I would ever decide how I should look based on anyone else's approval again, but still, it was nice to have him look at me with so much admiration in his eyes, like the sight of me pleased him as much as the sight of him pleased me.

"I built this place believing there would never be anyone else to—"

"Khamai!" a feminine voice suddenly shrieked from inside the pod attached to the balcony where we stood.

My chameleon stiffened at that sound, then spun around to stare into the pod, just as I did, seeing for the first time that it appeared to be a sleeping chamber, complete with leaf-softened bedding.

Bedding that a beautiful chameleon female was climbing out of it like she'd just been asleep, and we'd awakened her.

"Maika!" Khamai sounded as stunned as I felt as the other chameleon female—Prdayu was what his people called them-selves, I now knew—approached us warily, her gaze shifting from Khamai to me, then staying fixed on me, her expression unread-able as she stared.

Rudely, in my opinion, but I was sort of staring back, though the green-eyed jealousy monster was already poking its head up, demanding to know who the eff this pretty reptilian lady was living in *my* Khamai's tree house, saying his name like she knew him. Just like he apparently knew her, since he'd clearly called her by name.

Then he rushed to her and caught her up in his arms, embracing her like he'd never expected to see her again. "Maika!" he cried, clutching her close and leaving me stunned and maybe a little devastated.

Maybe a lot devastated.

She hugged him back just as fiercely, and I was ready to find myself a spear when Khamai suddenly pulled away from her to return to my side. He caught my hand and tugged me closer to the other female. "Maika, this is my skyfallen mate," he said excitedly, "gifted to me by the gods themselves, but I haven't had a chance to give her a beaded collar yet, but she's carrying my spawn already, and—"

Maika held up both hands, her tail coiling tightly behind her as her eyes widened in shock. "Your *mate*?"

Then her gaze lowered to my neck, like she was searching for a collar necklace like the gorgeous, netted bead collar that adorned her neck that I was only now noticing because it had blended so well with the rest of her vivid coloration.

Then she smiled, broadly, her sharp teeth flashing as she approached me, holding both hands out to me. "You've agreed to accept my brother's collar?"

Her gaze flicked to Khamai, even as I kicked myself for jumping to conclusions and not trusting my chameleon not to have another wife or girlfriend hidden away that he was eager to return to. Nate had left me with trust issues, but Khamai deserved better than such suspicion. He'd proven himself to me many times over.

"Does she... understand me?" she said in a whispered growl to him. "Does she know about...?"

Khamai wrapped his arm around my shoulders, his head

quills—he called them bristles—lifting with his distress. "Vera understands our language, Maika, though it is somewhat difficult for her to speak it clearly without a tongue-horn. I hadn't yet explained to her about... I haven't told her that I've been exiled."

He looked down at my face, and I turned my gaze from his sister to look up into his eyes. "I have been alone for many turnings of the seasons, my Dayglow, and I had expected to be alone for the rest of my days." His scales darkened to the dullest colors I'd ever seen as he lowered his arm from my shoulder and caught my hands with his. His tail that was coiled around my calf as usual tightened as if he feared that I would break away from him. "I've been exiled from my village, because I killed the chief who attacked my sister."

I let out my held breath in a relieved whoosh, though I shot a sympathetic glance to Maika, who was glancing from Khamai to me as if waiting to see how I responded to such news. "Good riddance to bad rubbish, like my daddy always said." I lifted a hand to his face, tracing my fingers along his cheek as the colors of his scales beneath it brightened slightly at my response.

Then I realized Maika wouldn't understand my words the way Khamai now did and tried to repeat the sentiment in Prdayu, realizing that speaking his language was much harder than simply understanding it.

She looked more than a little confused by my butchery of her language, but she also appeared to be considering my words.

Then, I realized I still had a confession to make to him, and it seemed appropriate at this time, though if I'd had scales like his, they would be black as pitch right now. "I killed the man who shot you, Khamai." I bit my lip as he scowled at the mention of Nate. "But I was also foolish enough to marry that bastard in the first place."

His scowl deepened. "You accepted the collar of that creature?" His gaze shifted to my neck.

I really wondered about this collar thing. Did he have one like

Maika's to give me? Because I was already coveting it, and I couldn't even feel guilty for wanting one of my own.

"More like a ring." I held up my bare fingers. "But I took that off and threw it away before I even met you, my love. He'd lost any right to call me his the moment he stuck his tongue down another woman's throat."

I heard an outraged huff from Maika, like she was offended on my behalf and realized that I had continued to speak in their language rather than my own, as if subconsciously, I wanted to be polite.

This translator the Lusians had implanted was unnervingly good at reading my mind, even when I didn't know what I was thinking yet. It was even better at putting the right words in my head to communicate with those who didn't have one.

It was little wonder Khamai thought Cupid was a god who wielded magic.

"Beneficial disposal of rancid leavings," she growled in an approximation of the saying I'd used earlier. When I glanced at her, she nodded her head her head once in an approving way.

I was already starting to like this lizard lady.

"So, you are free to accept my collar now, my Dayglow?" Khamai's hesitant voice brought my focus back to his face.

From my peripheral view, I saw Maika walk away, and figured she was giving us some privacy, but I remained intent on Khamai. "I am freer than I've ever been, Khamai, and I would love to 'accept your collar.' Nothing would make me happier than to become your mate."

Khamai's scales brightened to his happiest colors as he embraced me, holding me close against his chest so I could hear his heart pounding beneath my ear. "I love you, my brightest Dayglow! I will love you for the rest of my days, and when Tytonid comes to claim my spirit, I will fight him to remain by your side."

"I love you too, my beautiful chameleon," I said fervently, my arms around his waist hugging him even tighter as his tail coiled up my leg to my thigh. "I will love you forever and always, to the end of my days and beyond. I would travel a million light years to be with you, and I'd do it all over again a million times as long as you're there at the end of my journey."

"Your devotion is *so* romantic," Maika's happy voice broke in, causing us to reluctantly put some distance between us.

Khamai chuckled at his sister's exclamation, then she handed him the most beautiful, netted bead necklace I'd ever seen. A true work of art that reflected my chameleon's brilliant eye for color and pattern.

He took it reverently, then presented it to me, laid over top of his palms as he spread his hands slightly to show the entirety of the repeating pattern.

The necklace had many carved beads in the same blues, yellows, reds, grays, and greens that adorned my chameleon's scales at their brightest. I also spotted more muted beads, some in their natural tones of wood or bone, and some given a very subtle graduated dye job.

I raised my awestruck eyes from the collar to meet Khamai's expectant—and clearly anxious—gaze. "It's stunning!"

He unhooked the collar, then placed it around my neck, the weight of it settling over my collarbone, yet still feeling surprisingly comfortable. Then he stepped back to study his handiwork. "Now, my Dayglow," he said in a soft growl, his eyes lifting to meet mine. "*Now*, it is stunning.

Epilogue

Vera

MAIKA HAD COME to the Dense, as my Khamai called the thick jungle that was his home, in search of her exiled brother, because she wanted to bring him back home. She'd found this tree-net after many weeks of searching the one place she suspected her brother would have gone, but it was empty, though signs of Khamai were everywhere.

So, she'd settled in to await his return, admitting sheepishly to us that she'd freely explored the place while he was gone. She was very admiring and told him how proud their parents would be to see him living in such a sprawling and beautiful home.

Apparently, the elders who had been adamant about his sentence—despite how his sister had been attacked, and he'd only been defending her honor from a monster—had finally passed away. A new chief and a new council of elders had unanimously decided that Khamai had been in exile long enough.

The fact that the chieftain had given Maika the beaded collar that she now wore so proudly as the only adornment besides her colorful scales—and that she was now his mate—probably had a lot to do with their decision. She told Khamai that she'd convinced her mate of what had truly happened that terrible day, and he'd been so outraged by the violation that he'd announced that he would have done exactly what Khamai had done had he understood the old chief's offenses.

Khamai wasn't as thrilled as one might expect him to be when presented with such a reprieve, though he'd expressed happiness for his sister's new mating. After a hastily prepared dinner where we all sat together, and I watched them discussing his exile and potential return to the village, I noticed that Khamai's scales had darkened.

I wasn't the only one who understood what that meant.

"This news doesn't please you, does it, my brother?" Maika cocked her head curiously, her bristles lifting in distress. "You haven't forgiven them for exiling you, have you?"

Khamai turned his head away from her, and me, staring through the open side of the eating pod we were in at the surrounding trees. "They expect me to return as if nothing had ever happened, but I can't do that." He turned his gaze to me, and his scales began to brighten as he reached for my hand, his tail tip that was coiled in its place around my calf tickling the sole of my foot. "I've found my home, and it isn't in that village."

Maika slowly nodded her head. "I wouldn't wish to leave this tree-net behind either, brother." She grinned at me. "Nor would I want to leave my beloved mate behind. But you could still visit the village, could you not?" Her gaze lowered to my stomach. "You could formalize your mating in the Life Tree, and when your spawn comes—"

"Our spawn will be born beneath the watchful eyes of the god, Cupid." His hand rested on my stomach, his expression as wonderstruck as it had been the very first time we'd made love. "He will ensure that our son is born healthy, and that my mate is safe in the delivery of our young. This, he has promised—and the promise of a god of love is not to be taken lightly."

I inwardly rolled my eyes but let Khamai live with his illusions a little longer. Someday, maybe he would see the larger universe for what it was.

Or maybe he would still believe in magic, because I realized that I was beginning to again as I gazed lovingly at my handsome, scaled Prince Charming, while sitting in this amazing tree castle with a beautiful, beaded collar fit for a princess as the only thing I was wearing. The only thing I wanted to wear.

Khamai

RETURNING to my village was not a prospect I had looked forward to, but with the birth of my son, who was hale and hearty and had a set of lungs on him that rivaled my Dayglow's loudest squawks, but also carried the distinct vibration of a developing tongue horn, I felt like it was finally time to make that journey.

With the help of Cupid's magic.

Suddenly appearing in the center branch cluster of the main village tree gave us quite the entrance, leaving the villagers awestruck as they stared at the three of us.

My arm wrapped possessively around my skyfallen mate, as her arms cradled our perfect son. He was scaled like me, with hints of the same coloration already forming, and he had a tail, hands and feet that would aid him in the trees, but he had her blue eyes, and soft, downy golden head furs that stuck out from his tiny head behind the beginnings of a crest. He also had a little, flat bump of a snout that Cupid said would someday grow into a beak like my Dayglow's, and miniature versions of my Dayglow's ear flares on the sides of his tiny head.

He had already begun to suckle from my Dayglow's chest rounds, which were swollen now with food for him. Vera called it "milk." It was most curious to see her feed our spawn and watching them together made me feel so joyful that my colors were vivid almost all the time now.

Now, I got to show him off to the villagers who had once turned their back on me, and I couldn't be prouder as they stood around us, awestruck and terrified because we'd just appeared in their midst.

Maika was waiting for us, since I'd told her we would come here after our son was declared strong enough to leave Cupid's Arrow, and she rushed from the chieftain's tree pod, climbing rapidly down to the branch platform where we stood.

My mate snuggled against my side as I held her with my arm and my tail, my other hand lifting to stroke the soft head furs of our son while I watched the villagers gather with a warning expression both on my face and in my wary coloration.

Let them attempt to harm one head fur on my mate or my spawn, and I would bring the wrath of Tytonid down upon this village.

Then my sister's mate joined her as she reached us, swinging down from the highest tree on a thick vine. I sighed, shaking my head. Parsonii had always been a show-off. Still, of all the males in the village, I was grateful it was this one who'd gifted my sister her collar and had taken her as mate.

He had been one of those who'd sided with the old chief's mate in pleading for leniency from the elders, though he'd been too young back then for his words to have much of an effect. He'd changed much in the following season-turnings, growing strong enough to claim the title of chieftain for himself from the weak-willed one that had replaced the chief I'd killed.

Now, he settled an arm over Maika's shoulder much like I had my arm over Vera's, his fingers stroking the beads of her collar reflexively, like he still couldn't believe he'd convinced her to wear it, and he was checking to see that it was actually there, and she truly belonged to him.

I understood the feeling because I did that often with my own mate. It still seemed like some beautiful dream to see her in my home, wearing my collar, and I still worried from time to time that I would wake up to find myself alone again. Only, it would be much worse this time because there was nothing on this world that could ever compete with my skyfallen mate. If she was just a dream, I never wanted to wake up.

"I asked her fourteen times to accept my collar before she said yes," Parsonii admitted with a sheepish grin after greeting us, when he noted my gaze shifting to the collar my sister wore. "She refused everyone who offered their collars to her, saying she would never climb the Life Tree until her brother was here to witness it."

And Maika hadn't climbed the Life Tree with Parsonii yet. Just like I hadn't climbed the tree with my mate. My sister had insisted on waiting until she could find me and bring me home, after Parsonii had convinced the elders to rescind my exiled status.

Now, we were here to witness my sister finally formalize her mating with Parsonii, and as the last of her bloodline, I gave my formal blessing to him to climb with her into the Life Tree. Maika hugged me tightly before she made the climb with her mate, pausing to nuzzle the soft hair of our son, Calum.

"Have a nice climb, May," Vera said to her in a knowing tone, her pronunciation of our language much better now, even if her words still lacked resonance.

Maika grinned toothily, then winked as she'd seen Vera do. "It's not the climb that matters, but what we do at the top."

Parsonii's scales turned darker in embarrassment as my Vera cackled and Maika glanced over her shoulder at her chieftain.

Many people came up to us later as we sat at the feast table beside my sister and her mate during the after-climb celebration. All of them wanted to meet Vera and gaze upon our son, having been informed of both from Maika, though I let no one stray too close to him save for Maika and Parsonii.

The villagers were more than convinced that Vera was godsent to me as a consolation for being unjustly exiled, and they treated her with awe and reverence, and gazed upon our son with wonder.

I also believed she was godsent. Had I not seen the wonders

and magic of Cupid's Arrow with my own eyes? My Vera insisted that it was only "science" that I was witnessing, and that there was no magic in it, but I couldn't understand how she didn't recognize magic when she saw it. Maybe because her own world had been a magical one, and she'd grown up believing such things were commonplace, she was unable to view them with the same wonder I felt.

She'd told me much about her world that seemed impossible to believe, but she also said she never wanted to return to it. Remarkably, she insisted that it was *my* world that was the magical one, and that our ordinary home in the Dense was the true wonder.

As I presented her with the wrist collar of faceted Urcifa's scales that I'd secretly traded for, going through my sister to acquire the stones from the village stonemaster, my colors glowed as brightly as those stones glittered when the collar poured from the bag into her palm. She loved her beaded collar so much that she'd insisted she didn't want another, claiming it was perfect, so I'd decided to make her a wrist collar instead with the glitterstones.

"This is...." Her eyes widened as she stared at the glitterstones. "These are *diamonds*!" She glanced up at me, her mouth gaping as she held out her palm with the wrist collar still pooled in it, Calum cradled in her other arm against the chest round he suckled from. "This is... there's so *many* of them, it's-it's so expensive!" She stared down at the sparkling stones in her palm. "I've never been given a gift so expensive, Khamai. I don't even... I'm not even sure I dare wear this without fear of losing it."

"You don't like it?" I felt a stab of disappointment. I'd hoped she would be excited about the gift. Urcifa's scales were rare and highly prized, and any Prdayu female would be immediately extending her wrist to have it attached, eager to show it off to everyone.

Her gaze jerked up to meet mine. "I *love* it! This bracelet is so beautiful! I just didn't expect this!"

I took the wrist collar from her palm and clasped it around her wrist, smiling as it caught the light and reflected it over her skin. The stonemaster had formed soft metal around the stones instead of piercing them through to put them on the cords, but the metal links were so discrete that the glitterstones claimed all the eye's attention.

But not *my* eyes, which never strayed from my mate for long. "My Dayglow, Urcifa's scales are beautiful on your wrist, but they lack your brilliance."

Her stunned expression shifted to a slow smile as she turned her wrist to admire the sparkles. "Diamonds are forever," she said softly, then looked up from her wrist collar to meet my eyes. "I can't think of a more appropriate sentiment. I'll love you forever, Khamai."

"And I you, Vera."

❧

CUPID

I FLIPPED through the well-worn copy of "Priscilla's Neanderthal," which was one of my favorite paranormal time-travel romances. I knew every word inside the book by heart, but I still pretended to read it, simply for the joy of holding the book and turning the pages.

"So, the spawn is delivered," the orb floating nearby suddenly said, perhaps growing impatient with my slow perusal of a story I already knew well. "Do you think it's time to move on?"

I glanced up from the printed words written by a human who had dared to dream of a "happily ever after" and pondered the bookshelves lining the walls of the cabin around me. So many love stories, and I knew them all by heart. Every book in this cabin had been archived in a digital format, but I preferred the printed copies. The breaks in the spine, the dog-eared pages, the worn edges of the covers, all showed that the stories were well-loved by the humans who had created them and collected them.

I'd been sent to Earth to observe and study the human obsession with love and romance and had ended up growing obsessed myself when I'd started analyzing their romance novels. They were fiction, stories told that didn't align with the reality the humans experienced, yet somehow, so many humans still had hope for those happy endings.

They still believed in them.

The orb made an unnecessary throat-clearing sound—an affectation, like many it had taken on—and I finally relented and glanced its way.

Arrow Two, I'd initially dubbed the virtual clone of my ship's AI, but it had decided that it now wanted the crew to refer to it as "Snarky."

"So, are we moving on, or what?" Snarky flashed blue, then did a slow rotation in the air, just for fun, I suspected.

AIs. They were so illogical sometimes.

"I have been considering which case should be our next Happily Ever After." I studied the images projected onto one of my bookshelves. The only one that wasn't stuffed full of romance novels.

That bookshelf was reserved for the true stories of love. It held only a few at the moment, but I intended to add to my collection. Vera and Khamai's story had just joined the others on that shelf that looked so empty in comparison to the other shelves.

I had many human lifetimes to grow my collection.

"That last one got a little dicey." Snarky flashed red, bobbing in the air with distress it didn't normally allow to show. It was still feeling guilty about Khamai getting shot before it could intervene. "Almost lost the Prdayu."

I stroked my chin, though I didn't need that affectation to slip into a thoughtful state. It was something I'd picked up from watching rom-coms. I'd picked up many human gestures from watching rom-coms, as had the entire cohort. "We will be more careful next time, but we were in time to save him."

"If that bullet had hit him a little further to the left—"

I lifted a hand to cut Snarky off. "It didn't."

And now, Vera and Khamai would have their happily-ever-after, and all would be well for the Prdayu, according to the flux. There were even ripples suggesting there would be more happily-ever-afters for this world and its people that I might collect in the future.

This was a primitive world, guarded by Syndicate drones to keep prospectors and other exploitative efforts from interrupting the development of its civilization. I might have interfered with the drones a bit in order to slip the escape pod past their scanners —and then keep them from detecting the Arrow—though that second task was a small thing for a Lusian saucer to achieve.

Other cohorts knew what we were doing, because they viewed the flux as well, but the changes I made to the currents of time were insignificant to the wider galaxy.

But not to the people we brought together.

My gaze shifted from the list of case files to the bookshelves again.

The humans still dreamed of a happily-ever-after to complete their stories, despite the grim reality that surrounded them. All these stories showed how often they thought about it.

I had decided to use my ability to view the flux to make those dreams a reality.

Author's Note

Thank you for reading My Chameleon Mate! I hope you enjoyed reading this story as much as I enjoyed writing it.

I will be posting my more lengthy and involved Author's Note on my blog (https://susan-trombley.com/category/authors-notes-potential-spoilers-ahead/) for this book rather than fill out a bunch of pages in this book with it, but I will take a moment to say that this story arose from my need for a lighter project after completing a very high-pressure, compelling project that took a lot out of me emotionally.

This story was great fun to write and allowed me to dive back into the language barrier trope that I had fun writing with my Into the Dead Fall book, along with a primitive environment, which was another favorite part of writing that book (which I initially wrote strictly for myself and hadn't planned on publishing at first)

I really enjoyed spending time with Vera and Khamai for this book, and Cupid and his crew are an exciting development for me, since I think it's time for some lighter HEAs in the Iriduan Universe, and he's determined to bring them, making only small changes in the currents of time. His love for romance is a reflection of my own, and his desire to bring happiness to a universe that has experienced so much misery also reflects my own.

I hope these characters and this book brought a smile to your face as you read it (despite the few darker moments I tried to make brief), and I hope you will be interested in reading more in this series. I have other stories for Cupid the gray to collect, if my readers are interested in reading them, including a certain Okihan ex-pirate (we're-called-privateers) with a bushy fox tail who's looking to retire from the mercenary life. (If you've read The Fractured Mate, you've met him 😊)

If you enjoyed this story, I hope you'll leave a rating before you go, or even a review, no matter how short it might be. Reviews and ratings really help a book gain visibility and find more readers, and I usually base my decisions on what books to write on what books my readers are most interested in reading, so ratings and reviews are extremely useful. I also want to add an extra heaping helping of thanks to anyone who has ever left a review or rating on any of my books. It really does help tremendously.

I really appreciate all of you who have taken the time to read this book and spend some time in the worlds I create. You make it possible for me to continue creating these stories and characters, and I am deeply grateful for that!

As for my current WIP, I am eyeballs-deep in a reread of my Iriduan Test Subjects series, which spawned this universe, for those who are unfamiliar with it. My goal is to have everything fresh in mind when I sit down to work on The Director's Mate, which I intend to be book 9 in that series (assuming all goes well!) For those who *are* familiar with the series, that would be Ava's book, with Roz and crew, the gray aliens who have been up to their elbows in manipulating galactic events in my ITS series.

Ava is an optimistic romantic, so I'm definitely looking forward to writing her story! And Roz and crew are grays, with some interesting adaptations. :D

I'm still not sure when that book will be ready, but know that it's on my priority list, and I'm doing the reread of the series specifically with the goal of writing it.

That being said, please let me know what other characters you'd like to see get their own stories. I have story ideas for every character I ever mention by name, believe it or not. If they get a name, ideas immediately start forming for their stories (yes, even those background characters only seen briefly in my stories have their own stories :D), so I love to know which ones readers want more of, because if there's enough interest in a character or characters, I will usually develop those ideas I have into a complete novel.

You can contact me on either one of my Facebook pages:

Susan Trombley Author

The Princess's Dragon

Or send me an email directly to: susantrombleyauthor@gmail.com

Also, be sure to subscribe to my newsletter (if you're 18 years or older) for updates and announcements I have added a section to my newsletter where I feature exclusive content for my subscribers, such as sneak peeks, excerpts from unpublished or pre-published works, character art (commissioned and my own, sometimes includes links to the NSFW version) and interviews, and anything else I think my fans will enjoy. I only send out a once-a-month newsletter, and additional newsletters only when I have something to announce (i.e. new release, sales, giveaways), so you won't be spammed. You can sign up at this link:

Susan Trombley Newsletter

Other Links to keep updated on news (and be sure to check out my other books, links on the next page):

Blog: https://susantrombley.blog

Website: https://susan-trombley.com/

Instagram: www.instagram.com/susan_trombley_author

TikTok https://www.tiktok.com/@susantrombleyauthor

Bookbub: https://www.bookbub.com/authors/susan-trombley

Goodreads

Amazon author page: https://www.amazon.com/Susan-Trombley/e/B003A0FBYM

Other Books by Susan Trombley

Iriduan Universe Love Stories
    My Chameleon Mate (This book)

Iriduan Test Subjects series
    The Scorpion's Mate
    The Kraken's Mate
    The Serpent's Mate
    The Warrior's Mate
    The Hunter's Mate
    The Fractured Mate
    The Iriduan's Mate
    The Clone's Mate

Into the Dead Fall series
    Into the Dead Fall
    Key to the Dead Fall
    Minotaur's Curse
    Chimera's Gift
    Veraza's Choice

Children of the Dead Fall series (Spin-off of Into the Dead Fall series)
    Vincent's Resolution
    Sherakeren's First Date
    Alexander's Nest
    Friak's Spark

Shadows in Sanctuary series
    Lilith's Fall
    Balfor's Salvation
    Jessabelle's Beast
    Executioner's Grace
    Uriale's Redemption

Children of the Ajda series
    Guardian of the Dark Paths

Fantasy series—Breath of the Divine
    The Princess Dragon
    The Child of the Dragon Gods
    Light of the Dragon

Standalones or Collaborations
    Rampion